DEATH OF A BIRD EXPERT

I drove back to Bookarama. This time I was fortunate enough to find a parking slot right in front. Everyone seemed to be gone. The sign over the door was turned off, and the street was dark. Was I too late?

I shut off the ignition and hurried to the entrance. A couple of lights were still on inside toward the back. The door was unlocked.

I went inside. Several paperbacks were scattered on the floor between the door and the sales counter. The folding chairs were just as they had been. I couldn't see the signing table because the projector display screen had been moved in front.

"Rose?" I called. There was no sign of her or her daughter or any of the other clerks.

I headed for the table to look for the books Derek had purchased, thinking that maybe Mason had left them there. He'd obviously returned to the campground.

Rose came from the storeroom, pulling a long, rolled-up rug the color of a purple finch. She dropped the heavy rug at her feet when she saw me. The plank floor shook. Her eyes flew to her right, and my eyes followed.

Mason Livingston was seated at the signing table. His torso drooped forward and his head rested on the table. A pair of scissors protruded from his neck.

Rose bit her lip. "He's dead. I killed him. And I'm glad he's dead."

Books by J.R. Ripley

DIE, DIE BIRDIE

TOWHEE GET YOUR GUN

THE WOODPECKER ALWAYS PECKS TWICE

TO KILL A HUMMINGBIRD

Published by Kensington Publishing Corporation

To Kill a Hummingbird

J.R. Ripley

LYRICAL UNDERGROUND
Kensington Publishing Corp.
www.kensingtonbooks.com

LYRICAL UNDERGROUND BOOKS are published by

Kensington Publishing Corp.
119 West 40th Street
New York, NY 10018

All Kensington titles, imprints, and distributed lines are available at special quantity discounts for bulk purchases for sales promotion, premiums, fund-raising, educational, or institutional use.

Special book excerpts or customized printings can also be created to fit specific needs. For details, write or phone the office of the Kensington Sales Manager: Kensington Publishing Corp., 119 West 40th Street, New York, NY 10018. Attn. Sales Department. Phone: 1-800-221-2647.

Lyrical Underground and Lyrical Underground logo Reg. US Pat. & TM Off.

First Electronic Edition: July 2017
eISBN-13: 978-1-5161-0310-0
eISBN-10: 1-5161-0310-6

First Print Edition: July 2017
ISBN-13: 978-1-5161-0311-9
ISBN-10: 1-5161-0311-4

Printed in the United States of America

1

"Amy, what are you doing up on that ladder?" asked Kim. I jolted, and the ladder's legs wobbled precariously. "Don't do that!" I had a hummingbird nectar feeder dangling from my index finger by the ring at the end of the metal rod attached to the round base. The rod was for hanging the feeder from a tree or hook.

Kim scratched her head. "Do what?"

"Scare me like that. I could fall." I looked down at the ladder's feet to make sure I was safe. "And to answer your question, what I'm doing up here is hanging a hummingbird feeder."

"Why?" Kim's my best friend and partner in Birds & Bees, my bird-feeding and bird-watching supply store in Ruby Lake, North Carolina. She only works in the business part time. She's employed as a Realtor the remainder of her working hours. Still, for all her time spent in the store, she's far from an expert on bird feeding or bird watching.

"To feed the hummingbirds, for one thing."

I hung the distinctive red plastic hummingbird feeder on the steel hook my cousin Riley had attached to the porch eave. The red-topped feeders have a clear shallow base that holds the sugar water the birds favor. "How does it look?"

"Okay, I guess." Kim didn't look impressed. The truth was, she wasn't as into birds as I was.

Esther poked her head out the front window of the shop. "Her ex-professor, Mason something, is coming, and Amy's trying to impress him."

"Thank you, Esther." I frowned at her and climbed down. Ladders make me nervous. People sticking their faces out windows while I'm teetering at the top of one downright scare me. "And that's Mason

Livingston." I dusted off my khaki shorts, part of the Birds & Bees uniform. That and the red T-shirt I was wearing with our store's name and logo embroidered on it.

Kim removed a hummingbird feeder from the cardboard box on the front porch. I saw her lips moving as she counted the rest of the feeders in the carton. "Yeah, but *six* hummingbird feeders?"

I laughed and pushed a curl behind my ear. "I want to impress him *a lot!*" I grabbed the feeder from Kim's hand. "Help me with the rest of these, would you?"

"Sure thing." Kim grabbed a suction cup hanger and stuck it to the front door.

"Not the door." I pulled it down and moved it to one of the front windows opposite the cash register inside. That way we could watch the hummingbirds come and go while ringing up the sales. "It will only get spilled. Besides, the hummingbirds may not like the door opening and closing all the time."

"Okay," said Kim, snatching another from the box. "What about the rest of these?"

I looked around the porch. "Let's put another on that side of the door." I pointed to the window Esther had stuck her head through. "The rest can go in the garden."

"You must really like this guy." Esther stepped out on the porch. She had balked at the idea of wearing shorts around the shop but had finally agreed to wear a pair of khaki slacks and had opted for a robin's-egg blue T-shirt.

I'd ordered her several colors of the shirts and made her promise to wear them. I was tired of seeing her around the store during business hours in her raggedy old housedresses that smelled of cigarettes and looked like a cat had been snoozing on them—both of which were forbidden items in my business-slash-home.

The policy was no reflection on cats. I'm a big fan of the felines. Unfortunately, I have a strong allergic reaction to them. Esther Pilaster, aka "Esther the Pester" or "Esther Pester," as I was wont to call her on days when she was especially annoying and I was especially short of patience, wasn't much for following my rules about either. Not that I had caught her smoking or frolicking with a cat, but all evidence pointed to the existence of both. One of these days, I was determined to prove it.

Since my mom had unilaterally given Esther a job in my store and she was already renting a room here, I could only make do until her lease was up.

"Mason Livingston was one of my college professors." I had attended the University of North Carolina at Chapel Hill on the other side of the state. "I admire him."

"I thought you were an English major? Not an ornithologist." Kim hung a feeder in a small Japanese maple just inside the white picket fence that hugged the sidewalk. "This okay?"

"Yes, fine. And yes, I was an English major. But I took a Birds of North America class from Mason as an elective. You know birds have always been my passion." Now they were my job.

"Esther, would you mind running over to Otelia's Chocolates and picking up a pound? I remember Mason was a fanatic about chocolate," I called as I carefully maneuvered the wooden ladder between the flowers. Otelia's chocolate shop sits catercorner to Birds & Bees and is within shouting distance of Ruby Lake and the marina.

"Sure. Anything special?" she asked with peppermint-scented breath. I was sure she sucked on the hard candies to cover the smell of tobacco.

"Something fun. Use your best judgment." I'd give Mason the chocolates later at the book signing. "My purse is behind the counter."

Esther went inside and returned with my credit card. "I'll be right back. Either of you ladies want anything for yourselves?"

"I wouldn't say no to a half pound of maple fudge," Kim answered quickly.

"What about you, Amy?" Esther hollered as she started down the brick path to the sidewalk. Bright red salvia and yellow coreopsis bordered the edges and were alive with bees. I was hoping to attract at least one hummingbird to my yard while Mason was in town.

"I wouldn't say no to some maple fudge either," I said. I laid the ladder down along the edge of the sidewalk and moved to a feeder pole I had asked Cousin Riley to place in the center of a bed of hummingbird sage, formally known as *Salvia spathacea*.

"That's my problem." I ran my fingers over my tummy. "A half pound of fudge seems to equal about four pounds of body fat. So nothing for me, thanks."

"How is that even possible?" Kim chuckled as Esther crossed the street, ignoring the crosswalk and the moving vehicles and their blaring horns. Like I said, Esther is not big on rules. Even rules of the road.

"Must be my metabolism."

"I'll leave you to finish hanging the last couple of hummingbird feeders. I'm going to run upstairs a minute." I wanted to get the sugar water I had prepared earlier for the feeders.

"Okay, I'll top off the regular birdfeeders while I'm at it," Kim answered. We have several birdfeeders outside the shop. We keep them filled mostly with unshelled black oil sunflower seeds but occasionally offer treats like peanuts or safflower seeds. The idea was to attract the birds to the feeders and the customers to the birds and then to Birds & Bees. So far, it seemed to be working fairly well. Business had picked up since opening several months back. With summer in full swing, I was hoping that upward trend would continue.

I climbed to the third level of the old Queen Anne Victorian-era house where I lived with my mother. The second floor was occupied by my current renters, Esther Pilaster and Paul Anderson. The business occupied the entire ground floor.

Some say the old house is haunted. I like to joke that it will cease being haunted once Esther moves out. She was on the last year of her legacy lease, and I, for one, was looking forward to her moving on.

"Hi, Amy," said my mother, looking up from the English countryside mystery novel she was reading. "Everything okay in the store?"

"Fine, Mom." I crossed the apartment to the kitchen on the other side of the small flat. We shared a two-bedroom, open-concept apartment. Open-concept because there was one bathroom, two bedrooms, and the living-area-slash-kitchen; we lived our lives in the open, like it or not. I pulled the plastic jug from the fridge and set it on the counter. "I came back for the hummingbird nectar."

"Anything I can do to help?"

"No, thanks. I've got it." I yanked open the freezer. "Thanks for boiling it up for me though." Hummingbird feeder food is easy to make at home: four parts water to one part dissolved sugar. We melted the sugar in a saucepan of boiling water, then stored it in a glass juice container in the fridge. Mom had prepared a batch for me the night before while I'd been out on a date.

I pulled the ice tray from the freezer and stabbed a cube with my finger. "Solid as a rock." I grinned with satisfaction. Mom had made up such a big batch of sugar water that I'd had the idea to freeze the extra in an ice cube tray.

Mom looked up from her book. She appeared tired. Mom suffers from muscular dystrophy. She'd been getting worse there for a while, but the disease seemed to be in check now, which was a great thing. Still, she wears out easily, and I do my best not to be a source of stress or worry for her. Sometimes I succeed. "How did it turn out?"

"Perfect. I'll use the liquid now, and the frozen cubes will be ready the next time our little friends need their feeders refilled."

The sugar water only lasted in the feeders for about three days tops. That wasn't necessarily because the birds drank it all, but because the liquid tended to get a bit funky out in the hot sun, not to mention the effects of the insects that sometimes got trapped inside the water and decomposed therein. For the health of the hummingbirds, it was always best to clean the feeders and refill them every third day.

"Do hummingbirds really live on sugar water?" Mom asked. "It doesn't seem possible."

"It isn't. The sugar water is a nectar substitute. Hummingbirds also eat a lot of spiders and other insects. Sometimes when you see a hummingbird hovering over a flower, it isn't because it's about to feed on nectar—it could very well be that the bird has spotted a tasty spider or even an insect trapped in a spider's web."

"I never knew that."

"It's quite common. They also perform hover-hawking and what's called sally-hawking."

"Hawking?"

"Yes." I grabbed a bowl from a shelf, set it on the kitchen counter, and twisted the frozen cubes of sugar water free, then dumped them in the bowl. "Hummingbirds might fly through a swarm of insects, like gnats, and snatch them as they pass. Kind of like swifts do. That's called hover-hawking. Or they might sit on a branch, spot their prey, and make a beeline for it. That's sally-hawking." I jiggled the bowl of cubes.

"I don't think I'll ever learn everything there is to know about birds," sighed Mom.

I smiled. "That makes two of us!"

Hoo-hoo-hoo-hoo!

The distinctive dog-like hooting of a barred owl sounded from outside. But there was something funny about this call; it sounded a bit . . . metallic. Not to mention I'd never seen a barred owl hanging around the Town of Ruby Lake in the middle of the day.

Mom turned her head toward the front window. "What on earth is that?"

"I don't know. It sounded like it came from the street." I slid the ice cube tray back into the freezer. "I'll take a look." I crossed to my bedroom from which I have a great view of Lake Shore Drive, the main road that sweeps along the lake and into town. The busy street is home to much of the tourist industry and shopping in our fair burg. It was the perfect location for Birds & Bees.

"What is that thing?" Mom had come into my room, and she peered over my shoulder to the street below.

I cocked my head. "If I didn't know better, I'd say that was a giant birdhouse!"

2

I ran down the two flights of stairs as fast as I dared. Esther was at the front counter. "What do you want me to do with these chocolates?" She held up a white bag, nothing more than a blur in my peripheral vision as I flew past like a hawk pursuing its prey. "I got chocolate-covered cherries. Otelia was running a sale on them."

"Perfect. Leave them behind the counter, please, Esther. I've got to see what's going on out there!"

Esther dropped the bag, leaned over the counter, and looked out the plate glass window. "Looks like the circus has come to town."

Hoo-hoo-hoo-hoo!

I threw open the front door and marched toward the street. A bright red pickup truck sat at the curb. Behind it, attached by a trailer hitch, was a tiny house. I'd seen tiny houses on TV—they had become something of a fad—but never one quite like this.

Kim stood at the edge of the street gaping, hummingbird feeders forgotten. "Have you ever seen anything like it?"

"It's a giant birdhouse," I said, stating the obvious. The adorable house on wheels was, indeed, shaped very much like a tall, skinny red birdhouse with a cedar shingle roof. I saw a pasty white face peek out the side window, then disappear.

A moment later, the door at the back opened, a small step was lowered, and Mason Livingston alit on the street.

"Amy!" he called, seeing me standing on the sidewalk next to Kim. He beamed. "Wonderful to see you!"

He whipped off a pair of tortoiseshell sunglasses with greenish lenses and thrust them in his breast pocket.

"Professor Livingston!" We met halfway, and I gave him a friendly hug. "How are you, Professor?"

"Very well, thank you. Please, it's Mason, darling." He shook his finger at me. "I'm no longer your professor."

"Thank goodness for that. I mean, no offense, but I'm glad my college days are behind me."

He turned his attention to Kim. "And you are?"

"Professor Livingston—Mason—I'd like you to meet Kim." I waved my hand toward my friend. "She's my best friend and a business partner."

"Wonderful to meet you," said Mason. He took both our hands. "Frankly, I can't decide which of you is more beautiful."

"That's easy." Kim fluffed her hair. "It's me."

I laughed. "Come on. Let's go inside. I've got some refreshments, and we can get caught up."

"Of course," Mason said, bright brown eyes gleaming beneath bushy brows. He turned toward Birds & Bees. "Quite a place you've got here."

"Thank you," I said.

"Plenty of hummingbirds, I see." He nodded appreciatively. "Did you know that, to survive, a single hummingbird will drink twice its body weight in nectar each day?"

"Interesting," said Kim. "And not an ounce of body fat on them. I wish I could get away with that."

Mason started toward the shop, but Kim held me back.

"Tipsy," whispered Kim.

"What?"

"I think your old college professor has been dipping in the sauce."

I cocked my head as I watched Mason start up the walk to Birds & Bees, arms swinging. His gray flannel suit hung loosely from his shoulders. His tie was half undone. "Mason does seem a bit unsteady, doesn't he?"

Kim giggled. "I've seen steadier rowboats out on the lake. In a thunderstorm."

"Let's go. Mason's waiting." He'd already disappeared inside. That meant he'd be facing Esther alone.

"Hold on, Amy. I want to get a picture."

"Of what?"

"This giant birdhouse, of course." She thrust her phone at me. "Here, take my pic so I can post it online on my page."

"Oh, brother." I took the phone and aimed while Kim posed mischievously in front of the tiny quirky house on wheels.

"Did you know he was going to be showing up with this thing?" Kim smiled broadly.

"Not a clue," I replied. "Now turn the other way. The sun was in your face in that last shot."

Kim turned her head. "Do you think your old professor would mind if we take a look inside?"

"I'd mind. That would be trespassing." Not that I hadn't done a little of that myself. All in the name of truth and justice, of course.

"But I want to pose in that window." She pointed to a rectangular window with white trim and a window box that held some faded plastic flowers. "It will be fun."

"Maybe later," I said. I handed Kim her phone and gave her a nudge. "If Mason gives his permission."

"Fine," grumbled Kim, following me up the walk.

Inside, Mason had cornered Esther in the small first-floor kitchenette in the back corner of the shop. I always tried to leave out snacks and drinks for the customers. There were chairs where they could linger with their refreshments and read from a selection of bird-, plant- and bee-related literature.

"Are you sure you don't have anything stronger?" I heard Mason ask Esther.

Esther gave me the stink eye. "My fist's pretty strong." She waved her clenched hand at the professor's nose.

"Now, now, Esther." I grabbed Esther's hand and lowered it. "Care for some lemonade, Mason?" I pulled the glass pitcher from the fridge and set it beside the sink.

"Thank you, Amy. I am a bit parched."

Using a pair of stainless steel tongs, I dropped ice in each of our glasses, then poured a round of lemonade. Esther chugged hers down, then helped herself to seconds and a chocolate chip cookie. Mom had baked the cookies in advance of today's event. Nobody made a chocolate chip cookie like Mom. I heard the tinkle of the door opening. "Could you go assist our customer, please, Esther?"

Esther muttered something under her breath but said she would.

"I'll go, too," said Kim. "I can finish setting things up for the kiddies."

"Kitties?" Mason looked at me inquiringly. "Are you selling cats here now in addition to birdseed?"

"Not kittens, kiddies." I spelled the word. "We're having a group of day-schoolers in. I try to hold special events for the children on a fairly regular basis. It's a way of teaching them something about birds and bees—"

"Oh?" Mason wiggled his eyebrows in a lascivious fashion. He swirled the ice around in his glass, then drank.

"Nothing like that!" I touched his arm. "I'm pretty sure every parent in town would be out for my blood if I tried to teach their children the facts of life. Not that I'd want to."

"So you teach them a thing or two about our avian and apian friends."

"That's right. It's as much fun for me as it is for the kids." I offered Mason a cookie from the tray, and he ate it greedily. "Would you care to stick around for it? I know it's sort of last-minute, but I'm sure the children would enjoy hearing you speak, especially about hummingbirds."

"Thank you. Thank you, Amy." Mason yawned. "But I really am rather tired. It's been a long drive, you know. A long trip."

"I can imagine." I set down my glass. "How long is your book tour?"

"Another month. I've been on the road for two months already. I'm looking forward to this book-launch tour coming to an end."

"We're thrilled that you decided to make our little Town of Ruby Lake one of your stops. I'm sure it's not quite the big-city event you're used to, but I'm hoping for a good turnout. I know Rose Smith, the bookstore owner, has been making plans like crazy. She put up flyers and has advertised your book signing at her store in the local paper and has been running some radio spots." All of which had to be costing a pretty penny. I knew what it cost to advertise just in our local newspaper.

"I'm looking forward to it. And to your little, what was it? Birds and Brews gathering?"

"Yes. That's tonight. I host that jointly with Paul Anderson at Brewer's Biergarten next door. He's the owner."

"Is he as enamored of birds as you?"

"No, Mister Anderson is enamored of beer."

"I see." He scooped up another cookie.

"I can't tell you what an honor it is for us that you've agreed to speak." I was gushing like a schoolgirl but couldn't seem to stop.

Mason laughed. "You know how much I love to talk. And I adore the spotlight. How could I resist?"

"Then why not stick around and meet with the children?"

"I don't know, Amy . . ."

"We're going to be having a class on the mason bee along with a hands-on demonstration."

"*Mason* bee?"

"I thought you'd get a kick out of that," I said with a grin. "As I mentioned, the kids should be arriving within the hour." I tapped my watch crystal. "The children will be making mason bee nests. Are you sure you wouldn't like to stay? It's a group of youngsters from the daycare center. They're adorable and full of energy. It should be a lot of fun."

Mason shuddered and yawned once more. "No, thank you. I'd really like to get settled. It's been a long drive." He touched my wrist. "I'll come by later." He fished his keys from his pocket. "In time for the lecture."

"Okay, I understand. Will you have some free time tomorrow? I could show you the sights."

He shook his head sadly. "I'm afraid not. My publisher keeps me quite busy on these junkets. I have interviews and meetings all day tomorrow, including dinner with a newspaper editor who's driving over from Charlotte."

"That's too bad."

Mason patted my arm. "We'll have time the day after that. I've nothing on my schedule but the book signing that night."

"Perfect. I'm going to hold you to it. There's a lot to see and do around here."

"I'm sure there is." The professor tugged at his sleeve. "Do you know a facility where I might park my vehicle?"

"You mean like a recreational vehicle park? You won't be staying at a hotel?"

"No. The publisher had offered to set me up, but I prefer my tiny birdhouse."

"It's fantastic," I said.

"The best little birdhouse in Texas!"

"I'll bet." I knew Mason was a tenured professor at a private university in Texas.

"I'll have to give you the grand tour. Not that it will take long," Mason said with a laugh and a wink. "So is there an RV park nearby?"

"There's a public campground adjacent to the marina across the street—the Ruby Lake Park and Marina. You may be able to get a spot there if the campground isn't full. Summer is the busiest time of year here in town."

"I saw the sign for the marina as I was coming in." Mason nodded. "I'll check it out."

I walked Mason to the street. "You'll have to register at the office and get an overnight camping permit." I gave Mason directions to the lakeside marina office. "You can't miss it." We hugged briefly, and Mason promised to return at seven for dinner at Brewer's Biergarten and the Birds and Brews meeting afterward.

"The professor's leaving already?" Kim asked.

"He wanted to rest."

Kim nodded as she counted out bamboo shoots. "Every time we're finished with a group of kids here in the store, that's what I want to do, too."

The children arrived shortly thereafter, nearly twenty of them. Kim and I got busy. "Where's your bee guy?" Kim looked frazzled already as she set out stools for the teachers and pillows and rugs for the kids to sit on.

I set a five-gallon bucket down in the middle of the open space we had created for the event near the front of the store. "He should *bee* here any minute."

Kim groaned. "Must you?"

I heard the sound of the buzzer announcing someone was at the delivery door. "Mom, could you please see who's at the back door?"

"Of course, dear."

My mother had come down to assist with the kids. She's a former teacher and is great with them. I'm also sure she misses teaching and can't pass up the opportunity to spend time with children, especially when they are as young and bright-eyed as these daycare kids. Mom had taught high school or, as she liked to call it, high anxiety school.

As the two daycare teachers herded their kids and got them

seated, I finished setting up the materials. The bucket was filled with six-inch pieces of bamboo that Cousin Riley had sawn to length for me. I also had several balls of twine. The children would be building mason bee nests, which are made by bundling a handful of the thin bamboo shoots and tying them together with twine.

"Sorry I'm late." Mitch Quiles, a squat man with tight black curls, bushy eyebrows, and a crooked nose, had arrived, and his hands were full. Mom's hands were full, too.

"Good to see you again, Mister Quiles." I grabbed a box of display materials from Mom and set them at the front of the group. Mitch Quiles owned Quiles Apiary outside town and was the most knowledgeable person around on bees. I introduced him to the school group and let him do his thing. He had brought samples of honeycombs and a small case filled with twenty of the many species of bees that could be found in the Carolinas.

With the kids sitting on the floor and the teachers on the stools, attentions rapt, I passed out paper cups of lemonade and chocolate chip cookies on napkins.

"Although the mason bee is a spring pollinator and we're a little late for this time of year, you'll each be making your very own mason bee nest to take home. How do you like that?" Mr. Quiles asked his audience. There were murmurs of appreciation.

"Will we get honey, Mister Quiles?"

"Sorry," said Mr. Quiles. "The mason bee is a solitary bee. They do not live in hives and do not produce honey. They are great pollinators though." He looked toward the two teachers. "Maybe you would all like to see an actual honey-producing hive sometime?"

Several kids answered yes.

"Well, if it's all right with your teachers, I'm sure we can arrange for you to come out to my place one morning. I have a dozen hives you can view."

"I had hives once," Kim said out of the side of her mouth. "I wouldn't have wanted anybody to see them."

"Quiet," I whispered.

"What do you say, class?" asked one of the teachers. "Would we like a field trip to Quiles Apiary?"

The vote was unanimous.

We broke up into small groups. Mom and I started handing out bamboo sticks, and Kim and the teachers cut lengths of twine. Mr. Quiles went from group to group, checking out the children's handiwork and lending a hand.

"How exactly does the bee make babies in here? It doesn't look like a nest," a young boy asked, peering into a hollow tube.

Mr. Quiles held up a length of bamboo. "The female bee forms a small ball of nectar and pollen at the farthest end of the nesting tube and lays an egg on the ball.

"Next, she collects mud to create a cell partition and repeats the egg-laying process until she reaches the mouth of the tube, which she caps with mud for protection. Interestingly, the female mason bee controls the sex of her eggs, laying female eggs toward the back of the nest and males toward the front."

"Why does the mother lay the girl eggs in the back?" asked a girl with short blond curls.

"To protect them," replied Mr. Quiles.

"Hey, that's not fair," complained a boy.

Mr. Quiles patted his shoulder. "Better get used to it, son."

Kim and I laughed.

After the demonstration wrapped up, I walked Mr. Quiles out to his van and thanked him for coming.

"Anytime, Amy. Thanks for having me."

"You know, we're having a Birds and Brews get-together at Brewer's Biergarten next door this evening. Maybe you'd like to come?"

"Birds and Brews, you say?" Mr. Quiles jiggled his car keys. "I am rather fond of both."

"Mason Livingston has agreed to talk to our group, so it should be especially interesting."

Mr. Quiles rubbed his chin. "Mason Livingston, you say? I'd say that could be very interesting indeed." With that, the beekeeper got in his van and drove off.

3

"Where's this professor friend of yours?" Paul sounded annoyed. He had reserved half of the outdoor seating area, the space between his *biergarten* and my bird store, to host this month's Birds and Brews gathering with its special guest of honor, Professor Mason Livingston.

The only problem being that our esteemed guest of honor was a no-show. He'd already missed dinner. Now he was missing the very lecture he was supposed to be delivering.

I pulled out my cell phone and checked the time. "I don't know. Mason should have been here by now." I'd changed out of my normal work clothes and into a blue dress and low heels.

"You want me to go check on him?" Derek started to rise from his seat.

"No, you stay here. Enjoy the game." I pecked his cheek. "I'll go." There was a big-screen TV playing silently in the corner near the bar. Derek didn't put up an argument. He and Paul had a wager going on a baseball game.

Paul had arranged several tables in a semicircle. Paul, Derek, and I sat at a table facing the others clustered around us. The empty seat beside me was for Mason.

"I'll be right back, everyone," I called out to the group as I stood. "I'm going to go see what's keeping Professor Livingston. Perhaps he got lost," I suggested, though it seemed unlikely.

"Maybe he should've brought along a guide *owl*!" hooted Derek.

"Very funny."

"Need some company, Amy?" That was Karl Vogel, former police chief of the Town of Ruby Lake. He pulled the thick, black-rimmed glasses he always wore from his nose and wiped them on his shirttail.

"No, thanks, Karl. You stay and enjoy yourself. I'll be right back." Floyd Withers was with him. Floyd and I were old friends. Karl and Floyd lived in the same senior facility and had become best of friends themselves. "Good to see you, Floyd. Spot any interesting birds lately?"

"We spotted a red-winged blackbird the other day," answered Floyd, looking dapper in a button-down shirt and slacks. His thinning white hair was combed straight back, and his bushy moustache was freshly trimmed. Karl, by contrast, was slowly going bald with a shock of long and unruly white hair that stuck up from the top of his head.

"I want to hear all about it later," I said, kissing his cheek. "In fact, you should share with the group."

Floyd agreed.

It wasn't far from Brewer's Biergarten to the marina, so I walked. I crossed through the marina and docks to the park that runs along the lake's edge. The campground was crowded with tents and campers of all shapes and sizes, but it wasn't hard to find Mason Livingston's trailer. It was the only bright red, human-sized birdhouse for miles—to say the least.

The campground was filled with people gathered around small fires or at picnic tables, all enjoying the lovely evening air and the spectacular scenery, with the lake in the foreground and the forested mountains in the background.

As I approached Mason's trailer, I saw a figure I recognized rounding the corner of the tiny house on wheels. It was Lance Jennings, a local reporter for the *Ruby Lake Weekender*, the town's local paper. Lance is about forty years old and forty pounds overweight for his six-foot frame.

"Amy." Lance rubbed his thick nose. "What are you doing here?"

"I came to get Professor Livingston. He's speaking to our group tonight." I glanced at the closed door. "Were you interviewing him? Is he here?"

Lance gulped. "N-no. I don't think so." He had a computer tablet in his hand, his version of an old reporter's notebook. "I just got here myself." He glanced back at the professor's trailer. "Well, I've got to go."

"Bye." I frowned as Lance wandered away. "What was that all

about?" I muttered under my breath. I approached Mason's trailer, climbed the two steps to the door at the rear, and knocked. "Professor? Mason, are you in there?" I pressed my ear to the door. Nothing. "Professor? It's me, Amy." Was he in? Could he be in the shower? Assuming the odd trailer home had such conveniences. "Mind if I come in?"

"I saw him go in a while ago," offered a man at a nearby Winnebago. He sat under the RV's awning playing cards with a woman I took for his wife.

The woman nodded in agreement. "Of course, we've been in and out. We only got back from supper at the diner a little while ago."

"That's right," agreed the man, returning his attention to the cards in his hand.

"Thanks. I'm Amy Simms. I run Birds and Bees in town. The owner is a friend of mine," I explained.

"A bit of an eccentric, isn't he?" the man called.

His wife nodded her agreement. "You don't see a lot of holiday campers pulling up to a campsite in a giant red birdhouse."

"Maybe he's asleep." I tried the door. It was unlocked. "Mason?" The interior was cramped and filled with shadows. Only a bit of light spilled through the curtained windows. A single bed was pressed up toward the front end of the trailer nearest the pickup truck.

I gasped and felt a sudden chill.

Mason Livingston lay sprawled out on his tiny mattress.

I hurried to the bed. He was in the same clothes he'd worn when I'd met with him earlier in the day, though his tie hung loose around his neck. "Mason?" I touched my hand to his chest and felt a heartbeat.

Mason stirred, sluggish as a honeybee on a cold spring morning. "What?"

I smelled alcohol on his breath. "Mason!" I gasped. "Are you all right?"

He sat up, looking groggy and pale. "Yes. Amy?" His eyes flitted around the cramped space. "What are you doing here?"

"I came to get you. It's time for your lecture. Everybody's waiting."

"Oh, dear." Mason dropped his feet over the side of the bed. "I am so sorry. I must have dozed off." He rubbed his hands over his face. "I drove all the way from Nashville today."

"Here," I said, handing the professor a glass of water from a tiny table beside the bed. "Of course, you're tired. Drink this, get freshened up, and we'll walk over to the *biergarten* together."

Mason nodded and lurched to his feet. He pulled open the narrow door to a tiny bathroom and disappeared inside. Minutes later, he came out looking somewhat refreshed and semi-alert.

I hadn't made up my mind whether he was sober. A bottle of tequila lay on the floor within reach of the bed. It was three-quarters empty.

"You know," I chuckled as I led him back through the marina and over to Brewer's, "I don't mind telling you that you gave me quite a scare back there."

"How's that?" inquired Mason, adjusting his tie.

"When you didn't answer your door for me or Lance—"

"Lance?"

"Lance Jennings. He's a local reporter."

"Ah, yes, Mr. Jennings."

"You know him?"

Mason's lips curled. "Let's say we've had some communications."

That was an odd remark and an even odder look on his face, but I didn't pursue the matter. "I saw Lance outside your door . . ."

"Yes?"

"Then I saw you sprawled out on the bed, and I—" I hesitated.

"You what?" We stood at the edge of Lake Shore Drive, waiting for traffic to clear before crossing.

"You'll think it's silly."

"Tell me, Amy. We're friends, aren't we?"

I nodded as we stepped into the street. "I thought you were dead."

Mason threw back his head and laughed. "Oh, Amy. You always did have quite the imagination!"

I waved to my mother and Esther, sitting in a pair of rocking chairs on our front porch. "That's my mother," I explained to Mason as we passed. "I'll introduce you to her later. She's dying to meet you."

"I'll look forward to it," replied Mason. We entered Brewer's Biergarten and joined the group in the courtyard. I introduced the professor to Derek and Paul. "Pleased to meet you, gentlemen," said Mason.

"Likewise," said Paul. He wore jeans and a crisp black T-shirt with his business's logo discreetly placed on its left sleeve. "Try the lager. I brewed it specially for the event."

Mason accepted his glass and sipped. "This stuff tastes like cat urine." He spat and set it down quickly on the table, then drank from the first glass of water he could find.

Paul forced a smile and shoved his hand through his wavy brown hair. "Isn't this going to be fun," he mumbled to Derek.

Derek patted him on the shoulder and came to take his seat beside me. Unfortunately, Mason had taken his spot. Derek was forced to sit at the end of the table, and he shot me a bemused look.

Rose Smith, owner of Bookarama on the town square, was among those in attendance. She approached our table the minute we sat down. "Good evening, Professor Livingston." She held out a hardcover copy of his latest tome, *Hummingbirds and Their Habits*. "I'm Rose Smith, from the bookstore?" She seemed nervous and hesitant to speak. "I got your email and brought the book for you. You said you wanted a copy for tonight."

Mason took the book with a smile. "Thank you so much."

"Good evening, Rose," I said. I introduced her to Paul and Derek. Out of the corner of my eye, I spotted Mitch Quiles at the farthest table and shot him a wink.

"We've already met." Derek shook her hand. "I'm a frequent visitor to your bookstore."

"Yes, you do look familiar."

Derek looked around. "Where's your lovely daughter, Amber?"

"She's working tonight. Plus, she's busy making last-minute arrangements for Professor Livingston's book signing. There's so much to do." She turned to Mason. "It's going to be wonderful, I'm sure. I can't thank you enough for agreeing to come to my humble little store and speak to us." She smiled at me. "We expect quite the turnout. You are coming, aren't you, Amy? Both of you?" She was looking at Derek.

"Of course, we will," I said for both of us.

"And you, Mister Anderson?" she asked hopefully.

Paul's lip curled. I had a feeling he was still smarting from the professor's cat urine comment. "Maybe."

"Wonderful," said Rose. She was a small, fiftyish brunette with a pageboy haircut and green eyes. I remembered seeing her daughter a time or two at the bookstore, a lovely young blonde in her twenties. "And don't worry," she told Mason. "I got everything on your list that you requested. The wine, the cheese, the special signing pen."

He patted her arm solicitously. "Splendid." He turned to me. "Shall we get started, Amy?"

"Just a minute." Lance Jennings pushed his way between us as Rose slunk away to a table at the far end of the courtyard.

"Lance," I said, startled. "We're about to begin."

"Lance Jennings. *Ruby Lake Weekender*." He stuck out his hand and offered a business card, but Mason ignored it or didn't see it. "I was wondering if you might have time for an interview afterward."

I looked at the professor. I knew how tired he was. "I'm not sure tonight is a good idea, Lance. Maybe tomorrow?" I looked from the professor to Lance and moved to get Lance away.

"Hold it!" called a voice at the edge of the courtyard. We all turned. A woman stood on the sidewalk, looking in over the brick pony wall that separated the sidewalk from the courtyard.

"Now what?" I muttered. The woman wore tight blue jeans and a white shirt. She lifted her leg and deftly climbed over the wall. She waved impatiently for a pimply faced kid, who looked like he'd just barely finished high school, to follow. He hesitated, struggling to balance the ungainly camera on his shoulder, then did as she ordered.

She hurried over, oblivious to the stares of our Birds and Brews gathering. "Violet Wilcox," she declared. "*AM Ruby.* How about a quick interview for our listeners, doc?"

Mason looked like a deer caught in the headlights.

"Listeners," sneered Lance. "What listeners?"

"Excuse me," I said, putting myself between her and Mason. "Who are you exactly?"

She looked at me like I was a total fool. Her platinum blond hair, milky complexion, and hour-glass figure had clearly caught Paul Anderson's attention.

"Your friend, Mason, appears to be as popular as a rock star." Derek leaned toward me. "Should I be jealous of this guy?"

"Never," I assured him. I turned to Ms. Wilcox. "I'm sorry, but both you and Lance will have to wait until tomorrow."

"Why don't we film your talk now, doc?" Violet Wilcox ignored me and focused on Mason.

"I really don't know—" The professor was holding his book up against his chest as a shield.

"What do you need film for, for crying out loud?" Lance cast a disparaging look at the hapless cameraman. "You run a radio station."

The blonde turned on Lance. "For your information—"

Paul took action. I wasn't sure if it was for Mason Livingston's benefit or his own. "Listen, Violet, isn't it?" He laid a hundred-watt smile on her. "I'm Paul Anderson, owner of Brewer's Biergarten." He left out the part about being one of two owners of the business, the other being my lousy ex-boyfriend, Craig Bigelow. "Professor Livingston is rather busy at the moment. How about if I buy you a drink?"

She hesitated.

"Have you ever had a behind-the-scenes look at a brew pub?"

"No, I haven't." She blinked. Apparently he was having some sort of effect on her.

"Great." He laid a hand on the small of her back and led her away. "Then you're in for a treat. I'll bet your listeners," he glanced at the kid with the camera, "or viewers would love to learn more."

She nodded and waved for her pimply faced assistant with the camera to follow. That was the last we saw of them that night.

4

On the morning of the professor's book signing, Mom and I were enjoying breakfast at Ruby's Diner across the street from Birds & Bees when Paul Anderson showed up. He was heading for a stool at the bar but came to our table at the window when he spotted us sitting with the sun in our faces.

I hadn't been in Ruby's much lately. The diner's owner and I had had a bit of a falling out, but our relationship seemed to be on the mend. At least she was allowing me in the diner.

I had missed the diner's onion rings almost as much as I'd missed my rapport with its owner.

"Good morning, Paul," Mom said, ever cheerful. "Join us."

"Don't mind if I do. Morning, Amy."

"Good morning, Paul." I raised my brow. "We missed you last night. You and Miss Centerfold have a nice time?" He and the woman from the radio station had disappeared, and Paul had never reappeared to talk to our group about the beer like he was supposed to. Fortunately, Mason liked to talk and was an accomplished speaker. He'd held most everyone's rapt attention.

"Who?" asked Mom, lowering her coffee mug.

Paul chuckled. "Violet Wilcox. What's wrong, Amy? Jealous?"

I pulled a face. "You wish." Nonetheless, I dug into my stack of buckwheat pancakes with renewed interest. "We are supposed to be hosting Birds and Brews jointly. The whole thing was your idea, as I recall." I cast a critical eye his way.

He couldn't stop beaming. The waitress came and took his order of ham and eggs and coffee. "What can I say? I'm a popular guy. I couldn't get away. Besides, I was trying to keep her from interfering in Livingston's talk." He dumped too much sugar and too much cream into his coffee. "How did it go?"

"Great," I answered. "Though, truthfully, I thought a number of people looked a bit out of sorts or put off by the lecture. Maybe it was just one of those nights." Mr. Quiles, for one, had barely said a word the entire evening. I ran a forkful of pancake through a puddle of syrup. "Rose Smith certainly seemed enraptured. She couldn't keep her eyes off him."

"Yeah, after everybody left, I saw her hanging around inside with your pal, Mason, sharing a couple of *bottled* beers."

I could tell that Mason's remark about his in-house brew still stung. "Interesting. Could romance be budding for Rose?"

"Oh, Amy," Mom groaned.

"Where is the professor, anyway?" Paul looked across the diner and waved for more coffee.

"Beats me," I answered. "He was supposed to be here." We had made plans to meet that morning for breakfast. "He knew Mom was coming and wanted to meet him."

"You always spoke so highly of your old college professor," Mom said, folding her napkin and tucking it under her plate. "I suppose I will have to wait until the signing tonight." Mom had said she was going to come and buy a copy of his book, not that she was as into birds as I was.

"What time did Mason leave the *biergarten*?" Remembering how tired he had looked yesterday afternoon and how long he had been on the road with the book tour, I expected he was tucked inside his trailer, fast asleep.

Paul rubbed his chin. "I'd say about ten thirty. Violet left right after that. I didn't even get her phone number."

"You mean the two of you didn't do the horizontal tango?" I teased.

"Amy!" said my mother.

"Sorry, Mom." I grabbed my wallet from my purse and placed some cash atop the bill.

"For your information, Ms. Wilcox was still antsy to get an interview with Livingston. The woman never gives up. I think she just wants to scoop Lance and the paper."

"From what I've seen of her so far, that sounds about right." I described Ms. Wilcox to Mom and explained how she worked for a local AM radio station.

"How on earth did this Ms. Wilcox expect to find Professor Livingston so late at night? Didn't you say he was staying at the campground, Amy?"

"Are you kidding?" Paul replied. "How can you miss him?" He reached across the plate and helped himself to a slice of my toast. I wasn't going to eat it anyway—not that he'd asked. "Everybody's talking about that crazy red birdhouse he came rolling into town with behind his pickup truck."

"True," said Mom, having seen the tiny trailer house with her own eyes.

"This from a man who spent his first days in town living out of a dilapidated camper parked outside my store."

"I remember it fondly," said Paul as he dug into his eggs the minute the waitress set his plate down.

"I don't. I guess you'll have to wait until the book signing to meet Mason, unless he stops in the store before that, Mom."

But he didn't.

Derek picked Mom and me up a half hour before the book signing and drove us down to Bookarama. What with it being the middle of the tourist season and the evening of a special event at the bookstore, he'd had to park a block away in the public lot.

Rose and her daughter, Amber, stood just inside the door, greeting customers as they filed in. Rose wore a red-and-yellow flower print dress, while Amber had opted for jeans and a long-sleeve black sweater.

I had tried calling Rose earlier in the day but had gotten her store's answering machine. I'd wanted to find out if she had been in touch with Mason. I hadn't heard a peep from him all day, and that had been concerning. The last thing I wanted was for him to miss his own signing, not only for his sake but for Rose's and the Bookarama's.

It was with relief that I waved to the professor, seated alone at a six-foot-long table set up at the back of the store. Row after row of beige folding chairs had been placed in front of him, and nearly every seat was filled.

"Hi, Amy, Derek. And Barbara." Rose hugged my mother. "So

glad you could make it. How are you?" Everybody in town knew about Mom's MD. Mom said she was doing fine. Rose pushed a hand through her hair. "I'm so glad to hear it."

"Congratulations, Rose," I said, meaning it. "It's quite a coup to get a well-known expert like Professor Livingston to do a signing at your store."

Rose giggled. "I don't know about that. If you ask me, he came more because of your relationship with him."

"Don't sell yourself short," I replied. "He's lucky to have devoted independent bookstore owners like yourself to promote his books."

"Thanks, Amy." Rose stepped aside as three more people, including one with a guide dog, came through the door. She looked harried. "Amber, would you please show Amy, Derek, and Barbara where the refreshments are?"

Amber agreed.

"You two go ahead," I said. "I want to say hello to the professor and give him these." I waved the box of chocolates I'd been meaning to give him.

Derek left with my mother, and I walked over to Mason, who was chatting with an older woman who appeared to be bending his ear with a story about the birds she had seen on her adventures in Africa.

An ordinary-looking woman I judged to be in her late forties stood behind Mason. She wore a simple cream-colored blouse and a long, pleated brown skirt with low heels. Her shoulder-length brown hair was pushed back behind her ears, held in place by a pair of thick glasses.

"Good evening, Mason. Am I interrupting?"

"Certainly not." The professor stood as I handed him the chocolates. "What's this?"

"I know what a sweet tooth you have, so I brought you a little something from one of the local chocolatiers, Otelia Newsome. You met her last night at Brewer's."

I looked around the crowded store for her face so I could introduce her formally but saw no sign of her. "I don't see her, but I know she'll be here. She promised she would. Don't let that stop you from enjoying the chocolates in the meantime."

Mason beamed. "I couldn't stop myself if I tried." He set the box at the edge of the table, rubbed his hands together, then looked at his watch. "I believe it is nearly time to get started." He touched the spacebar of the silver laptop at his side. A white display screen had been set up behind him and to his right.

"I've prepared a presentation. Nothing tells a story like a picture." A bottle of wine and a cheese-and-cracker tray rested beside the computer. The cheese and crackers looked untouched, but the bottle of wine was nearly empty. That probably explained his reddish eyes and nose. Kim wasn't the only one to notice that the professor liked to drink a little more than I had remembered.

Mason turned to a woman hovering behind him. "Amy, I'd like you to meet Cara Siskin."

Cara smiled briefly and shook my hand. Her cheeks were flush. "My pleasure." Green eye shadow accentuated her emerald eyes.

"Ms. Siskin works in my publisher's publicity department." He winked at me. "She keeps me in line."

"I try to." Cara rolled her eyes in mock exasperation. "Speaking of which, we should be getting started. Your fans are waiting."

Mason beamed. "Of course. Forgive me, Amy. I wouldn't want to disappoint."

"No problem," I replied. "Don't let me keep you. I came to listen, not talk."

"Good luck, Mason." Derek appeared at my side. He held three copies of *Hummingbirds and Their Habits*. "Can we get these signed now, or do we have to wait in line with the rest of the masses?" he joked. The books had been stickered with the Bookarama logo on the back to show they'd been purchased.

"Leave them with me," Mason said with a smile. "I'll have to think of something very special to write."

I wished the professor good luck and took a seat between Mom and Derek.

"You bought three copies?" I said. Mason's newest book was a forty-dollar, full-color, hardcover edition.

Derek shrugged. "What can I say? One for each of us: you, me, and Barbara. He's your friend. I wanted to be supportive. Besides," he said, casting a glance at Rose, who stood nervously behind the sales counter, "it helps Mrs. Smith, too. I have a feeling this little soiree is costing her a bundle. She told me she had to rent the projection screen, and I saw that bottle of wine Mason's drinking. That stuff's seventy dollars a liter."

I whistled and reached for Derek's hand. I'd noticed two more bottles on the floor beneath the table. "You're a good guy."

"Shush," Mom said. "Professor Livingston is about to begin."

Rose gave Mason a glowing and perhaps overlong introduction. Nonetheless, he seemed to relish every word. I wondered again if anything special had happened between the two of them last night. Rose had been the ex-Mrs. Smith for a very long time, ten years or more from what my mother had told me.

A small smile passed my lips. Maybe that was why Mason hadn't shown up for breakfast. Maybe he'd had company, and maybe that company had been Rose Smith. I remembered Paul describing the two of them drinking together last night at the *biergarten*. It could also explain why I had been unable to get a hold of either Mason or Rose today. They could have been together the entire time.

"What's so funny?" whispered Derek.

"Nothing." I squeezed his hand. "I'll tell you later."

Mason's presentation went over very well. After speaking for nearly an hour and showing numerous slides taken from his new book, Rose announced that the professor would stay and sign everyone's copy.

"Wow," I said, looking at the line that had formed versus the small number of people heading for the exit, "by my guesstimate, more than three-quarters are staying to buy books and get Mason's autograph."

"Good for Rose," Derek said. "Are you ready to get out of here?"

"What about the reception?" Mom asked, glancing toward the crowded signing table.

"We can stay if you like," Derek said, shooting me odd signals with his eyes. "I don't know about you two," he stretched his arms over his head, "but I'm worn out." He nodded toward my mother.

Mom said she was fine with staying, but I could tell by the look on her face just how tired she was. Crowds wear her out. Derek must have noticed even before I did.

"Mason looks pretty busy over there." I took Mom's hand. "He won't mind if we leave. Besides, I don't think he'll even know we've gone."

"Are you sure, dear?" Mom asked.

"I'm sure."

Derek pulled the car around so Mom wouldn't have to walk. Despite her fatigue, Mom insisted on treating us to hot fudge sundaes at Sugar Mountain, a small ice-cream shop a mile away. Neither Derek nor I could say no to that.

After finishing, I was on a sugar high, but I could see the bags under my mother's eyes. "Time to go home, Derek. And no more stops, even if they do involve hot fudge and whipped cream."

He agreed and drove us straight back to our place.

"Care to come inside for a nightcap?" I asked Derek as he dropped us off at the curb outside Birds & Bees.

"Don't worry," Mom smirked. "I have no intention of staying up and watching TV." The only television in the apartment was in the living room. "I, for one, am exhausted and intend to go straight to bed."

Derek turned off the engine. "I'd love to come up," he said. He jumped out of the car and came around to open my mother's door first. The man is such a gentleman. "And you, young lady, are more than welcome to join us."

Mom giggled. "I know better than that."

I climbed out of the backseat. "Oh, shoot."

"What is it?" asked Derek, leading my mother up the walk by the arm.

"We forgot our signed copies of the book back at Rose's."

"Can't it wait until tomorrow?" asked Mom.

I shook my head. "I promised Mason I'd start reading tonight and tell him what I think. Give him my first impressions when we meet for coffee tomorrow. I know he'll be disappointed if I don't."

"It's late," said Derek, looking at his watch. "The store's probably closed by now."

"Maybe." I pulled out my cell phone. "I'll give Rose a call." I dialed. "The line's busy." Maybe Rose was busy with Mason, I thought with a smile. "I'll just run over. It won't take long."

"I'll go with you." Derek looked from my mother to me. "Are you going to be all right, Barbara?"

Before she could frame an answer, I said, "No, that's okay. I'll go, Derek. Would you mind seeing Mom upstairs?" It was late and she was tired and there were two flights of steep stairs to climb. It was a pity the old house didn't have an elevator—except for a dumb one, which I'd had sealed off because of a past incident.

Derek reluctantly agreed. He fished in his trouser pocket and pulled out his key ring. "Here, take the Civic. It will be faster."

"I promise I'll be right back."

Derek grinned. "I'll start the popcorn."

I knew I was in for a treat. The man loved his butter.

I drove back to Bookarama. This time I was fortunate enough to find a parking slot right in front. Everyone seemed to be gone. The sign over the door was turned off, and the street was dark. Was I too late?

I shut off the ignition and hurried to the entrance. A couple of lights were still on inside toward the back. The door was unlocked.

I went inside. Several paperbacks were scattered on the floor between the door and the sales counter. The folding chairs were just as they had been. I couldn't see the signing table because the projector display screen had been moved in front.

"Rose?" I called. There was no sign of her or her daughter or any of the other clerks.

I headed for the table to look for the books Derek had purchased, thinking that maybe Mason had left them there. He'd obviously returned to the campground.

Rose came from the storeroom, pulling a long, rolled-up rug the color of a purple finch. She dropped the heavy rug at her feet when she saw me. The plank floor shook. Her eyes flew to her right, and my eyes followed.

Mason Livingston was seated at the signing table. His torso drooped forward and his head rested on the table. A pair of scissors protruded from his neck.

Rose bit her lip. "He's dead. I killed him. And I'm glad he's dead."

5

I felt my mouth go dry and my heart turn to warm jelly. "Rose?" I took a half step closer. "What—I mean—what happened? Are you okay?"

The bookstore owner nodded. She looked slightly disheveled but otherwise okay. "I'm fine, Amy." She smoothed her skirt, then cast a long look at the professor. "Will you help me get rid of the body?"

"Help you—" I stuttered. Had the woman gone mad? What on earth had happened after everyone had gone? My box of Otelia's chocolate-covered cherries lay open near Mason's right hand. The books Derek had purchased sat askew at the edge of the table with the signing pen atop them. Several other copies of the book were stacked at the edge of the table.

Rose sighed heavily. "I suppose we'd better telephone the police then." She pointed to the sales counter. "The phone's over there."

I glanced over my shoulder. The store phone was at the end of the counter, near the wall. I eased my way over without taking my eyes off Rose. My hand fumbled for the phone. It was one of those old-fashioned ones attached to an answering machine.

I dialed the police station. "Hello?" I said. "Anita?" Anita works the switchboard there. "This is Amy Simms." It was then that I noticed that every paperback on the floor had had its cover torn off.

"Good evening, Amy. How are you? How's Barb?" Anita and my mother were very good friends.

"Not so good," I said. I kept my eye on Rose, who stood near the professor's body, her arms limp at her sides. "I'm at Bookarama." I gnawed at my lip before saying, "There's been a murder."

"A murder? Are you sure?"

If she'd seen that pair of scissors jutting out of Mason Livingston's neck and the pool of blood dripping from the wound, she wouldn't have had to ask that question. "I'm sure."

"Are you okay, Amy? Are you hurt? In any danger?"

"I'm fine, Anita. I-I don't think I'm in any danger." I hoped that was true. Rose looked docile enough.

"What about the perp? Did you get a good look at him? Do you know where he went? Jerry's going want to know so he can issue an all-points."

"Yes, I got a look at them, and it's a her. And there's no need to send out an alert. It's Rose Smith, and she's right here."

"Amy!"

"It's okay, Anita."

"I'm going to dispatch the troops and an ambulance."

"Yes, I suppose you should." I glanced at Mason's lifeless form. The ambulance wasn't going to do the professor much good now, but at least he wouldn't be left lying in so undignified a fashion too much longer. "But not for me."

"Hold on and don't touch a thing," Anita said calmly. "I don't want you hanging up. I'll open up another line and call Jerry. He's at his lodge." She clicked her tongue. "He's not going to be happy."

And he wasn't.

"Confound it, Simms!" Jerry bellowed as he came strutting through Bookarama's front door. He was dressed in civilian clothes. "What the hell are you up to?" He cast a curious look at Rose.

Jerry is about my size with blond crew-cut hair that makes him look about twelve years old, a squat nose, freckles, and dark jade eyes. We'd dated once in high school. Once was enough.

Jerry claims he was born with his distinctive nose, but I think he was punched in it—not by a culprit but by a girl he had made a clumsy pass at in high school.

I told Anita the police had arrived and hung up the phone. "What's that supposed to mean, Jerry?" I'd tried to speak with Rose while we waited for Jerry and his force to show up, but she had refused my overtures.

The bookstore owner had taken a chair near the door with her back to Mason's body and not said a single word after stating, "We'll wait here quietly for the police, Amy." Then she had sat with her hands folded primly in her lap, remaining as quiet as a nesting wren.

"I mean, don't you have anything better to do than stick your nose in police business, Simms?" Chief Jerry Kennedy slapped his lodge cap against his thigh. The cap was a ratty-looking bit of brown leather and fur. "Sutton, Reynolds! Don't either of you touch anything until we get photos and prints."

Both officers promised to obey. Dan Sutton was speaking with Rose, who had remained seated in the last row of chairs. Her hands were still folded in her lap. Larry Reynolds began taking photographs of the crime scene with a fancy camera.

"Look, Jerry, Mason was a friend of mine. He was here at the bookstore for a signing of his latest book."

"What sort of book?"

"What does that matter?" When he ignored my question, I continued. "A book about hummingbirds."

Jerry snorted. "A book about hummingbirds? What for?"

"Yes, Jerry, a book about hummingbirds. Some people like them. We left our copies here at the store, and I came back for them."

"Who's we?"

"Mom, Derek, and I."

Jerry nodded. "Then what?"

"Then I came back by myself to pick up our books." I explained how the lights were on in back and the door was open. "So I came in."

"And saw the dead man."

"Not right away. As you can see, the screen hides the table. I didn't see him until I got closer."

"And you saw Mrs. Smith at that time?" Jerry eyed the bookstore owner.

"Pretty much."

"And she confessed to murdering the guy?"

I sighed. "Yes, pretty much." The question was why.

"Sutton!" hollered the chief. "Take Mrs. Smith down to HQ. Hold her until I get there."

Dan said a few words to Rose. She stood and complacently placed her hands behind her back. Officer Sutton pulled out a pair of cuffs and snapped them around her wrists.

Chief Kennedy and I stepped away from the door as Dan and his prisoner passed. "Are the cuffs really necessary?" I asked.

The corner of Jerry's mouth turned up. "Why don't you ask the dead man that question?" he quipped. "Oh, no, wait." He snapped his fingers. "You can't." Jerry stood on his tiptoes just so he could loom over me. "He's dead." The chief waved at his officer. "Take her away, Dan."

Jerry waved at me. "You can go, too, Simms. I'll call you if I need anything further."

"Can I have my books?"

He looked confused. I pointed to the table. Mason hadn't yet been moved by the waiting EMTs. "Evidence. You'll get your bird books back if and when I release them."

"Fine." I pushed open the door.

"Wait."

I wheeled around, tugging at the strap of my purse over my shoulder. "Yes?"

"What time did you get here?"

"About ten fifteen, I'd say. The signing was over just after nine. We went for ice cream, then returned to Birds and Bees." I nodded my head. "Yes, I'd say I arrived here just a little after ten."

Instead of thanking me for the information, Jerry shooed me away with his fingers.

I stifled the urge to give him a piece of my mind and walked to Derek's car. A voice from the shadows startled me.

"Hey!"

I turned. In the space between the buildings, a dark shape lurked. My blood froze. I glanced back at the bookstore. The sight of uniformed police moving purposefully about inside calmed my nerves to a degree, as did the flashing lights of their police cars outside.

I now noticed that Jerry had parked in the street, blocking me in. Great, now I'd have to ask him to move his vehicle.

"Hey!" A shadowy arm waved for me to come closer.

I remained where I was. "Can I help you?" I strained to see into the shadows. All I could make out was a tall, lean man in a short denim coat. His hair hung over his ears.

"What's going on in there?" There was a whispery, raspy tone to his voice, as if his vocal cords had been rubbed with sandpaper.

"There's been an accident," I said. I wasn't sure if I should say more. Especially to a stranger.

He bobbed his head, and his shoulders moved with it. "Yeah, accident." He took a couple of steps until he could see into the front of the store at an angle. "He's dead, isn't he?"

I swallowed hard. "You'd have to ask the police that. They're here, you know. I'm sure they'd like to talk to you." I turned my head toward the police cars in case there was any way he might have missed them. Their blinking lights lit up the quiet street. "Who are you, anyway? What are you—" I turned back to my mysterious visitor.

He was gone.

As more vehicles arrived, including Greeley's big black hearse—Andrew Greeley's the local mortician and medical examiner—I asked a passing officer if he would mind getting the chief to move his car so I could go home.

The sooner, the better. The police officer came back out from the bookstore a moment later jingling some keys and moved the car himself. I thanked him and headed for home, but not before checking the backseat for lurking passengers. I'd seen scary old movies before. I knew what to look for. Fortunately, I had no stray riders.

Back at Birds & Bees, I hurried inside—being certain to lock the door behind me—and up to our apartment. Derek was on the sofa, his stocking feet atop the coffee table, watching a movie as I burst in and bolted the door.

He straightened. "Where are the books?" His brow furrowed as he looked at me. "Everything okay, Amy? You look like you've seen a ghost."

"Worse," I answered, hanging my purse on a hook on the wall behind the door. I flopped down onto the couch beside him. "I saw a dead body."

"A dead—"

I grabbed his hand as if to hold on for dear life. "A dead body." I squeezed Derek's fingers so hard he yelped. "And it was Mason. Mason Livingston."

I didn't know if it was the thought of Mason dead or the memory of Rose Smith standing over the body and calmly declaring that she had murdered him or both, but I suddenly broke down in tears.

Derek wrapped his arms around me and let me cry.

After several minutes of nestling, I went to the bathroom for some tissues and to freshen up. When I returned, Derek had made us chamomile tea. I took a cup gratefully and snuggled up beside him once more.

"Are you ready to talk about it?" He melted a spoonful of honey from Quiles Apiary into each of our mugs.

"I think so," I said between sips.

He patted my knee. "Tell me what happened."

"When I got to the bookstore, the door was open. I called Rose. I didn't see anybody." I hesitated, collecting my thoughts. "When I got farther inside, I could see that Mason was seated alone at the table where he had been speaking and signing books. There was—" I swallowed hard. "There was a pair of scissors . . ." My hand went to my neck. Derek eyed me intently. "Sticking out of Mason's neck."

Derek flinched. "That's—" He struggled for words.

"Vicious?" I finished.

"Yeah," he said, running the tip of his tongue over his lips. "I was going to say terrible, but vicious says it all. If you had gone to the bookstore earlier, you might have been a victim, too." He held me tighter. "You didn't see Mason when you entered Bookarama?"

I shook my head. "No. I couldn't see the signing table because the projection screen was in the way. Somebody had moved it."

"That might not mean anything. It could have been moved as a first step in putting it away. Then again, it could have been meant to hide the body."

"That's what I was thinking."

"Where was Mrs. Smith?"

I folded my legs up underneath me. "That's the weird part. She came out of the storeroom lugging a big area rug."

"Did she appear surprised to see that Mason was dead?"

"No," I answered. "In fact, she told me that she killed him."

"What?" Derek stiffened.

"And that she was glad he was dead." I let the words sink in.

Derek drank his tea. "I don't get it," he said finally. We both followed the action on the silent TV. Derek had muted the sound. Men and women danced gaily on the screen in all their black-and-white glory. Derek knew how I loved my musicals, and this was a Busby Berkeley extravaganza called "Dance Until the Dawn" from the 1931 musical *Flying High*.

"Do you think you could go down to the police station tomorrow?" I asked.

"What for?"

"To talk to Rose. Find out what's going on. Maybe you can help her."

"Help her?" Derek shook his head. "The woman's apparently admitted to cold-blooded murder. I am not a criminal defense attorney, Amy."

"Maybe she didn't do it," I countered. "Or maybe there were extenuating circumstances."

"Like what?"

I didn't know and said so. "Just go see her?" I planted a kiss on his chin. "Please?"

Derek frowned, and I knew I had him. "Fine." He kissed me back. "But you owe me."

"Don't worry," I replied. "I always pay my debts."

6

I filled Mom in on the murder over breakfast.

"I'm not sure I can even eat." Mom added a dollop of dark brown sugar to the oatmeal in the saucepan, then served it up.

I carried the coffee carafe to the table. It had rained in the middle of the night, but the sun was up bright and hot this morning. Steam rose off the nearby rooftops. "I know what you mean." I added some slivers of almonds and a handful of dried cranberries to my bowl. Mom enjoys her oatmeal plain.

"You must be feeling terrible this morning, Amy."

"I've slept better." The dark rings under my eyes were a testament to that.

"Why would Rose want to kill your friend Mason?"

"That's what I'd like to know. I asked Derek to stop by the police station this morning. Maybe she'll talk to him."

"Maybe," Mom agreed. "I wonder how her daughter is holding up."

I stopped, a spoonful of oatmeal halfway to my mouth. "Oh, my gosh. I hadn't even thought about Amber." My free hand flew to my mouth. "I can't imagine what's going through her mind. A man murdered in her store. Her mother in jail."

"We should prepare a basket of food and take it to her."

"That's a good idea," I said. When someone was down, Mom took them food. When they were dead, Mom sent flowers to their family. "Do you know where Amber lives?"

Mom pursed her lips. "I'm not sure. I believe she has an apartment near the shop. Rose lives above the bookstore."

There was a loud knock at the door. "I'll get it." I opened the door. "Amber? Mom and I were just talking about you!"

Amber Smith stood in the doorway. Her blue jeans and T-shirt were caked with dried mud. Her face was smudged, and her hair looked like she'd just rolled down a mountain. "Hello, Ms. Simms." She tugged helplessly at her mud-caked blond locks. "I hope you don't mind my coming up. The lady downstairs said it was okay."

I stepped aside. "That would be Esther." Sure, she complained every time she saw Derek come up to the third floor, but a muddied stranger was no problem. "It's fine. Come on in." I noticed her face looked drawn and her blue eyes were rimmed in red. There was dirt under her fingernails.

"Thanks." She slipped off her shoes, which were equally damp and dirty, and left them on the mat outside the door.

"I suppose you heard what happened last night..." My voice trailed off.

Amber nodded and bit her lower lip.

"Hello, Amber." There was a note of tenderness in my mother's voice. Mom came forward and gave Amber a squeeze of affection, despite the young woman's appearance and the grime on her clothes. "How are you holding up, dear?"

"Okay, I guess." Amber sniffed and rubbed her nose with the back of her hand.

We both refrained from asking Amber why she looked as bad as she did. The young woman had been through enough for one night.

"Would you care for a cup of coffee?" I asked, leading the way to the kitchen table.

"Yes, thank you."

I offered Amber a chair, and she sat with her back to the fridge. Mom cleared the breakfast dishes and rinsed them in the sink while I poured Amber a fresh cup of coffee. "Cream or sugar?"

"No, thank you." Amber cradled the cup in her hands.

"Honey?" I pushed the jar of Quiles toward her, but she shook her head. "How about something to eat?"

Her eyes lit up for the first time since arriving. "I am a little hungry."

I offered her a choice of cereal, both hot and cold, and sourdough toast. There was little else available.

"I need to go down and get to work," Mom said, hanging her apron over the handle of the oven door. "If I'm late, the boss gets on my case."

I grinned. "Sounds like you've got a smart boss."

Mom smiled back. "She's got a smart mouth, that's for sure." She gave me a peck on the cheek and squeezed Amber's shoulder. "Let me know if there's anything you need, you hear?"

"I will," promised Amber, her voice low.

Amber settled on a couple slices of sourdough bread with peanut butter and jelly. I dropped the loaf on the table and carried over a plate and the jar of peanut butter. I grabbed the strawberry jam from the fridge. "I'm afraid strawberry is all we've got."

"That's perfect," said Amber, pulling the tie off the plastic surrounding the loaf.

I watched while she slathered on the peanut butter and jelly then wolfed down her sandwich. After what she'd been through, I didn't know if I could have eaten a thing. But each person handled adversity in their own way.

"Mom says you have an apartment near downtown."

"I did." She folded her hands in her lap. "I did have an apartment. I live with Mama now."

I smiled. "Hey, just like me. People tease me now and then, but I love it."

"Me too." Her finger played with the handle of her cup. "I heard that you were the one who found Professor Livingston dead." She eyed me timidly.

"Yes. So you know everything?"

She nodded.

I refilled our mugs and took a seat. "How did you hear?"

"It was on the radio."

"If you don't mind my asking, Amber, where were you last night when . . ." My voice trailed off, unsure how to frame the rest of that sentence.

"I was out."

"You weren't upstairs from the bookstore when it happened?"

She shook her head. "No. I went camping down by the lake."

"Camping?"

Amber nodded. "I like to do that sometimes. Just to get away. Lie out under the stars and enjoy the night sounds."

That explained her appearance. "So you didn't even know about the murder until this morning?"

"That's right." Amber sighed deeply. "I was sitting at a picnic table near the lake. Some campers had a radio on." She shivered. "At first, I couldn't believe it. First, that the professor was dead. And then . . .

and then when the woman on the radio said that my mother had admitted to killing him . . ." She shook herself again. "I couldn't believe it."

Amber reached across the table for my hands. "You've got to help me, Amy. Mama couldn't possibly have killed him. It's inconceivable!"

"I don't know what I can do, Amber." She looked at me with big, hope-filled eyes. "But I'll do whatever I can to help," I answered sincerely. "Have the police told you anything?"

"I haven't spoken with the police yet."

"Then you haven't talked to your mother either?"

"No." The beginnings of a tear formed in the inner corner of Amber's right eye.

"Amber, do you have any idea why your mother might have done this? Could it have been self-defense? Might Mason and your mother have had an argument of some kind?" Something that would lead to rage and murder, as impossible as it would have seemed.

"I-I can't imagine." Her voice was soft and plaintive as a hungry baby songbird's.

"Neither can I." Though I only knew Rose casually, she seemed sweet and harmless. And Mason, while he had his quirks, had never so much as raised his voice in all the time I'd known him. "Are there any security cameras in the bookstore? Maybe they could tell us something."

Amber shook her head. "We don't have anything fancy like that. There's never been any need."

I understood and said so. I didn't have security cameras in my store either. The only thievery I had to suffer was Jerry Kennedy constantly helping himself to the peanuts in the bin at the front of the store. "You need to go talk to the police. And see your mother. I'm sure she's very concerned about you. I asked my friend, Derek, to go down to the police station this morning. He may have been there already."

"Mr. Harlan? An older man with black hair with some silver in it? I've seen him in our store. He buys a lot of legal thrillers."

I shook my head. "No, that's Ben Harlan, Derek's father. They're both lawyers. And good friends. Now," I said, rising from the table, "why don't you go get yourself washed up and change clothes and go see your mother? She must be scared stiff."

Amber rose and took her plate and cup to the sink. "I'll do that."

She turned to me suddenly. "Do you think the police will let me in the house?"

"Oh. I hadn't thought of that." With the Smiths living upstairs from the bookstore, would the entire building be off limits?

"In fact, now that I think about it, I wonder if we'll even be able to open the bookstore today. I'll have to let the others know."

"Others?"

"Our staff."

"Do you have much staff?"

"Only a couple of part-timers. A high school girl and a woman who's retired from the library."

"You could get cleaned up here, if you'd like. Then give them a call. Use my phone." I looked her up and down. "We're about the same size. You could borrow some clothes."

Amber plucked at her muddy nylon jacket. "No, thank you. I'm sure the police will let me into the apartment. It's not like anything happened there. Besides, if they don't, I can borrow something from one of my friends." She started for the door.

"If you're sure—"

"I'm sure." Amber opened the door and slipped into her shoes.

"Can I give you a lift?"

"No, thanks. I've got my bicycle downstairs."

"Okay. I'll walk you out."

"You don't have to bother, Ms. Simms."

"It's Amy. And I was going that way anyway." We went down the steps together. Esther gave us a funny look and opened her mouth to speak, but Mom drew her attention away by asking Esther to give her a hand in the storeroom.

I pulled open the front door. "I'm sure everything will sort itself out, Amber. Please, see your mother as soon as you can."

Amber nodded and picked up a unisex bicycle that leaned against the wall on the porch. The teal bicycle also looked like it had been through a mud storm.

She pushed the bicycle down the path to the sidewalk and climbed on. A sleeping roll and a small knapsack were strapped to a carrier over the rear tire.

"And don't judge your mother too harshly!" I shouted as her feet pushed down on the pedals.

She turned her head in my direction, looking quite serious as she said, "I won't, Amy. Believe you me, I won't."

Back inside the shop, I dialed Derek's cell phone to see if he had paid a visit yet to Rose Smith. I got his voicemail, and my call to his office was answered by his secretary, who said she had no idea where he was. Ben Harlan was in conference with a client, so he couldn't help me either.

As soon as I could get away from the store, I went to Professor Livingston's trailer to poke around. Maybe there was something in his camper that would give me a clue as to why Rose Smith would have wanted him dead.

The first thing I noticed were the eggs. Hands on my hips, I gaped up at the giant birdhouse or tiny house or whatever Mason might have called it besides "the best little birdhouse in Texas."

"I know this is supposed to be a birdhouse, but aren't the eggs supposed to be on the inside?" I muttered.

The outside of Mason's birdhouse was splattered with broken eggs, all around the sides and up on the peaked roof. Mason's un-hitched red pickup truck appeared unscathed.

I examined his pickup truck first. The front seat of the pickup was littered with old newspapers, magazines, and fast-food wrappers and cups. The bed of the pickup was empty.

I turned my attention to the egged trailer. Balancing on my tip-toes, I peeped in one of the tiny house's windows. Nothing looked much different than it had when I'd found the professor dozing yesterday.

I walked around to the rear and jiggled the door handle. The couple I'd spoken with briefly outside their motorhome the other evening had set out a couple of chairs in the grass and were reading quietly.

I waved and walked over. "Good morning," I began. "Any idea who did that?" I looked pointedly at the egg-spattered house. The yellow yolk and bits of white eggshell contrasted vividly with the bright red paint job.

"Not a clue," said the man, looking up from his book.

"We're just glad they didn't egg us." The woman petted the collie at her feet.

"Yeah, that's going to be near impossible to wash off. If that fella's a friend of yours, you'd better tell him to get to cleaning it up before the sun bakes it on but good."

"Haven't you heard?" I asked.

"Heard what?" asked the woman.

"The owner was, well, he was murdered yesterday."

The woman's book fell from her hands to her feet. The collie bounced around it and barked once. "In there?" She appeared uneasy.

"No. In town."

The woman turned to her husband. "I'm not so sure this town is safe, dear."

He nodded. "It might be time to move on."

"I'm sure you don't have anything to worry about. I didn't mean to alarm you." I turned my attention back to the professor's eccentric camper. "You didn't see anybody hanging around, I suppose?"

Both shook their heads. "No," answered the man. "And whoever egged the place must've done it after we turned in last night."

The wife agreed. "We would have noticed. Believe me."

I thanked them for their time and explained once more that the camper's owner had been a friend of mine. "I came by to collect his things," I said, hoping that my excuse, vague as it was, sounded plausible. I did not want them reporting me to the campground's management or calling the police on me. I returned to the professor's home away from home.

The door was unlocked, so I ascended the stairs and pulled it open.

7

It was no fun stepping inside a dead man's home—albeit his traveling one—especially when that man was only very recently dead and had been a friend. More than dead, this was no simple heart attack; Mason had been stabbed savagely, his life taken from him way too soon. He'd only been in his fifties. That was far too young to die. What had possessed the bookseller to kill him and in so brutal a fashion?

Scrutinizing the tight space, I could see that Mason was clearly not a neat and tidy sort of man when it came to his housekeeping habits. Funny, because he had always taken such care with his personal appearance.

The narrow bed was at the far end of the trailer. There was a small kitchenette built in on the right side, across from the tiny bathroom. Clothes and personal items were strewn around or tucked away in any available cubby. There were also plenty of books. It was no surprise that most were about birds.

I lifted a well-worn copy of *Hummingbirds and Their Habits* and flipped through it. I didn't know if I'd ever get back the copy Derek had bought for me or if Mason had even had the chance to sign it for me. Why had he asked Rose to bring him a new one the night he spoke to our group?

Several pages contained highlighted text or circled passages. The professor had probably used the personal copy in preparing notes for his talks. A black laptop computer, several dirty paper plates, and a mug sat atop the small fold-out table that appeared to have served as his dining table and work desk.

A stack of mail lay on the floor beside the bed. I flipped through the pile—a few magazines, a couple of bills, and various letters, including one from Frank Duvall, a local businessman. I remembered seeing him at our last Birds and Brews meeting and later at the bookstore for the professor's book signing. I could not remember if the two men had spoken to each other at either event. All the pieces of mail had been addressed to Mason via a post office box address in Texas.

A phone number with a local area code had been scribbled in pencil on the back of another of the envelopes. I made a note of the number on my cell phone, curious as to who Mason might have been calling. It wasn't my number. I didn't think it was the number of the bookstore, but I'd check. Mason hadn't mentioned knowing anyone else in Ruby Lake.

I opened the letter from Frank Duvall and began reading. I knew little about Mr. Duvall, but from the Duvall's Flower Farm letterhead, it was clear what he did for a living. I also saw that the telephone number scrawled on the outside of the other envelope was not the number for the flower farm.

I read further. The grower had contacted the professor concerning a flower he had developed. Duvall was looking for Mason's endorsement in taking the plant to market. That was interesting. Why hadn't Mason mentioned it? Was it all hush-hush, or had he merely considered it unimportant and unworthy of his time?

I returned the letter to the envelope and the envelope to the pile. As I did, my eyes caught a glint of something shiny between the mattress and the wall. I dropped to my knees and pried it out. It was a woman's mini makeup kit. I turned it over in my hand. Apparently Mason had had company at some point. In our correspondence before his arrival, the professor had said that he was separated from his wife. I flipped open the cover. The kit held several shades of concealer, blush, eye shadow, and two tiny brushes. The makeup kit could have belonged to anyone—and it could have lain hidden there for any amount of time, from last year to last night. Did it belong to Rose Smith, perhaps?

I slipped the small makeup kit in my pocket and left.

I returned to Birds & Bees but didn't go inside. I wanted to see if Derek had returned to his office yet so I could ask him whether he'd gone down to the police station as promised. If he had, I wanted to learn if the police had allowed him to see Rose Smith and what she might have said.

I found a parking spot directly in front of Harlan and Harlan, the law practice Derek shared with his father. Through the window, I saw Ben sitting behind his desk, reading something on his computer monitor.

It was what I saw on the sign above the display window next door on the left that took me aback. Soft pink letters against the white brick building read DREAM GOWNS.

Derek had told me that his ex, the other Amy, was planning to open a bridal salon with some of her friends. I'd been hoping that meant somewhere far away, like Charlotte or Raleigh. Los Angeles would be nice. But here? Next door to Derek's office? Not to mention, he lived in a one-bedroom apartment over the law offices.

That wouldn't be a dream. That would be a nightmare.

I told myself not to panic as I shut off the van's engine and popped open my door. After all, just because a bridal salon was opening next to Derek's place of business didn't mean he knew the owner—or had once been married to her.

The front door of the salon opened, and a man in a brown suit stepped out, holding the door open with his back and clutching a big cardboard box. He turned as he came out and headed up the sidewalk.

"Derek?" I joined him on the sidewalk.

Derek lowered the box in his arms. "Amy!" His cheeks were red. "I wasn't expecting you."

"I can see that. I can also see that you're busy." I eyed the box. "Moving in or moving out?" I looked from him to the ghastly pink signage on the building next door.

He cleared his throat. "Actually, I was just lending, uh . . ."

"Your ex-wife, Amy?" I said when he seemed determined not to finish.

"Yes." He set the box on the ground and tugged at his shirt collar. "She asked me to give her a hand. I was helping her move a few things." He leaned forward and kissed my cheek. "How have you been? How are you holding up?"

"Fine," I said. "I wanted to ask you what you'd learned about Mason's murder and find out if Jerry let you talk to Rose. But if you're busy . . ."

"No," Derek grabbed my wrist. "Not busy at all." He retrieved the box from the sidewalk. "Let me take this around back. Maybe we can go get some lunch and talk there?"

I arched my brow. "Talking sounds like a good idea." It sounded like a very good idea.

Derek glanced guiltily up at the new store's sign. Two lovely gowns, one white and the other blush with lace appliques, stood in the front window. Amy the Ex was nowhere to be seen, not that I was complaining. "Great, wait for me in the office. I'll be right back."

I went inside the offices of Harlan and Harlan. The receptionist-slash-secretary was nowhere to be found. Ben was on the phone, so I simply stuck my head in the door and waved hello. I sat in the visitor's chair near the door, and Derek returned a couple of minutes later with his hands free.

"Let me grab my keys and we can go." He started up the hall toward his office in the back. "Some Southern comfort food okay with you?" he called.

I said it was, and he turned around. "I guess I don't need my car keys then. We can hit Jessamine's Kitchen."

"Jessamine's Kitchen? I'm game," I said, having never been.

"Trust me," said Derek, holding the office door open for me. "They've only been open a couple of weeks, but I've been a few times already. They're convenient, and the food's great."

We crossed the busy town square to the restaurant and were seated immediately. As the waiter filled our water glasses, I looked Derek in the eye. "I've been looking for you all morning. You're a hard one to pin down."

"Sorry." Derek massaged his temples. "I've been putting out fires all day."

"Like your ex?" I smiled at him. "Sorry, it's none of my business."

"Trust me, I'd rather she opened up across town," Derek said with a heartfelt sigh. "And she was all set to. Then Robert LaChance offered her and her partners a great deal on the space next to mine, and as Amy, my ex, says, it was just too good to pass up."

So Robert LaChance was the reason that Derek's ex was opening a business right next door to his law office. Wasn't that interesting? My fingertips drummed the tabletop as Derek ordered the grilled okra appetizer for us to share.

Robert and I had had our differences. He had tried to get the better of me on more than one occasion. Heck, he'd tried to put me out of business. I knew he owned several properties around town in addition to his car dealership. He'd even tried to get me to move out of my current house and into one his properties. Was it a coincidence that Derek's ex had ended up in one of his buildings, or had he done it to annoy me?

"You okay, Amy?" Derek had caught the curious expression on my face.

I didn't want to bother Derek with my insecurities and possibly misplaced suspicions, so I determined not to let our discussion go there. "Yes, just thinking." I grinned. "I'm afraid that happens once in a while." The waiter returned with a shallow bowl of grilled okra and a lemon-basil dipping sauce. I dipped a piece of okra in the bowl and tasted it. "This is delicious."

"I told you."

I grabbed a second pod and scooped up some more sauce. I'd stop at three. I was counting my calories. "Did you get a chance to speak with Rose Smith?"

"Yes. Sort of."

"Sort of?"

The waiter interrupted before Derek could explain. I ordered the pecan, cranberry, and turkey salad and Derek the shrimp and grits.

"She didn't want to talk to me," Derek explained.

"Didn't want to, or Jerry wouldn't let you?"

"Chief Kennedy seemed fine with it. He said he wasn't getting much out of Mrs. Smith himself."

"He wasn't upset that you were interfering with police business by going down there?" If it had been me, he would have told me to mind my own business.

"Nope. Besides, I was down at the police station to see a client anyway."

"Oh?"

"Yeah." Derek paused as our lunches were served. "Thanks," he said, picking up his napkin and draping it across his lap. He picked up his fork. "I had to bail out Packard Mulligan."

I leaned back against my chair. "Wow. Pack Mulligan. That's a name I haven't heard in a long time."

"You know him?" Derek shoved a forkful of shrimp-covered grits into his mouth.

"Not really," I said. "His family lived on the outskirts of town. I had a friend who lived out that way on a small farm. We used to play out there sometimes after school and in the summer." I grinned at the memory. "We were all scared of Pack back then."

"Scared how?"

I shrugged. "You know how kids can be. Pack was several years older than us. His family kept to themselves. We thought they were all hooligans, thieves, and cutthroats."

Derek chuckled. "Unfortunately, that still seems to be the general opinion around town."

"Small towns can have long memories," I said.

"Are you saying he or his family had some history of trouble with the town? Because I haven't found any legal history to speak of."

"No, nothing that I know of. All rumors and innuendo."

"Such as?"

"You'll laugh when I tell you this . . ."

"I could use a good laugh."

"Kids used to say that he murdered his own father and put his preserved corpse on display in the parlor."

Derek laughed.

"I know, it sounds silly now." But back then we had considered the possibility.

"Please don't spread stories like that around." Derek buttered a biscuit. "Innuendo and rumors are what's got Packard Mulligan into trouble this time."

"Can I ask what he's done or is accused of having done?"

"I don't think he'd mind. Besides, it's public record. There has been a string of home robberies, plus a few shops around the downtown area have reported things missing. Nothing serious. Small items taken when folks are out during the day. Store owners say whoever the perpetrator or perpetrators are, they're coming in through the rear entrances."

Derek patted my hand. "You should do like the police have suggested to the business owners and keep your back door locked during the day."

"I'll try to remember that."

Derek continued. "The chief says Mister Mulligan has been accused of all kinds of petty theft over the years, including stealing chickens, but nothing that's ever amounted to anything. He's never even been held over for trial."

"Stealing chickens? As I recall, the Mulligans had a good-sized chicken coop of their own."

"So I hear. And you know what Packard Mulligan said when I asked him about that?"

"What?"

"He said he doesn't even eat chicken, only beef and pork."

I couldn't help chuckling. "Why lock up Pack now?"

"The chief said somebody saw Mister Mulligan near one of the downtown shops that was robbed about two days ago."

"Does he have any evidence? Was Pack caught with anything taken from the houses or stores?"

"Not a thing. Pack was taken to the station in the morning and is now back home. He was very cooperative, in fact."

"It sounds to me like Jerry shouldn't have locked him up in the first place."

"He was only doing his job. Keeping the good citizens of the Town of Ruby Lake happy can be a big part of that."

"I suppose. What does Pack do to provide for himself?"

"Mister Mulligan is an egg farmer. He runs a stand down at the farmer's market. Sells direct to some of the regional mom-and-pop stores."

"That figures." After that, the conversation shifted to topics more idyllic.

We finished our lunch and Derek called for the check. "Sorry I can't linger. Duty calls."

"Same here." I needed to get back to the store. "It's too bad you weren't able to chat with Rose. You know, her daughter came by the apartment this morning."

"Amber?"

I nodded.

"What did she want?"

"Mostly I think somebody to talk to. She's really shaken up by this whole thing."

"Of course. Nobody wants to think of their mother as a murderer."

8

"What are you doing here?" Kim asked the minute I stepped through the back door of Birds & Bees. She was sitting on a stool in the corner of the storeroom sorting through a box of birding and gardening books that had come in.

I hadn't ordered any copies of Mason's book out of respect for Rose's book signing. I didn't want to cut into her sales. I had thought I would stock *Hummingbirds and Their Habits* afterward. Now I wasn't so sure I wanted the book—a sad and gruesome reminder of the professor's ugly end—on our shelves.

"It's my place of business," I quipped. "Where else should I be?" I headed upfront and tossed my purse under the sales counter.

Kim followed me. "At the police station, making your official statement like you're supposed to be." Kim shook her head as if disgusted with me.

I frowned. "Supposed to be? Jerry told me he'd call me when he was ready for me to come in." I folded my arms across my chest. "He hasn't phoned me yet."

"Uh-oh." Kim's hand went to her mouth.

"Uh-oh what?"

"Uh-oh, Larry told Dan, and Dan told me . . ." Kim and Dan had started seeing each other socially. Nothing serious yet, as far as I could tell, but there appeared to be some sparks. Kim pointed her finger my way. "And I was supposed to tell you . . ."

I closed my eyes and counted to ten. "So now the chief of police thinks I'm playing hard to get. He's probably fuming and cussing me out six ways to sundown."

Kim smiled weakly. "Probably."

I snatched my purse from behind the counter and headed for the back door and my van. "If anybody's looking for me, you know where to find me!"

As I expected, Jerry was happy to see me but annoyed that I was late.

Jerry sat toward the back with his feet on his desk. "You took your own sweet time getting here, Simms."

"Sorry." I shot a look-what-you've-done-to-me-now expression at Sutton and Reynolds, who were practically cowering in the opposite corner of the police station.

Jerry dropped his feet to the floor. "Come on over here and let me get your statement." A ratty tweed suitcase sat at the side of his desk.

"Going somewhere?"

"Huh?"

I pointed to the suitcase.

"Never mind that," he snapped. "It belonged to the victim."

"Sorry I asked." I took a seat across from him. "Have you spoken to Mason's wife and family? The university where he teaches? Everybody must be in shock."

"We're handling it, Simms. It's our job. Your job is to answer my questions."

I crossed my legs. My right foot jiggled of its own accord. "What do you want to know?"

"I want to know exactly," he reached for a pencil and pointed the sharp end at me, "*exactly* what you saw and what you heard over at Bookarama." His eyes bored into mine. "Before *and* after the murder." He tapped his notebook against the desktop and wriggled his fingers in a come hither fashion. "Go ahead and start." He reached over and hit the Record button on a small digital recorder that he slid toward me.

"Give me a minute," I replied, shutting my eyes and trying to recall everything I'd seen and heard. "This isn't easy. I mean, I wasn't expecting to have to remember anything in particular. I couldn't know there was going to be a murder."

Jerry eyed me impatiently. "Come on, Simms. I haven't got all day."

I rubbed my temples. "What about Rose? What's she told you? Anything?" I glanced toward the hall. I couldn't see the cells from where I sat, but I knew where they were. I knew exactly where they were. I'd been in one of them—briefly, but it still gave me sweats whenever I thought of it.

"She ain't here."

I cocked my head. "She isn't? Where is she? County lockup?"

Jerry sighed. "You're sorely trying my patience, Simms." He rolled the pencil over his desk. "If you must know, we let her go."

I straightened. "You let her go? Why?"

"Because she has an alibi, that's why."

"Alibi? But I saw her kill Mason."

"What?" Jerry leaned closer.

"Well, I didn't see her do it exactly." I turned to Officers Sutton and Reynolds for support, even though I knew none would be forthcoming. "Jerry, Rose admitted to killing Mason. I told you that. She said she killed him and that she was glad. Glad he was dead." I shook my head in disbelief. "And you let her go? What was her alibi? What did Rose say?"

"Rose is saying nothing. Refuses to talk. Period." Jerry was clearly disgusted. "No matter. I know for a fact she was talking to John Moytoy at the time of the killing."

"From the library?" I knew John. He was a friend of mine. "But he's out of town. He couldn't possibly—"

"Will you stop running off at the mouth?" The chief gripped his skull. "You're giving me a headache. He's back now, and he says she was on some video chat thing with him. They use their computers to talk to one another."

"That doesn't make sense. She must have killed him before or after talking to John."

"We have a time of death, Simms. A bunch of folks stuck around after the signing for snacks and refreshments. Afterward," he dug unsuccessfully through a stack of papers, "around ten, Livingston was on his cell phone with his attorney in Houston.

"According to Mister Castillo—that's the attorney—they were on the phone when your professor friend shouted, sounded scared. A minute later—" Jerry snapped his fingers, "the line went dead. Mister Castillo says he tried calling back and got no answer. Livingston's phone log backs that story up.

"And Rose was talking to Mister Moytoy at that exact time. Now," the chief said, perhaps feeling like he'd shared too much and clearly determined to take control of the conversation, "tell me what you saw, who you saw, and every little thing in between."

I know I talked, and I suppose some of what I said made sense, but I couldn't remember a word of it afterward. All I could think about was how I had seen Rose Smith standing over Mason Livingston calmly professing to having murdered him.

And now she was free.

Before I knew it, I was free to go, too. I rose and started for the door. I wanted to have a word with Dan Sutton, but it would have to wait until we were out of his boss's earshot.

"Just a second, Amy." Chief Kennedy swaggered toward me at the front of the station.

Amy? It wasn't often that Jerry called me by my first name. "Yes?" I asked.

He fidgeted in the doorway, his hands on his black leather belt. "You know the wife."

"Sandra? Yes, of course. What about her?"

"Well, she's got this silly idea in her head that she wants to renew our wedding vows." He looked like he'd bit into a lemon.

"Really? How fun." Though I often wondered what she saw in Jerry Kennedy, I realize it takes two to make a pair, and Jerry did adore her. "That's a wonderful idea. What made the two of you decide to do it now?"

"I don't know about wonderful." He turned a quieting gaze on Sutton and Reynolds, who were snickering at their desks. "But I know what got the idea in her head. It's that new wedding dress store opening up on Main."

I couldn't help smiling. "You mean Dream Gowns?"

"That's the place."

"Why are you telling me all this, Jerry? Do I get to be a bridesmaid? Walk you down the aisle, perhaps?" I winked at Sutton and Reynolds, who were trying with little success to smother their laughter with their hands over their mouths.

"Very funny. I was wondering . . ."

"Yes?"

"Maybe you can get me and Sandra a discount on the wedding gown. Darn things are crazy expensive. And seeing how you're friends with Amy Harlan—"

My brow shot up. "Friends with Amy Harlan?! Believe me, Jerry." I dug in my purse for the keys to my van. "It would be a big stretch to call me and Derek's ex friends."

Jerry was clearly disappointed.

"Fine," I said, knowing I'd regret my words. "I'll ask." I waggled my finger at him. "But that's all I'm going to do. No promises."

"Thanks, Amy. I'll let Sandra know. She'll be tickled." He rested a hand on my shoulder. "In fact, it wouldn't surprise me none if she did ask you to be one of her bridesmaids."

Oh, great. I pictured a horrible, ill-fitting, eggplant-colored bridesmaid dress in my future. "Now that I've done you a favor, how about doing a little one for me?"

"Such as?" Jerry asked, eyes narrowing.

"Such as telling me if you have any other suspects in Mason Livingston's death?"

Jerry beamed. "Oh, I've got me a real good one."

"Do you mind telling me who?"

Jerry remained silent a moment, toying with me, no doubt. "Amber Smith."

"Rose's daughter? But she couldn't have done it. She was camping out by the lake last night."

Jerry cleared his throat. "Amber Smith was also in attendance at the book signing and reception. And the security camera over at Lakeside Market's got her on tape buying two cartons of eggs."

"So? People do eat eggs, Jerry."

"Yeah, but did you know that your professor friend's birdhouse-camper thingamajig was egged last night?"

Yes, I did know, but thought it best not to admit it. "Really? Why would Amber want to egg Mason's trailer?"

"That's what I'd like to know," answered Jerry. "I've invited Amber down to the station to tell me."

9

"Why would she lie?" I asked Kim later that evening as we sipped glasses of white wine in my apartment.

"You've got me," Kim replied, sloshing her wine around. "Maybe Rose was covering for somebody." She gulped and swallowed. "Maybe she's nuts."

I leaned forward and set my glass on the coffee table. I sat on the sofa, and Kim was in my dad's favorite old chair. Mom and I had never been able to let the chair go. We never would. The way Kim was waving her glass around, Dad's chair was likely to get a soaking.

"Who would she be covering for? Amber?" I asked.

"Who's Amber again?"

"Rose's daughter."

Kim nodded sagely. "Bingo."

"Jerry considers her his number-one suspect." I explained how Amber had been caught on security camera videotape purchasing eggs at Lakeside Market sometime after Mason's death. "And Mason's trailer house had been heavily egged."

"Two dozen eggs?" Kim chuckled. "Yeah, I'd call that heavy. Sorry. But it does sound rather childish."

"I agree. But Amber is past the teenage stage. She must be twenty at least. Besides, throwing eggs at somebody's place doesn't sound like the act of someone who's just committed murder."

"Maybe," Kim said.

I shook my head. "But why?"

"You mean why cover for Amber, or why would Amber want to murder your old college professor?"

"Both," I answered with a frown. Kim held out the wine bottle, and I didn't say no to a refill. It had been a long day. "I can see why Rose might want to cover for her daughter if she thought Amber had stabbed Mason."

"It's only natural, I suppose," agreed Kim.

"What I don't get," I said, "is where was Mason the day before he was killed? Where did he go? Who did he see? He lied to me about having interviews and appointments arranged for the day. And he lied to me about having a dinner scheduled that evening with a newspaper editor from Charlotte."

"Why did he lie to you about it?" asked Kim. "Do you think he had something to hide?"

I could only shrug. "I can't think of any other good reason for the lies. Can you?"

Kim said she couldn't.

"That still leaves one big question. If Amber really did kill Mason, why? Why would Amber want him dead?"

The room was silent as we each gave this some thought. Unfortunately, neither of us could come up with an answer, at least not one that made sense. When Kim suggested that perhaps Amber's mind had been taken over by a superior alien race that was bent on collecting samples of ornithologist Earthlings, we called it a night.

The following morning after breakfast, I left Kim and Mom in charge of the store and stopped at the public library. I pinned down John Moytoy in the biography section.

"Good morning, Amy." He slid a thick book about Lady Bird Johnson back on the shelf. "How are you? How's business?"

"I'm good, and business is chugging—or should I say chirping?— right along. How was your trip to Asheville?" I rubbed my nostrils with the back of my finger. The dust rising from the shelves tickled my nose.

"Nice so far as library meetings go." John is of the Cherokee tribe, and his family has lived in the Carolinas for generations. He was an old classmate of mine and seemed unchanging, ever cherubic in body and disposition. His hair remained jet-black, while several gray hairs had already crept into mine. Life could be so unfair. "We didn't exactly turn Asheville on its head with our late-night revelry."

"There's always next year, John." I motioned John to follow me to a study table by the window. "I hear that you were Rose Smith's alibi in Mason Livingston's murder."

John nodded somberly. "That's right. I'm so sorry." He pulled off his glasses, wiped them on his sleeve, then returned them to his nose. "I know he was a friend of yours."

"Thanks. I'm still trying to process Mason being gone. It seems so impossible."

"I know, but Rose couldn't have done it. Like I explained to Chief Kennedy, Rose and I were video chatting at the time it appears Professor Livingston was murdered. Heck, I could barely get a word in edgewise. She couldn't have done it."

"Why do you suppose she would say she did then?"

"I don't have a clue. You wouldn't catch me admitting to murdering somebody, especially when I hadn't."

"Would you mind telling me what the two of you were talking about, John? I didn't even know you were friends."

John shrugged and pulled up a chair. I joined him. "Sure, Rose and me go way back. It's no secret what we were talking about, so I don't see the harm. We were talking about Mason Livingston."

"Oh?" Alarms went off in my head.

John smiled. "Relax, nothing nefarious. I knew I was going to be out of town for the book signing, and Rose knew how much I regretted that I couldn't be there. I'm always eager to meet authors. We don't get many of them passing through Ruby Lake. I made Rose promise to have him autograph a copy of his book for me and a second one for the library collection and to fill me in the minute the event was over."

He shrugged. "And she did. Rose sounded so happy. She said the signing had been a huge success. They sold dozens of books, and the professor signed them all, including yours." John paused in his thoughts. "Who could have imagined that it all would have ended so tragically afterward?"

I sighed heavily, drawing an angry stare from a nearby patron. I lowered my voice to a whisper. "How did you hear about the murder?"

John replied, "Jill Church told me."

"The librarian?"

"Former librarian," John said. "After she retired, she got a job working part time at Bookarama. She says once books get in your blood, you can never get them out."

What John said about Jill Church made sense. I remembered Amber telling me that one of the part-timers used to work in a library.

"When she told me Professor Livingston was dead and that Rose Smith had done the deed, I rushed right back." He scratched his head. "I mean, I couldn't believe it. I had to tell the police what I knew."

"What about Rose? Were you able to talk to her and ask her why she'd said such a thing?"

John shook his head. "I tried. Chief Kennedy told me she was refusing to see anyone, even a lawyer."

I left John to his library duties and headed out to Rolling Acres, a senior living facility on the other end of Ruby Lake. I had made several friends at the retirement home since returning to town. Many attended my occasional bird-watching hikes. Some also showed up for our monthly Birds and Brews gatherings at Brewer's Biergarten.

Birds & Bees had also started a Seeds for Seniors program. We supplied birdfeeders and seed to several senior facilities in the region, and I hoped to make it more. I had a bag of mixed seed in the back of the van. I parked in front of Karl Vogel's bungalow, thankful that I didn't need to go through the reception area of the main building. The woman in there had a dim view of me, and I wasn't sure why.

I was about to ring the bell on Karl's bungalow door when I heard him wheezing out on his deck. I left the bag of seed on the mat and went around to the patio.

"Hello, Karl. What are you doing?" I asked, looking over the gate.

Karl sat in a lounge chair in a T-shirt and baggy tan shorts. My other good friend at the center, Floyd Withers, snoozed in the chair beside him. A burp-like snore erupted from his nose.

"Hey, wake up, Floyd!" Karl kicked Floyd's lounger. "We've got company."

Floyd slowly opened his eyes. "Hi, Amy. Come on in."

"Hello, Floyd." I grinned as I pulled open the gate and let it shut lazily behind me. "Taking it easy, huh?"

Floyd rubbed his face. He had thinning white hair and a bushy moustache. "I was bird-watching," he said. He pointed to a nearby oak. "There was a real nice grosbeak in that there tree just a little bit ago."

Karl snorted. "Bird-watching!" He sipped from a can of beer he kept between his knees. "With your eyes closed?" The former chief of police had dazzling gray eyes behind thick, black-rimmed glasses and beneath a shock of white hair.

"You've still got your ears, haven't you, Floyd?" Though he didn't need it—he and Karl were tight—I couldn't help coming to the old gentleman's defense. "It is important that you use all of your senses when bird-watching, Karl. Not merely sight. Hearing, smell, touch . . ."

"Even taste?" quipped Karl. "Because I am feeling a mite peckish."

I smiled. "Very funny, Karl."

"Hey, I try."

"Speaking of birds, I left a bag of seed by your front door."

"Me and Floyd will take care of it," said Karl. "The feeders are getting low."

The former lawman rose and fetched me a can of beer from a small cooler next to the sliding glass door.

"Thanks." I popped the tab and took a small sip. "Of course, the two of you have heard about Mason's death."

"Somebody practically scissored his head off," Karl said, none too sensitively.

Floyd turned to Karl. "Didn't you say the kid did it?"

"Kid?" I took a chair at the outdoor dining table. I closed my eyes, enjoying the warm sun on my face and the sweet scent of jasmine coming from the flower garden on the other side of the wall.

"Amber Smith," Karl replied. "The bookstore lady's daughter."

I looked at Karl. "I heard Jerry wanted her to come down to the station, but is it official?"

Karl shrugged a bony shoulder. "She's a suspect, if that's what you mean. I don't believe Jerry's officially charged her with the crime yet." Karl coughed. "But to hear Jerry tell it, she isn't denying she did it. In fact, she dared him to prove it."

"I don't believe it!"

"It's true," replied Karl. "According to Jerry."

I thought a moment. "You know, Jerry believes Amber egged Mason's trailer the night of the murder. He says the market's security camera shows her buying two cartons of eggs that very night."

"I heard that," replied Karl. "People do crazy things."

"But does somebody who just murdered a man then go throw eggs at his trailer? What would be the point?"

"Could be they do. I've seen some wackos in my time."

I was sure he had.

He chuckled. "We had a couple one time call nine-one-one to report their cat was holding them hostage."

"Oh, come on," said Floyd.

"It's true," replied Karl. "They said the cat was going crazy and they were scared for their lives."

"What did you do?" I couldn't help asking.

"What could I do? I was forced to drive out to the house. I pounded on the door, and when no one answered, I opened it. Darn cat flew out faster than greased lightning."

"What did you do then?"

"I turned around and went home," Karl said matter-of-factly.

"Have the police told you anything else, Karl?" As the former long-time police chief, he had a real in with Chief Kennedy. There were things Jerry would tell Karl that he wouldn't dream of sharing with me.

Karl took a long pull of his beer and fetched another. "Anybody else need a refill?" Floyd and I declined. "I haven't heard much else, but if I do, I'll let you know."

"Thanks." I rested my head in my hands. "What do you know about Packard Mulligan, Karl?"

"The Mulligans?" Floyd said with surprise.

"You know them, Floyd?"

"Knew them," he admitted. "Tyler Mulligan, Packard's dad, once worked as a janitor at the bank." Floyd was a retired banker. He'd worked for a spell in a branch of the local bank that had operated out of the space Birds & Bees now occupied. "Not a bad sort."

"Really?" I replied. "Derek tells me the Mulligans have quite the reputation. And not a good one. In fact, he's representing Pack now. Derek says he's been accused of some local thefts."

"Pish!" spat Karl. "Old man Mulligan was ornery to be sure. He drank too much, and he cussed too often. But I'd never known him to hurt a soul."

"He'd never been arrested?"

"There were some complaints, but nothing was ever substantiated and Mulligan was never charged," said the retired chief.

"Why all the rumors about him and the rest of the Mulligans then?"

"Because the Mulligans were different," Karl said. "People don't like people who are different. People get suspicious of such folks."

Truer words had probably never been spoken.

"You know," I began, "when I was a girl, we heard that Pack had murdered his father, embalmed him, and kept him on display in the parlor."

Karl and Floyd howled with laughter.

"Okay, okay." I slapped my knees. "I had that coming. I was a kid, what can I say?" It was time to change the subject. And I really needed to stop telling that story. "What about the Smiths?"

"What about them?" asked Karl.

"It seems unlikely and it sounds silly to even ask, but have Rose or Amber ever been in any trouble with the law that you know of?"

"Not while I was chief, and I don't recall anything since then either."

"I didn't think so."

"I've never heard a bad word about them," put in Floyd.

"I hadn't either," I replied. "Not even a whisper. And yet bad is pretty much all townspeople are saying now, I'll bet."

"Too bad," said Floyd. "The Smiths are nice people. The bank loaned Rose the money for Bookarama a dozen or more years ago. Her husband left her and Amber when Amber was just a babe. They've had it hard."

"I can imagine. And things have gotten harder now with Mason's murder in the bookstore." I balled my hands into fists. "But I just can't figure out why either of them would kill Mason or be covering up for whoever did."

Karl leaned closer and tapped my knee. "Think about it, Amy. If you were Rose and thought your daughter killed him, wouldn't you confess?"

I nodded. "I'd been thinking the same thing."

"And if you were the daughter and thought your mother was guilty, wouldn't you do the same?"

I nodded once more.

"You two are forgetting," barked Floyd.

"What's that?" demanded Karl.

"What if neither of them did it, but they each *think* that the other offed the guy?"

"What's your point?" Karl pressed.

"My point is, you old goat," Floyd turned to me, "who *really* killed Professor Livingston?"

10

Floyd was right. I had been such a fool. "That has to be it. Of course, Rose is covering for Amber, and Amber is covering for her mother. But the truth is neither of them killed Mason Livingston." I couldn't stop talking. "I mean, why would they? They wouldn't, right?"

Kim nodded. Birds & Bees was closed for the day, and Kim had come up for supper in the apartment. Over chicken potpie, I'd filled her and Mom in on what I'd learned about Mason's murder.

"So that means somebody else killed him." I banged my fists against my thighs. "But who? Who, who, who?" I accompanied each "who" with a bang on my legs.

"It had to be somebody who was at the signing that night, right?" Mom called from the kitchen. She was mixing up another trial batch of her homemade suet. Having given up on the idea of making breakfast cookies, she was now determined to perfect the perfect suet cake.

"Well, you didn't hear this from me," Mom's friend, Anita Brown, said. She'd come over after dinner to help my mother with the suet cake recipe. Anita, in addition to being a part-time dispatcher for the Town of Ruby Lake police and fire departments, was a whiz in the kitchen, particularly with pastries. Maybe she could work her wonders on bird suet cakes, too.

"Hear what?" I asked, turning my head her way.

"Well . . ." Anita hesitated.

"Spill it, girl," ordered Kim.

Anita seemed to give it some thought. She dropped the wooden rolling pin she'd been using to crush peanuts on the counter and hurried over to the couch.

"This will only take a minute, Barb. Do you mind?"

"No," Mom said. "I'll pop this first batch in the oven."

"Okay." Anita waved her hand. "No more than three hundred degrees."

"Got it," replied Mom.

"Okay, now, like Kim said, spill." I scooted over on the couch to make room for Anita.

"Well," Anita said, pressing her knees together and clasping her hands in her lap. "You should ask Jerry about the toxicology report."

"Toxicology report? Mason was stabbed with a pair of scissors. What's with the toxicology report?"

"Standard procedure," Anita answered.

"It seems odd to me that—"

"Never mind," interrupted Kim. She was sitting on the floor with a glass of wine and waiting for her phone to ring. Dan Sutton had promised to call. "Tell us what was in this toxicology report, Anita."

"Tsk-tsk." Anita shook her head. "You know I'm not privy to such things, and even if I were—"

"Anita," Kim said more sternly.

Anita shifted her position. "Okay, okay." She made calm down motions with both hands. "But like I said before—"

"We know, we know, we didn't hear it from you," I said. "Right, Kim?"

Kim eagerly agreed.

"Well . . ." Anita looked around the room once more as if to check for unwanted listeners. Satisfied that there were none, she said, "Jerry says the lab report came back showing signs of something in Professor Livingston's stomach called bisacodyl."

"Bisacodyl?" Kim scratched the top of her head. "What the heck is that?"

"Some sort of laxative," Anita replied. "A real strong laxative. I looked it up."

"So your friend Mason had constipation," Kim said. "What's the big deal?"

"The big deal is that the police think it's suspicious that he had such a large quantity in his stomach." Anita arched her brow. "It's very fast acting."

"Even if Mason had constipation, why would he drink or eat this bisacodyl right before a book signing?" I asked. "Wouldn't that be rather inconvenient?"

"Maybe he didn't," Mom offered from the kitchen.

"Exactly." Anita stood and held her forefinger to her lips. "Mum's the word, ladies."

The telephone in the kitchen began ringing. "That's the store line," Mom said, stealing a glance as she pulled a tray of hot suet cakes from the oven. Thankfully, they smelled mostly like peanut butter rather than salmon, which was what her last recipe had reeked of. Believe me, there isn't much that can upset the stomach more than a salmon-flavored breakfast cookie.

"That's okay." I stood. "You're busy. I'll get it."

"The store's closed," whined Kim. "Let it ring."

I shrugged and picked it up anyway. "Hello, Birds and Bees. How can I help you?"

Kim rolled her eyes at me. I ignored her.

"Is this Amy Simms?"

"Yes, but I'm afraid the store is closed now. We're open tomorrow from nine in the morning until eight in the evening. If you'd like to come by first thing—"

The man on the other end cut me off. "This is Herman Kotter."

"Do I know you, Mister Kotter?"

"Sort of. My wife and I are staying out at the Ruby Lake Park and Marina. We talked."

"We talked? You mean you and I spoke?"

"That's right. You were telling us about that friend of yours, the guy with the big birdhouse who was murdered. Say, we read about that in the papers. That was some nasty business."

"Yes, it was." I was beginning to wonder what Herman Kotter was doing phoning me up at ten at night. "I remember now. You were in the motorhome in the next space."

"That's us. I wanted to get a spot nearer to the lake. I mean, we have no water view at all. All we can see out our windows is more motorhomes." He paused. "And tents. Lots of tents. The wife and I like camping, but we have never been into living in a tent. I did enough of that in the Army. Back then, we had to squeeze—"

"Was there something I could do for you, Mister Kotter?"

I could hear whispering in the background.

"Shush," said Mr. Kotter.

"What's that?" I said. I pressed my ear against the receiver.

"Not talking to you. I was talking to the wife." His voice dropped as he said, "I'm getting to that, dear. I'm getting to that."

I waited.

"Anyway . . ." He sounded rather annoyed now.

"Yes?"

"You asked if we'd seen anybody hanging around the guy's birdhouse . . ."

"And did you?"

"We sure did. You see, the wife was looking out the window. She was washing the plates and cups in the sink. I tell her she ought to use paper. Saves water."

"But wastes paper!" I heard her muffled retort in the background.

"Anyway, there's a little window over the sink in the motorhome so she can look out while she's washing." He cleared his throat. "In this case, outside toward this guy's birdhouse. It's quite a sight, I can tell you—"

"Who did you see, Mister Kotter?" I cut him off, figuring if I didn't now, we might be up all night.

"Who knows? Some lady."

"Some lady? Can you describe her? Was she tall? Short?"

"She was just some lady," he replied. "But since you were asking, the wife thought you might want to know that she was in there. I mean, seeing as how you and the dead guy were friends."

"Wait," I said. "Are you telling me she's there now? In Mason's camper?"

"Sure," Mr. Kotter answered. "At least she was a few minutes ago. I told the wife to keep an eye on the place, but you know how she is. She always thinks she knows better, and then she—"

"Mister Kotter," I interrupted once more, "thank you for calling me. I'm sure it's nothing. Probably another friend of the professor's."

Mr. Kotter chuckled. "Sure, sure. Seems like the man had a lot of friends. A lot of female friends, if you don't mind my saying."

In the background, I heard his wife say, "Hang up the phone now, Herman. You'll talk the woman's ear off."

"Well, I've got to go, Ms. Simms. We'll be leaving town tomorrow. Too much excitement here for us. We'll be heading for Pigeon Forge. Bye, now."

"Bon voyage," I replied. I set the phone back in its cradle.

"What was that all about?" asked Mom.

"The man in the motorhome next to Mason's trailer called to tell me there's a woman inside."

"Inside the professor's birdhouse?" Kim shifted in my direction.

"You should call the police." That was Anita.

"Maybe," I replied. "But what for? It isn't exactly illegal for someone to be inside Mason's camper." If it were, I was in trouble. "The police haven't declared it off limits, have they?"

"Not that I'm aware of," admitted Anita.

I grabbed my purse. "I think I'll run over and take a look."

"Want me to come with you?" Kim climbed to her feet and dusted off her rear end.

"No, you stay here. If we both go, it might make whoever it is feel like we're trying to gang up on her. Besides," I said, slipping my feet into a pair of sandals by the door, "now that you're dating Dan, I wouldn't want you snitching to him about any of my, shall we say, less than one hundred percent legal activities."

"I agree with the ganging up thing," Kim conceded, flopping down on the couch and punching a pillow. "But I would never snitch."

"You're dating Dan, *our* Dan?" Anita said as she dumped a couple of cups of raisins into a bowl in preparation for another batch of suet cakes.

"One of Ruby Lake's finest," I said with a smile as I exited the apartment, knowing that I'd left Kim to one of the town's leading gossip hounds.

It was a brisk ten-minute walk to the campgrounds. Even in the twilight, Mason's trailer stood out like a sore thumb or, in this case, a giant red birdhouse.

I waved to Mr. and Mrs. Kotter, who were watching from their window. The door to Mason's trailer was closed. I put my ear to it and heard nothing. Placing my hand quietly on the handle, I pulled the door open.

Cara Siskin sat on the edge of the bed, feet on the floor, arms pressed against the mattress.

"Ms. Siskin?"

She looked up, adjusting her eyeglasses as she did so. "What are you doing here?"

There was no point in lying. "One of the campers reported seeing someone in Mason's trailer."

"Who was it?"

"I don't know," I lied. I didn't want Ms. Siskin causing the Kotters any trouble. They'd be on their way tomorrow anyway. "I got an anonymous call."

"Good grief." The woman leapt from the bed and smoothed her violet pencil skirt. "This town is full of snoops." She looked out the window. "Snoops and creeps. Greedy little creeps."

I shifted uncomfortably. I had a feeling she was including me—in the first category at the very least. "Were you looking for something special?" The place was a mess, but it had looked like that from the very first time I entered.

"Nothing in particular. Mason was more than a client—he was a friend. I thought I would take a stab at going through his personal effects, get things organized."

"Had you known Mason for a long time?"

"We met a couple of years ago when Mason came to the publisher with the idea for the hummingbird book." She pouted. "Poor man. If he'd known that it was going to lead to his death, I'm certain he never would have written it." She pulled a bottle of rum from a cabinet above the small built-in fridge.

"You seem to know your way around the place."

She gave a little shrug and tipped a plastic cup from a sleeve on the table. "I ought to. I've been in and out of here enough."

"But you're not sleeping here?"

She smiled. "Define sleeping."

"Mason told me you were staying at a motel. The Ruby Lake Motor Inn?"

"That's the one. It's not much, but it beats this place." She extended the sleeve of cups my way. "Are you in or are you out?"

"Out."

"Your loss." She shrugged once more and filled her cup.

"You don't really think writing a book about hummingbirds got Mason killed, do you?"

The publicist riffled through a stack of correspondence on the corner of the table. "He's dead, isn't he?" She set down the papers and picked up the professor's notated copy of *Hummingbirds and Their Habits*. "If he hadn't written this book, he wouldn't have come to your town, and he wouldn't be dead." She slammed the book shut.

"Do you have any idea who might have wanted him dead?"

Cara Siskin paced to the end of the tiny trailer and back. "What kind of a stupid question is that? The woman from Bookarama already admitted to killing him." She gave her head a shake.

"Haven't you heard?"

"Heard what?"

"Rose Smith is innocent."

Siskin appeared dubious.

"It's true. She has an alibi."

"You don't say." She tapped the side of her chin. "Do the police have any other suspects?"

"The daughter," I answered. "But I don't think she did it."

Siskin grinned. "You think she's innocent?" She pulled a face. "Well, so do I."

"Why do you say that?"

"Because my money's on Frank Duvall." She poured herself a second very generous glass of rum.

"The flower farmer? Why would he want to see Mason dead?" I wasn't about to tip my hand and admit that I knew about Mason's correspondence with the grower. It would only lead to questions. The publicist would want to know not only what I knew but how.

"Duvall was trying to get Mason interested in some scheme of his. He claimed to have developed some hybrid flower that was especially attractive to all species of hummingbirds. A real magnet, so he said. As if there really was such a thing."

"Mason didn't believe it?"

"Truth?" I nodded, and she continued. "I think Mason wanted to believe it. Personally, I think it's about as real as leprechauns."

"What exactly did he want from Mason?"

She pressed her fingers into the fold of her skirt. "He was begging Mason to endorse the flower. Mason said Duvall offered to make him a full partner if he did.

"Duvall had some grandiose idea that it would make the two of them rich. I can't imagine there could be that much money in some stupid flower."

"I don't know," I said. "The flower industry is huge, so is birding. A flower like that might be worth millions of dollars."

"Maybe." She didn't look like she believed it. "In any case, Mason is dead."

"And you think Frank murdered him? Why? As you say, he wanted Mason's endorsement and help marketing his flower. Mason dead wouldn't do him much good. In fact, it might have squashed his plans." At the very least, it would be a big setback.

"So maybe they had a falling out? Argued. Mason told me Frank was greedy. Maybe he got too greedy."

"Maybe."

She arched her brow. "You don't believe it?"

"I don't know what to believe." I ran my fingers down the sleeves of one of the professor's tweed sport coats hanging from a hook near the door. "I do find it hard to believe that Mason would have gotten himself in some scheme simply for money. He was a tenured professor in addition to being a published author and speaker. His wife's a professor, too. How's she taking Mason's death? Have you spoken with her?"

Cara Siskin's laughter filled the tiny space. "I expect she's dancing on his grave."

"Excuse me?" I was aghast at the woman's lack of compassion.

"Didn't you know?" I shook my head, and the publicist continued. "Mason and his wife split a couple of years ago. The divorce has turned quite nasty."

"Mason told me they had been separated, but he seemed to imply it was only a trial separation."

"According to his wife, living with Mason was a trial unto itself." The publicist grinned wickedly. "And the divorce has been proving expensive. In more ways than one."

"How do you mean?"

"I mean it was driving Mason to distraction. He went a year over his deadline getting this latest book done. My editor was not happy and refused to advance him any more money until he turned in the manuscript."

"Mason was having money problems?"

"Why do you think he was living in this dump?"

"Living? Do you mean to tell me that Mason was living in this trailer full time?"

"Yep. This is it." She spread her arms. "Home, sweet home. Your dear professor was dead broke. And now he's dead period." She chuckled. Clearly the rum was beginning to influence her movement and words. "Mason was in deep guano. Lost his wife, his job. Everything but this silly birdhouse on wheels and a truck with three years of payments left."

"Did you notice anything suspicious that night at Bookarama? Did you notice anyone hanging around who shouldn't have been there?"

"The police already asked me, and I told them what I'm telling you—not a thing." Cara drank. "I didn't see or hear anything unusual, and I didn't see a murderer lurking in the shadows with a pair of scissors in hand."

"What time did you leave the bookstore?"

"A few minutes after the book signing."

"You didn't stay for the reception? Isn't that unusual? You are, were, Mason's publicist."

"I had a headache, so I left early. You were his friend. You left early, too. Should I accuse you of murdering him?"

"I wasn't suggesting you killed him, Ms. Siskin. I only want to find the truth."

"The truth can be overrated."

"That's an odd thing to say."

"This is an odd little town," she replied, her expression sour.

On a hunch, I opened my purse and extracted the makeup kit I'd found in Mason's trailer. "Is this yours?" Light from the small lamp beside the bed reflected off the kit.

She set down her drink and took it from my hand. "Yes. Where did you get it?"

I pointed to the bed. "There."

She shrugged and stuck it in a large black leather handbag at her feet. "Thanks."

"Do you mind telling me how it got there?"

"You're a grown woman," she scoffed. "Figure it out. Now, if you don't mind, I have things to do."

"Fine, I'll leave you to it. Will you be staying in Ruby Lake long?"

"As long as it takes to help clean up this mess."

I nodded, though I was unsure exactly what mess she was talking about—the mess that was Mason's death or the mess his death had created for her. "I do have one more question."

"Shoot."

"Was Frank Duvall the reason Mason came to Ruby Lake?"

"What?" She looked at me like I was a complete rube. "Did you think he came here to see you? Or to sign books at some tiny bookstore in this little one-horse town? I mean, no offense, but we're trying to sell books, and this burg doesn't have enough readers to pay our gas fare."

No offense? Cara Siskin had just offended me and the entire Town of Ruby Lake in every way possible. "Speaking of book sales, do you think the professor's death will hurt sales of *Hummingbirds and Their Habits* or help them?"

She snatched up her plastic cup. "It's the end of the line as far as the book tour goes, of course. As for sales, no one can say for sure," she answered with a glint in her eye. "But I'm hoping it gives sales a boost."

I was sure she was. I pushed open the door, anxious to leave the ugly woman.

"Hummingbirds," she snorted. "Nasty little birds. Flitting all around, barely stopping. They make me nervous the way they never keep still. I don't know what anybody sees in them."

"They're beautiful," I couldn't refrain from replying. "Haven't you ever taken the time to really enjoy them?" Hadn't she looked at the wonderful photos in the professor's book—the book she was charged with publicizing? "Their hearts race twelve hundred beats a minute. And they are the only bird that can fly backwards."

She tossed her free hand in the air, unimpressed. "My job is, was, to sell Mason. No offense—I know you run a bird store—but birds are nothing but a nuisance. They fly into windows willy-nilly and poop all over the place."

I turned on my heel. For a woman who kept claiming she meant no offense, I'd been offended more over the course of several minutes by her than I would have thought possible in a lifetime.

"Wait a minute, Amy."

I stood in the open doorway, one foot on the first step. "Yes?"

"If this bookseller is so innocent, why did she confess?"

"I'm not sure. It seems likely that she did it to protect her daughter—or someone else, perhaps."

"So she confesses to cold-blooded murder? What did I tell you?"

spat Siskin. "This town is not only full of snoops and creeps—" She tipped back her cup and downed the remains of her drink. "It's full of kooks."

I refrained from replying, but one thing I knew for certain—there'd be one less "kook" in Ruby Lake the day Cara Siskin left town.

11

I was finishing a slice of buttered sourdough toast and washing it down with a cup of coffee when Mom came out, still in her housecoat. "Morning, Mom." I rose and bussed her cheek. "I've got to get downstairs and open up. There's coffee in the pot."

"Thanks." Mom yawned and held her hand to her lips. "Sorry."

It wasn't merely the yawn. I could tell from the way Mom moved that she was tired from the night before. "Late night?" I'd gone to bed soon after returning from Mason's place.

"Anita and I stayed up 'til midnight," she said, "working on our suet cakes."

"If this batch turns out half decent, I'll test-sell them in the store and see what reports come back from our customers."

"That would be wonderful." Mom looked at the stack of fresh suet cakes on top of the fridge. "We wrapped them last night. Anita's going to print some labels for them with the computer and printer at her house."

"Okay. We can bring them down to the store whenever you think they're ready. Who knows?" I quipped. "If the birds really *flock* to them, you just might be the queen of suet!"

Mom groaned at my lame pun. "It doesn't sound like a very glamorous title, like Miss Ruby Lake, but I'll take it."

"I'll make you a Queen of Suet sash. You can wear it around the store. White satin with gold glitter letters."

"I think not." Mom turned serious. "I couldn't stop thinking about your Professor Livingston and Rose and her daughter after I went to bed."

"I know what you mean." When I had returned home from Mason's trailer last night, I had filled the ladies in on my conversation with

Cara Siskin before calling it a night. Although we all had theories and opinions about her relationship with Mason, we had no idea what any of it meant.

My mother pulled a cup from the mug tree and filled it with coffee. "How did everything get so complicated?"

"I don't know. I can't picture Rose or Amber as the killer type."

"Me either," replied my mother. "The thing is, the way he was killed, with a pair of scissors stuck in his neck like that . . ." She rubbed the back of her neck. "It must have been a crime of passion."

"I suppose so. I really hadn't thought about it." But now that I did, my mother had to be right. "I don't think it was a random robbery or anything like that."

"The police haven't said anything that would lead us to think so." Mom sat at the kitchen table and adjusted her robe. "So who in Ruby Lake could have been angry enough at him to have wanted to kill him?"

I shrugged helplessly. "That's the question. Mason wasn't from here and didn't really know anyone. Besides me. Though, like I told you, he had received a letter from Mister Duvall." I handed Mom the milk. "I sure hope Jerry doesn't start thinking along these same lines and end up accusing me of murdering Mason."

Mom added a dollop of milk to her coffee and took a sip. "I'm sure he won't, Amy."

"That makes one of us. Maybe it was Cara Siskin."

"His publicist?"

"Sure, they were clearly having an affair. Love and hate, it's a razor's edge, right?"

Mom's eyes grew wide. "I certainly would not want to think so. I adored your father. I never once thought of murdering him."

I patted her hand. "I know how much you loved him, Mom. I only meant that Cara might have had her reasons for getting, I don't know, jealous maybe? I told you how Mason and Rose were together at the *biergarten*. Maybe he took her back to his trailer afterward for a little romance. And maybe Cara Siskin didn't like it."

"Enough to stick a pair of scissors in his neck?"

"It's a theory."

"So who else might have felt that strongly? Mister Duvall?"

"Sure. I told you what Ms. Siskin said. If what she said was true, there could be some reason that he wanted Mason dead."

"A business deal gone bad?"

"It happens."

"I suppose." Mom's fingernails clicked against the kitchen table. "I wonder if Jerry has interrogated either of them."

"Cara Siskin and Frank Duvall?" I looked at the time. It was five minutes past opening time. "I doubt it. I expect he's got his sights on Amber Smith."

"I still can't believe she's guilty."

"Neither can I, Mom. But let's face it. Somebody stabbed Mason, and Rose and Amber both had the opportunity. Well, at least Amber did. Rose has an alibi."

"There were a lot of other people at Bookarama that night," Mom countered. "I'll bet lots of people had the opportunity. Frank Duvall was there, as I remember."

"You're right. There was a woman with him."

"That was his wife," Mom told me.

"Ms. Siskin was there, of course. I wonder if she's married."

"You think a jealous husband could have done it?"

"It's thin, I admit. If she is married, I expect her husband is far from here. I wonder where home is for Ms. Siskin."

"Aren't most publishers based in New York?"

"Most, I guess. But I'm not sure in this case."

"Isn't the publisher's address inside the book?"

"You're a genius, Mom," I said with a grin. "I'll check first chance I get." I paused and shut my eyes. "Now that I think about it, Frank Duvall and his wife were also at the Birds and Brews meeting in addition to being at the book signing. I didn't think anything of it at the time."

"Do you remember anyone else from the signing?"

"Lance was there. So was that reporter woman from the radio station. Karl and Floyd and a lot of other regulars from Birds and Brews. Mitch Quiles. But I can't imagine any of them wanting Mason dead."

I sighed in frustration. "I don't know, Mom. There had to be close to thirty people at Birds and Brews and fifty people at Mason's book signing."

"Fifty people with opportunity."

"So that means it comes down to motive," I said. I gave Mom a peck on the cheek and ran for the door. "Time to open up."

Mom promised to be down later.

* * *

Restless and tired, unable to focus on my customers, an hour after opening, I told Esther I was leaving her in charge of the store. I couldn't get Cara Siskin's accusations out of my head. It was time I paid a visit to Frank Duvall. "Cousin Riley should be in soon. He promised to mow and trim the front lawn and weed the flower beds."

"No problem." Esther strapped on her apron. "I've got it covered. Where are you going?"

"I thought I'd drive out to Duvall's Flower Farm. They may carry some varieties that would do well in the front garden, don't you think? I was thinking of adding some new things."

"If you say so," replied Esther. "Looks to me like you've got about every flower in the world out there now. But why not just drive to the farmers market? It's closer."

"That's not a bad idea. Do you think the Duvalls will be there?"

"They're always there. Every grower around participates in the farmers market. They'd be a fool not to."

As I peeked out the front window to contemplate what new flowers I might want to add to the landscape, the publicist's comment about hummingbirds, and birds in general, came back to me. How could she not adore the colorful, tiny flyers? Several hummingbirds flitted about our front feeders, their tiny wings a blur as they flapped them at a speed of approximately fifty beats per second. I'd refilled the nectar just that morning. All the birds were of the ruby-throated variety, not surprising since they were fairly common to the region this time of year.

A stranger sat in one of the rockers with his back to me. "Who's that sitting out there on the porch, Esther?"

"I forgot to tell you. That nice, young Lance Jennings came by to see you. He's been waiting on the porch for twenty minutes," Esther answered.

"Young? He's probably a decade older than me, Esther."

Esther cocked her head as she looked at me. "Really?"

"Really," I snapped and yanked open the front door.

Lance looked up from his electronic tablet when he heard me coming.

"Good morning, Lance. What are you doing here?"

"I've come to interview you, Amy." He motioned to the empty bench beside him. "Take a seat."

"Now is not a good time. I was on my way out, Lance. Besides, what's this all about? Why do you want to interview me?"

"Are you kidding?" Lance tapped the tablet screen. "Mason Livingston was a friend of yours. You can give me the inside scoop."

I frowned. "Inside scoop?"

"Yeah, you know. The story behind the man, the murder."

"If you want a scoop, try the ice cream parlor."

"Very funny." Lance tapped his foot against the porch. "Come on, Amy. You knew the guy."

I folded my arms over my chest. "There really isn't much to tell, Lance. I hadn't seen Mason in years. We corresponded a little, but that was it."

"There's got to be more to the story than that."

I started to walk past him. "Sorry, but there isn't."

"You share with me, and I'll share with you!" he called as I bounced down the front steps.

I paused and turned around. "What exactly have you got to share, Lance?"

He motioned to the empty bench once more and smiled seductively. "Have a seat, and I'll tell you."

I parked myself on the bench. "Go ahead. I'm listening."

Lance set his tablet between his legs. In his white polo shirt and navy cargo shorts, he looked more like a tourist at a tennis resort than a reporter. "I'd been doing a little digging on your pal, Mason Livingston."

"So?"

"When I heard he was coming to town and was something of a celebrity, at least so far as Ruby Lake goes, I started nosing around on the internet, trying to get some background on the guy before he arrived."

"Again, so?"

"I believe that he may have plagiarized portions of his book."

"The new hummingbird book?"

Lance nodded.

"I don't believe it," I said sharply. "Mason would never do such a thing. Why would he?"

"It's not the first time that the professor has been accused of plagiarism, Amy. Let me show you something." He picked up his tablet and scrolled through some pages he'd pulled up on the internet, finally landing on whatever it was he was looking for. "Take a look at this."

I frowned but complied as he handed over his tablet. "What am I looking at?"

"A couple of articles in which authors and web bloggers have accused Professor Livingston of having lifted portions of their material for his books."

I read a little, then handed the tablet back over. "It's all very circumstantial," I said. "Had he ever been charged with a crime?"

"No," Lance admitted. "He has not. But that doesn't make him innocent."

"It doesn't make him guilty of anything either, Lance."

"Lawsuits are expensive, and most authors are notoriously poor. You know the old saying: Where there's smoke, there's fire."

"When it comes to Mason, I'd say you're blowing smoke, Lance."

Lance ran his finger under his shirt collar. "Very funny. Now it's your turn to tell me something."

"Such as?"

"Such as why Amber Smith would want to murder your friend, the professor?"

"Why not ask her yourself?"

"I tried," admitted Lance. "She refuses to talk to me. Ditto her mother."

"Smart women."

"Smart or guilty? The two of them are holed up in Bookarama. I was hoping maybe you could speak with them."

"Why would I do that?"

"You want to find out who killed your friend and why, don't you?"

I did, but I wasn't going to let this reporter know just how badly. "Is that why you were skulking around outside Mason's trailer the day he arrived? You wanted to confront him about the charges of plagiarism?"

"I wasn't skulking." Lance stiffened. "I'm a reporter. I was doing my job or at least trying to. Your friend, Mason, refused to let me interview him. Even his publicist refused my request for information unless I agreed to her terms."

"Which were what exactly?"

A corner of Lance's mouth turned up. "I had to keep the story about birds and the professor. Nothing more, nothing less. She'd even written up a list of questions that were," Lance flashed a pair of quote signs with his fingers, "safe. Everything else was out of bounds."

"You were at Birds and Brews and the book signing."

"What of it?"

"You don't give up easily, do you?"

"No, I don't. I smelled a story, and I wasn't going to back down."

"It sounds like you and Ms. Wilcox have something in common. She strikes me as the type who never backs down either."

"Wilcox is a nuisance," spat Lance.

"What's wrong, Lance? Is the radio station giving the *Weekender* a little too much competition?"

"Not in a million years," Lance said strongly. "The *Ruby Lake Weekender* has been serving the community for fifty years. And we'll be around for another fifty if I have anything to say about it.

"*AM Ruby* has been around for, what? All of six months?" Lance stood and flicked a bit of lint from his shorts. "And from what I hear, the station will be lucky to last another six."

"Wow, the two of you aren't exactly comrades-in-arms, are you?"

"The woman will stop at nothing to get what she wants. My informer tells me that she was seen cozying up to the professor in a bar out along the highway."

"Was this informer Greg Tuffnall?" There was only one bar in the vicinity, between here and the highway, and Greg Tuffnall was known to spill the gossip as much as he spilled the drinks.

"Maybe. That would be confidential."

"Right, confidential. When was this?"

"The night Mason spoke at that last Birds and Brews event of yours at the *biergarten*."

"I thought maybe he spent the night with Rose Smith." I also thought it interesting that Cara Siskin had failed to mention Violet Wilcox at all. Was she unaware of Mason's rendezvous with the radio station reporter? Or was she too aware and violently jealous and angry?

It was Lance's turn to smile. "Maybe he did, but if he spent the night with anyone, I'd guess it was Wilcox. Like I said, she'll stop at nothing to get a story."

"Do you think she knew about the plagiarism rumors?"

"She most certainly did. Why do you think she wanted an interview with him so badly for her radio show? Did you really think she wanted to talk about hummingbirds?"

"Actually, I sort of did. I would."

Lance rolled his eyes. "You are way too naïve, Amy. You're like a . . ." He snapped his fingers several times. "Baby chick. The world isn't all birds and bees." Lance started down the path to the sidewalk. "Sometimes," he called, his back to me, "it's greed and violence."

As much as I hated to think so, I knew Lance Jennings was right.

12

The farmers market was a popular destination that brought locals and tourists alike to the town square. All summer long, the market was open daily. I parked around the corner in one of the public lots and walked over.

I'd made a point to stroll past Bookarama. The closed sign hung in the window. I crossed the street to the square where row after row of red tents had been erected. Local vendors selling everything from their artistic creations to the fruits of their farm labor greeted every passerby with a smile and sometimes a sample.

I'd tried a local, unfiltered apple cider, a spoonful of honey and grits, and a habanero-mango salsa that left my mouth feeling like I was walking around with a bonfire on my tongue. I was glad to stumble on Duvall's Flower Farm's setup before I could do myself any more harm.

Frank Duvall occupied a stall near the middle of a long row. Three six-foot tables formed a U shape, and indoor and outdoor plants and flowers of many varieties filled every inch of the tabletops. He was talking to a woman in tight jeans and a ball cap with her back to me. When she turned and walked on, I recognized her. It was Violet Wilcox from *AM Ruby*.

I stopped and inhaled. "Hello, Frank. Everything smells wonderful," I said, smiling. My eyes carefully scanned each table, wondering which, if any, of these flowering plants might have been the one Duvall had contacted Mason about.

Mr. Duvall stuck his thumbs behind his suspenders and greeted me. His dungarees were faded, and his white T-shirt spotted with soil—an occupational hazard, no doubt. "They are wonderful," the grower boasted. "In fact, I've never met a flower I didn't like." He winked at me. Frank Duvall is a rotund man with sloping shoulders, a shock of radiant black hair, shot through with gray at the temples, and hazel eyes. If I was right, he was in his early sixties. He had the ruddy complexion of a man who spends a lot of time outdoors.

"Wasn't that Violet Wilcox?"

"Yes, yes, it was." He glanced away and waved his hand in front of his face.

"What did she want?"

"Ms. Wilcox is always nosing around for news. I suppose she's preparing something on the farmers market for her radio show. I'm afraid I wasn't much help."

"I see." What I hadn't seen was Violet or her assistant holding a tape recorder of any kind. That made it rather difficult to conduct a radio interview.

Frank shouted out a greeting to a fellow stall owner as she passed. Then he sidled up alongside me. "Are you looking for anything special or simply enjoying this lovely morning?"

"Both," I said. It was a beautiful Carolina morning, and though it was warming, the humidity was, gratefully, low. "I was considering adding some more flowers to attract hummingbirds to the front yard.

"I enjoy watching them, and they're good for business. I can't tell you how many people walking by stop to watch the birds zoom about from flower to flower."

"I'll bet."

"What would you recommend?"

Frank did a turn around his stall. "The red lantana are always good." He ran his finger along the leaf of a bee balm. "These are nice." He continued on. "Daylilies. Anything in the sage family, of course."

"Yes, I have a number of those."

"That's right," said Frank. "I remember seeing some between your store and the *biergarten*."

I moved over to a striking red, star-shaped flower near the corner of the center table. "What's this one here?" I lifted the small quart-sized plastic pot and held it up to the light.

"Oh, that's nothing. Something I'm working on."

"It's beautiful. How much is it?"

He set the flower gently back in the corner. "Sorry, it's not for sale." He wiped his hands on the front of his dungarees. "Yet."

"Pity. It would make a great addition to my garden."

Frank laid a gentle hand on the small of my back and led me to the third table. "I'm running a sale on penstemon—or beardtongue as most folk know it. Five dollars each, or three for twelve."

I looked over the colorful, trumpet-shaped blooms. "Such a lovely shade of pink."

"They do well in full sun or partial shade."

"I'll take three," I agreed, pulling my wallet from my purse.

"Great. I'll write you up." Frank moved a tall thermos bottle sitting atop a thick ledger and wrote down the sale. He set the three plants in the sturdy lid of a cardboard box. "Remember, they don't like to be crowded."

"I'll remember," I promised. I brought the box to my nose and sniffed. "Mason Livingston would have loved these."

"Excuse me?" A guarded look came to the farmer's eyes.

"I'm just saying that Mason had a special fondness for flowers that attracted hummingbirds. It's no wonder, considering he wrote a book on them, right?"

"If you say so."

"Did you get to know Mason while he was here, before the—"

Frank waited for a pair of browsers to move on before replying. "Not really. I listened to the talk he gave. But you know that."

"You were at his book signing, too, as I remember."

"Yeah. What's wrong with that?"

"Nothing. I'm just trying to figure out what Mason did, who he saw, and where he went while he was in town."

"Heck if I know."

"You didn't meet with him?"

The farmer made a face. "Why should I? Nope. I saw him the same places everybody else did—the bookstore and the *biergarten*."

"So you didn't have any business with him?"

"Business?" Frank appeared surprised by the question. "I grow flowers, and he wrote books. What kind of business could we possibly have in common?"

"Sorry, you're right. Do you have any idea who else he might have seen or where else he might have gone, Frank?" I prodded. "There's an entire day that is mostly a blank for me, the day between the time he lectured to our group and the time he showed up for his book signing at Bookarama. Where had he been? Who had he seen and why?"

Frank chuckled. "You're asking the wrong person, Amy. Besides," he sat, hitching up his dungarees, "that sounds like police business. And the whole town is talking about how the police think Amber Smith murdered the professor."

"That's a nasty rumor, Frank. Please don't go spreading it. This is a small town, and a person's reputation can be ruined for life over such things." I balanced the box lid in my hands. "If the police really believed she was guilty, don't you think they'd have locked her up?"

"So she's got a good lawyer. That doesn't mean she isn't guilty."

"Amber Smith is a sweet young woman. Why on earth would she want to murder Mason, let alone actually commit the deed? She's a small-town girl, and Mason lived in Texas, for goodness' sake. What connection could she possibly have to the man? The fact that he was signing books in her mother's store? Big deal!

"You don't murder a man for nothing. She had no connection to him. None." I was getting worked up but couldn't stop myself. If anybody had a connection to Mason and a reason to kill him, it appeared to be the man I was talking to, but I wasn't about to accuse him without hard evidence. "I'm sorry to say it, Frank, but you're as bad as Jerry, jumping to conclusions. Conclusions that could embarrass and humiliate her."

Frank looked amused as he shook his head. "No connections, huh? I guess you haven't heard."

I scowled at him, unable to hide my anger. "Heard what?"

"Amber Smith and Mason Livingston were connected."

I arched my brow. "How?"

"The word is that the police have learned that she took a class with the professor when he was teaching a semester at the university in Chapel Hill some years ago."

13

My mind was reeling as I carried my awkward burden across the square. I ignored the honking cars as I darted across the street. Balancing the shallow box lid under one arm, I pushed open the door of Harlan and Harlan and went inside. I set the plants down on the table near the window where they could get some sun.

"Hello, is Mister Harlan in?" I asked.

The well-dressed woman in a peacock-blue jacket and skirt behind the mahogany desk looked me over and seemed to take me for a street urchin. "Which one?"

"Derek." I pointed to the logo on my shirt. "I'm Amy Simms, with Birds and Bees." Her brown hair looked sprayed into place, and she hadn't blinked once. She was so pale I wondered if she even knew what the sun looked like.

"Won't you have a seat?" She motioned to the plush chair at the window, then picked up the phone on the corner of her desk. Though she wasn't six feet away, I couldn't hear a word she said.

A minute later, Derek strolled up, dressed in his good gray suit and a red silk tie. "Hi, Amy. This is a surprise. What brings you here?"

"I was hoping for a word with you."

"You look upset." Derek came closer and took my hand. "Are you all right?"

"Yes," I nodded quickly. "I'm just a little shaken. Maybe I shouldn't have come." I pulled away, but Derek stopped me.

"Nonsense," he said. "I'm just finishing up with a client. It shouldn't take much longer. Wait for me?"

I nodded, embarrassed at the way I was acting. "Okay. If you're sure?"

He grinned. "I'm sure." He glanced at his watch. "If you'd like anything—water, coffee, anything at all—this is Mrs. Edmunds," he said, turning to his secretary. "Mrs. Edmunds, take care of Ms. Simms for me, would you?"

"Absolutely," the secretary replied smoothly, though I got the impression she'd more like to take a broom and sweep me out the door than she would provide me with refreshments.

Several awkward minutes later, during which time I squirmed in the chair, trying to ignore the sun beating down on the back of my neck and the sweat rolling uncomfortably down my back—and endured the occasional blunt scrutiny of Mrs. Edmunds—Derek returned. There was a stranger in baggy blue jeans and a light blue short-sleeve chambray shirt with him. The man made brief eye contact, keeping his gaze mostly on the carpet.

He nodded to Derek, then left.

"Who was that?" I whispered, turning to watch the tall man lumber along the sidewalk as if unsure what legs were meant for.

"You mean Mister Mulligan?"

"That's Pack?" I pressed my face closer to the glass. Packard Mulligan stopped at the corner and climbed into an antique black pickup truck loaded with boxes. "He looks so different."

Derek laughed. "When was the last time you saw him? Didn't you say you hadn't seen him since you were a kid?"

"Yes, that's right." I spun toward Derek and grabbed his arm. "No, it isn't right. I saw him again."

"Okay." Derek plucked my arm from his sleeve. "Listen, I don't have a lot of time. I've got another appointment in—"

"Twenty minutes, Derek," Mrs. Edmunds interjected firmly.

"Right. Twenty minutes. Come on back to my office."

"You don't understand," I said as I followed Derek to the rear of the space where his private office was located. "I saw Pack Mulligan outside Bookarama the other night."

Derek stopped in the middle of the hallway. "You mean the night of Professor Livingston's murder?"

I swallowed. "Yes."

"Are you sure?"

"Pretty sure."

Derek motioned for me to enter his office and patted the back of one of the chairs. "Have a seat." He took the chair beside me rather than going behind his desk. "So," he steepled his fingers, "you're pretty sure you saw my client, Packard Mulligan, outside Bookarama the night of the murder?"

"I think so. Remember I told you there was some man outside and that he asked me or said something about Mason being dead?"

"No, I don't recall you saying anything at all about that."

"Oh." I frowned. "I meant to. I guess I forgot. Anyway, it was Packard Mulligan."

"And he asked about the murder?"

"I'm not sure. He asked, I think, if somebody was dead."

"That's not unusual. There were police cars, flashing lights. Quite a scene, I expect. Anybody walking by would be curious."

"True."

"Did he mention Mason by name?"

"No. No, he didn't."

"What else did he say?"

"Nothing. And I really only barely saw his face. I'm sure it was Pack though. It had to be."

"But why?" Derek said. "I don't remember seeing Mister Mulligan at the book signing."

"Neither do I. So what was he doing hovering around outside?"

Derek could only shrug. "Going for a walk. People do stroll around the shops and the square at night."

"Maybe," I admitted grudgingly.

"And he does have a stall at the farmers market."

"It's not open at night."

"True. Listen, Amy, did you tell Chief Kennedy about seeing Mister Mulligan outside Bookarama that night?"

I shook my head. "Do you think I should?"

Derek pursed his lips. "I hate to say it, but, yes, I do." He stared into space. "Then again, I don't want to get Mister Mulligan into any more trouble than he's in now."

"Is he really in trouble? Maybe I should hold off."

"That's hard to say. There are a lot of homeowners and shop owners who would like to see him locked up. But, in my professional opinion, there's not enough evidence to convict. I'm hoping the county prosecutor feels the same way." Derek pressed his fingers into his knees. "You reporting seeing him outside the site of a murder isn't going to help his case or his reputation."

"I don't know about that. From what I've been hearing, half the town believes Amber Smith did it."

Derek looked doubtful. "That pretty little thing?"

I feigned jealousy and arched my brow. "Pretty, is she?"

Derek grinned. "You know what I mean. I can't picture her getting angry enough to grab a pair of scissors and stick them in the neck of a man she barely knew. What would be her motive?"

"I don't know, but I wish I did. Because to hear Frank Duvall tell it, Amber was a student at UNC when Mason was a visiting professor, just like I was years before."

"So? That doesn't give her a reason to hate the guy, let alone kill him. Even if he flunked her. Besides, hundreds, maybe thousands of students have had classes with Mason, including you. I'll bet dozens of former UNC Chapel Hill students live right here in the area.

"That doesn't make all of them," he grinned, "and you a suspect, too, does it?"

"No. I agree. Amber and Rose sure act guilty though. They've holed up in the bookstore, which has been closed since the murder, and are refusing to talk to anyone. At least, according to Lance Jennings."

"I disagree," Derek said. "I don't think they're necessarily acting guilty. Look at it from the Smiths' perspective. They're being accused of murder—first one, then the other—and hounded by the press. Wouldn't you hide out, too?"

"I suppose you could be right."

"I always am," he said with a gleam in his eye. "Trust me, they've lawyered up. I heard they consulted an attorney out of Greensboro. I'm certain that he's told them to do exactly what I would have told them."

"What's that?"

"To talk to no one. Especially the press. And nosy shop owners."

"Very funny. Do you think they'll talk to you?" I blinked my eyes at him disingenuously.

"Nice try. I'm not their lawyer."

No, he wasn't. But I wondered if they'd talk to me even if their lawyer, as Derek suggested, had told them to talk to no one. "Cara Siskin, Mason's publicist, told me that Mister Duvall wanted Mason to go into a business deal with him."

"What sort of a deal?"

"I don't know. Mason never mentioned anything like that to me. When I asked Frank Duvall about it, he seemed surprised and basically told me that the very idea was nonsense. I'm not so sure I believe him though."

"Oh?"

I explained about the flower that Duvall had purportedly developed and the part Mason Livingston was reportedly to play in marketing it.

"Do you really think a fancy flower could be worth enough money to cause a falling out and even lead to murder?"

"Hundreds of thousands? Millions? Your guess is as good as mine, Derek. As you know, people have killed for less."

"And you think this Mister Duvall has something to hide?"

"I got the feeling that he wasn't being totally honest with me when I spoke with him this morning at the farmers market. I asked him if he ever met with Mason, and he denied it."

"But Ms. Siskin says he did?"

I nodded. "The question is, who's telling the truth?"

Derek rubbed his chin. "And who has something to hide?"

I pulled out my phone and tapped the screen. "There's this, too."

"What am I looking at?"

I scrolled down. "I found this phone number written on the back of an envelope in Mason's trailer. I also found a makeup kit behind the bed that Ms. Siskin said belonged to her."

"What were you doing in Mason's trailer?"

"What can I say? I was curious."

Derek sighed. "You could be putting yourself in danger, Amy. I wish you would leave this matter to the police."

I ignored the remark and tapped the screen. "The phone number's local. It's not the bookstore, and it's not the Duvall's Flower Farm number either."

"No," Derek said quickly. I noted a hint of surprise in his voice as he straightened. "It's not, all right."

I stared at him. "You know it?"

"Sure," he said, taking the phone from my hand and chewing his lip. "That's Dad's direct line, not the main office number."

"Mason called your father? What did he want to speak with him about?"

Derek handed the phone back to me. "I have no idea. I didn't know they had been in touch."

"I wonder how Mason got Ben's direct line. They didn't know one another, did they?"

"Nope. Dad said he's never met the man."

"Doesn't that make you curious?"

"A little, I suppose. But anybody could get that number, Amy. It's posted on our webpage." Derek reached for his computer keyboard and tapped some keys. "Your friend Mason could have wanted legal advice about anything. Maybe he wanted to update his will or get something witnessed."

"Such as?"

"I don't know. A contract, maybe?"

"Like a contract between Frank Duvall and himself?"

Derek rubbed his chin. "Your guess is as good as mine."

"You're no help." I stood. "Let's go ask Ben what Mason wanted."

Derek shook his head. "Not now. I've got an appointment, re-member? And Mrs. Edmunds doesn't like it when I miss my appointments."

"I'm sure she doesn't." Derek and his father had been burning through temps in an attempt to find a permanent hire for the front desk. Mrs. Edmunds was the third in six weeks. "Can't we make an exception just this once?"

"Nope." Derek stood too. "I'd like to, but in this case, it wouldn't matter. Dad's not here."

Derek led me back up the hall. "I'd really like to know what your father and Mason talked about," I pressed as we reentered the reception area.

"Good afternoon, Mister Clemens. I'll be right with you," Derek called to a casually dressed elderly gentleman sitting next to my pink flowering plants. Derek turned to me. "Come back in about an hour, Amy. Dad should be back, and we can talk with him then."

Derek escorted Mr. Clemens to his office, and I was left alone with Mrs. Edmunds. "Have a nice day," she said, her eyes moving from me to the door in a clear attempt to get me moving.

"Actually," I began, "would you mind if I leave my flowers here a little while longer? I want to step next door to the bridal shop."

"I'm afraid," Mrs. Edmunds sniffed, "I am allergic to flowers."

"Oh. Sorry." Her eyes were starting to look a little puffy. I picked up the box lid full of plants and pushed the door open with my back. "Tell Derek I'll be back in an hour!"

I took Mrs. Edmunds's cool silence as a yes.

14

As much as I loathed the idea, it was time to bite the bullet and talk to Amy Harlan for Jerry. I wasn't sure what pull I had with the woman—other than her wanting to pull the trigger of a gun every time she laid eyes on me—but I had promised the man.

Besides, if I wanted to ply Jerry for more information, which I did, it would help if I had some leverage or some good news to report—like his wife getting a bargain-basement price on a wedding gown for her vow renewal ceremony. I'd never met a bigger cheapskate than Jerry Kennedy. He'd made me pay for my own snacks on our first and last date a million years ago—at least that's what my junior year of high school felt like these days.

Once more balancing the plants in one hand, I pulled open the door to Dream Gowns. As I did, a woman tried to get past me. "Sorry!" I dodged to the left, which was exactly the wrong thing to do. The box lid tipped, and one of my plants slid to the edge and tumbled over the side.

"I've got it!" I lunged for the plant, spilling the remaining two in the process. A slender woman in a peach-colored dress and pearls glared down at me. "Good thing these pots are plastic," I quipped.

I lined the three pots back together on the box lid, then fluffed the flower petals with my fingers. "They don't look any the worse." I smiled at the woman. Her skin looked like it had been formed with high-grade plaster. "Flowers sure are resilient, aren't they?"

She was staring at the carpet. Potting soil had spread everywhere. "Oops." I bent and quickly began scooping the damp potting soil back into the pots. Unfortunately, I was leaving brownish-black stains all over the pearl-white carpet. "If you've got some paper towels or a rag, I can clean this right up in no time."

"Will you use a rag to clean this, too?" The young woman reached over me and tugged at a beautiful white lace and taffeta ball gown.

That is, it had been beautiful. Now it was soiled from waist to hemline and looked like the bride who'd worn it had spent her honeymoon mudwrestling.

"What's going on?" I heard a soprano voice from deeper within the store call.

I cringed. I knew that voice.

"Some…woman selling plants door to door has ruined our new carpet and a Paul Duberg original," tattled the woman looming over me.

Amy Harlan marched to the front. "You!"

"Hello, Amy." I rose slowly, carefully balancing my flowers lest I spill them once more.

"What are you doing here? What do you want?" Before I could answer, Amy the Ex turned to the first woman. "It's okay, Liz. I'll handle this."

The woman named Liz hitched her designer purse over her bony shoulder and went out the front door to a polished black convertible.

Amy the Ex planted her hands on her perfect hips. She had gone blond, and her eyes were bluer and her figure even more voluptuous than the last time I'd seen her. How was that even possible? I wanted the name of whatever wonder pill she was popping or fountain of youth she was bathing in under a full moon.

"Is there something I can do for you?" She looked with distaste at the pink flowers. "You aren't really selling those hideous things door to door are you?" She shook her head. "They're hardly appropriate for a wedding ceremony." She wore a tight-fitting blue dress and matching heels. I was lucky on days I could find a matching pair of socks.

"No. I picked these up at the farmers market. Beautiful, aren't they? Have you ever been?"

"To the farmers market? No, I have not. I am rather busy, Ms. Simms. We're planning for our grand opening. There is quite a lot to do yet." She looked at the door. "So, if you don't mind?"

"Actually," I said before she could toss me out on my ear, "that's why I'm here. A friend of mine was interested in one of your gowns."

"You have a friend?"

I ignored the insult. "Well, sort of. That is, Jerry Kennedy, Chief Kennedy—"

Her nose wrinkled as if a skunk had just crossed her path. A telephone rang in the bowels of the store. "I have to get that. Follow me. And please," she said, pointing a manicured finger at the flowers, "put that box down and leave it here before you do any more damage."

I set the box just inside the door and followed. Though I tried, my hips didn't seem capable of sashaying half as well as Amy the Ex's did. I could have followed her with my eyes closed simply by following the scent of magnolia, honey, and lily of the valley that trailed in her wake.

I waited while Amy the Ex wrapped up a brief and mostly one-sided conversation with what sounded like a vendor of some sort. She seemed to be haggling over dates and prices.

I sensed that Dream Gowns was going to be very Southern in style and very hard on the pocketbook. The salon's walls had been painted off-white, and fashionable gowns hung on long, chrome clothes rods along the walls. Several low glass tables held a small assortment of accessories, including veils, belts, and crystal-covered shoes. There were two rows of pale pink satin-curtained dressing rooms toward the rear with a riser and three full-length mirrors between them along the back wall.

As I continued waiting, a man came in from the rear dressed in a green delivery uniform. "I've got a couple of boxes for you." He held out an electronic pad. "Sign here, please."

"I'm sorry, I don't work here," I answered.

Amy the Ex made a face at the two of us that clearly meant for us to keep our voices down. He extended the pad toward her. She held up a finger to indicate he should wait and she'd be done in a moment.

Three minutes later, during which the deliveryman and I spent awkwardly avoiding eye contact with each other, Amy the Ex hung up. She snatched the pad from the driver without a word and signed. "Leave the boxes in the storeroom, please. That's a dear."

I nodded toward the man's retreating back. "That's dangerous, you know."

"What is?"

Amy the Ex narrowed her eyes.

"That is, I heard that several merchants around town have had things stolen from their shops. The police think the perpetrator or perpetrators are coming in through the service entrances.

"There have been no signs of broken locks or busted windows. You should keep your back door locked, even during business hours. You have a lot of expensive-looking bridal wear here."

"I'll keep that in mind." Derek's ex took a seat in a black velvet chair against the wall and crossed her legs. She eyed me expectantly. Though several other chairs were spread nearby, I was not invited to sit.

I cleared my throat. "Speaking of police, as I said, Jerry Kennedy and his wife, Sandra—do you know Sandra?"

Amy the Ex shook her head. "We've not had the pleasure."

I cleared my throat once again. I felt like I'd swallowed a frog. Why hadn't I told Jerry to do his own dirty work? "They're planning a vow renewal, which I'm sure will be lovely, and of course, he expects Sandra will want to patronize Dream Gowns for her dress.

"I told him I would reach out to you." I smiled grandly, hoping she'd smile back, though I wasn't sure if such a thing were possible. "We business owners need to stick together, right?"

She looked down her perfect nose at me. "I'd hardly equate selling birdseed with selling couture gowns."

"No, of course not. The thing is, Jerry is really hoping you'll give him a professional discount."

She threw back her head and laughed. "And he sent you to ask me?"

I shrugged lamely. I was going to kill Jerry for talking me into coming down and asking a favor of this vile woman.

Amy the Ex stood, and I took a step back. She tilted her head, then paced the carpet a moment before stopping inches from me. "I'll tell you what, Ms. Simms. You can tell Chief Kennedy that I will be very happy to give him a professional discount." She grinned, but I sensed evil behind those perfect white teeth. "Shall we make it thirty percent?"

"That sounds wonderful," I said. Had she really agreed to give Jerry a discount? A thirty percent discount? Was the ice between us caused by me taking up with her ex-husband finally thawing?

"Chief Kennedy," I said, "and his wife will be delighted to hear it. I'll be sure to let them know. I can see that you aren't quite open officially to the public yet, but maybe Sandra could stop by sometime and discuss what she's looking for in her gown?"

"Of course," Amy the Ex said, folding her arms over her hard-to-miss bosom.

"Thank you, Amy. I can't wait to tell Jerry the news." I turned to leave.

"Oh, Ms. Simms."

I turned. "Yes?" I asked lightly.

"There is one little thing that I'll need you to do for me in return." She pinched her thumb and index finger together.

"Of course." I smiled. "What's that?"

"I'll need you to stay away from Derek."

15

"She really said that?" Kim looked at me in wide-eyed wonder.

"Yep. She really said that." I mounded some black soil beneath the plant with my bare hands and tamped it lightly. I had just finished telling Kim about my day and what Amy Harlan had demanded of me in exchange for giving Sandra Kennedy a discount on her gown.

"What did Derek say when you told him?"

"Nothing."

"Nothing?"

"Actually, I haven't told him yet. Frankly, I'm not sure if I'm going to." After my conversation with Amy the Ex, I'd been so flustered that I hadn't even gone back to Derek's office like I was supposed to. I'd come straight home and started planting the flowers Frank Duvall had sold me.

"Amy!" cried Kim, looking down on me from the porch. Her hands gripped the front rail. "You've got to tell him."

I glanced up at her, then grabbed the trowel and dug another shallow hole. "And have him think I'm some jealous little girl? No, thanks." I stood and wiped my hands. "They look nice, don't you think?"

"Yeah, yeah. More flowers, very nice. Don't change the subject." Kim followed after me as I picked up my trowel and gardening tray and carried it around to the small shed against the back of the house. "Your boyfriend's ex-wife just warned you to stay away from him. What are you going to do about it?"

"Nothing," I said. I set the gardening tools away and locked the shed. We went into Birds & Bees through the back door. It seemed we were just as guilty of leaving our service entrance doors unlocked as everybody else.

"Don't you think Derek's going to wonder why you never returned to his office as you said you would? I thought you wanted to talk to Ben Harlan to learn what Professor Mason had contacted him about?"

"I called their receptionist and told her to relay to Derek that something had come up. And yes, I do want to know what business Mason might have had that required him to contact a lawyer while here." I'd just been too flustered to deal with it then.

Kim followed me upstairs to my apartment. "By the way, Dan told me that Jerry wants to talk to you."

I went to the bathroom and turned the faucet on full blast. Kim leaned against the doorframe.

"Again?" I said, scrubbing my hands with soap and water. I toweled dry. "If it's about the dress, forget it. I'm done being his intermediary. If he wants a discount from Amy Harlan, he's either going to have to ask her himself or arrest her and force it out of her.

"Personally," I added, squeezing past Kim and heading to the kitchen, "I hope it's the latter."

"It's not about that," Kim said, gladly accepting the tumbler I handed her and holding it out while I filled it with chilled sangria.

"What's it about then?" I took my own glass and sat at the kitchen table. I was still upset over my encounter with Amy the Ex. What was I going to do about it? What was I going to do about her? And why did she have to open her bridal salon right next door to Derek's law office? Were there no empty storefronts available in Charlotte? Or on the moon?

"It's about that laxative found in Professor Livingston's stomach."

"Yeah, weird, huh?" I stood on tiptoes and rummaged through the cabinets. There was a bag of tortilla chips around here somewhere. I found it on my third attempt and ripped the bag open, setting it between us on the table.

"No salsa?" Kim asked.

"I'll look." I got up from my chair and threw open the fridge. I found an open jar on the middle shelf of the refrigerator door and took it to the table. It looked a little sketchy—a bit too green and goopy for a red salsa. I unscrewed the lid and took a sniff. "A little iffy maybe," I said, "but I don't think it will kill us." I pushed the glass jar toward her. "You first."

Kim shrugged off my concerns, dipped a chip, and took a bite.

"Seems fine." She chewed, and her eyes got all fluttery. A moment later, her hands flew to her neck, and she began gasping.

I folded my arms over my chest and rolled my eyes. "You're a worse actor than Cousin Riley."

"Fine," Kim said, giving up the act. "I can see I won't be able to count on you when some psycho poisons me."

"I guess we'll just have to wait and see." I dipped a tortilla chip in the jar. "Now, speaking of poisons, finish telling me what you started to say about the laxative that showed up in Mason's toxicology report."

"Dan says that Jerry says the laxative had to come from either the wine or . . ."

"Or what?"

"The chocolates you gave to the professor."

"Why my chocolates?"

"Because wine and chocolate-covered cherries were the only contents of the professor's stomach, according to Dan." I had to admit, having Kim dating Officer Dan Sutton was not only good for her love life, it was turning out to be a great way for me to glean inside information.

"Esther bought those chocolates for me at Otelia's. You know that. I can't imagine for one second Otelia suddenly taking to lacing her chocolates with—" I tapped my glass. "What was it Anita called it?"

Kim scrunched up her nose. "Biscuit something?"

"Bisacodyl," I remembered suddenly. "That's what it was."

"If you say so." Kim helped herself to a handful of chips, then leaned back in her chair. "All I know is, Jerry wants to talk to you about it."

"Fine. It can wait until tomorrow." I stood. "Don't fill up on chips."

"Why not?"

"Because I don't want you to spoil your appetite."

"Don't worry," Kim replied, shoving two chips in her mouth at once. "You know me, I can always eat."

I knew that. What I didn't know was how she maintained her figure. "Good, because I'm treating you to dinner." I selected a light green sweater from the coat closet near the apartment door and took my purse and keys from the table.

Kim followed me. "Great. Where are we going?"

"You'll see."

I drove. Kim played with the radio incessantly. I preferred Broadway musical show tunes. She preferred country and western. She won, if only because I had my hands on the wheel and my eyes on the road.

"Truckee's?" Kim gaped.

"Yep." Truckee's Road Stop sprawled over several acres of pitted blacktop and several more acres of gravel and dirt. The truckers came because it was close to the highway with easy on and off access.

I pulled into the lot. Lines of semis were idling at the gas pumps. As for the food, the servings were large and the prices were small. Truckers could park their long-haulers for as long as they liked, and there were free showers. And they only charged a buck for the use of a clean towel.

It didn't hurt that Truckee's also had a full liquor license.

I'd come once or twice when in high school and never since. But everybody in town knew Greg Tuffnall. The Tuffnalls had owned the highway rest stop for as long as I could remember. Greg's granddad had built the place by hand, and a Tuffnall had been running it ever since.

The bar had been added to the side of the diner in the sixties, and though the diner and bar shared a kitchen, the county had insisted at the time that it have a separate entrance.

"We're eating in the bar?"

"Didn't I mention? I'm treating you to drinks, too."

Kim hurried after me. "Aren't they ever going to resurface this parking lot?"

I stopped near a rust-pitted lamp pole and studied the complex. "Nothing much has changed in fifty years, has it?"

"Probably not even the grease in the fryers," Kim quipped. "Can we go inside?" She fanned her face. "It stinks of diesel out here."

"Don't worry," I said as I covered the last few steps to the bar's entrance, "I'll bet it smells just as bad inside."

16

The small bar was dark and crowded. I was right about the smell. Although smoking had long been banned, you would never have known it based on the smell of tobacco emanating from every inch of the place. The distinct odor of diesel also hung in the air like it was ninety percent of the atmosphere. Truckee's Bar was a relic of the sixties, in looks, furnishings, and aroma.

An American flag hung on the far wall next to a photograph of Richard Nixon. I led us to a couple of empty stools at the bar.

"Can't we at least sit at a booth or a table?" Kim complained as she sat down beside me.

"It's easier to talk here."

"We can talk just as easily in a comfortable booth as we can on these stupid stools." She swayed and bobbled uneasily on the loose stool.

"It's not you I want to talk to." I waved to the barmaid.

"What? You didn't invite me to Truckee's Bar to talk about my day and enjoy my scintillating conversation?"

"Is Greg Tuffnall here this evening?"

"Sure." The barmaid, a stout woman in her forties, planted her hands on the bar. "He's over in the diner. You looking for him or looking to avoid him?"

"I was hoping to speak with him. We're old friends."

Out of the corner of my eye, I noticed Kim's jaw drop.

"I'll tell him you're here." The barmaid wrung out her rag—which was cleaner than I would have expected—and ran it over the space in front of Kim and me. "Just who do I say you are?"

"Amy. Amy Simms. This is Kim Christy. The three of us went to high school together."

She seemed to take the fact at face value. "Can I get you two ladies anything to drink in the meantime?"

"What do you recommend?"

"We've got an IPA on tap that's good, cold, and on sale for two bucks a glass until seven."

"We'll take two of those," Kim agreed quickly. "And I'll have the cheeseburger basket with extra mayo."

I'd forgotten that I had promised Kim dinner. "Give me the same," I said, "but you can give her my mayo."

The barmaid scribbled our orders on a pad and poured and handed us our beer. "I'll let Tuff know you're here."

I tried the beer. "Not bad."

Kim drank hers half down. "Do you remember how everybody used to call Greg Tuffnall Tuff? I'd forgotten until she said it."

"Yeah. The guys in school used to say he was tough as nails." Greg Tuffnall had a reputation for getting into fights, and I didn't think he'd ever lost one.

Our food arrived with Greg Tuffnall. Each of his hands held a cheeseburger basket. "Well, well." He grinned as he placed the paper-lined baskets before us. "When Martha told me there was an Amy Simms and a Kim Christy here to see me, I almost couldn't believe it."

"Hello, Greg. It's been a long time. It's good to see you again."

He tipped back his head and looked me over in a way that made me uneasy. "It's been a long time all right."

Tuffnall leaned toward Kim, his stomach pressing into the counter. "It's been a long time since I've laid eyes on you, too, Kimmy." He batted his lashes and leered. He smelled of cheap cologne and day-old grease.

"Hello, Greg." Kim pulled the top off her burger, laid three French fries across the burger patty, squirted on some ketchup from a bottle Martha had left for us, then replaced the bun top. "Nice place you've got here. I'll have to tell my boyfriend about it." Kim had a way of putting men in their place, and she clearly wanted Greg Tuffnall securely in his.

"You haven't changed much, Greg." There was just more of him. Not that I was going to call that to his attention. Greg had always been a beefy guy, but some of that beef had now gone to a roll of fat around his waist, bulging over his gold belt buckle. Greg had short black hair. He always had. He called it a military cut, and the description fit. His eyes were dark blue and matched the dark khakis he was wearing.

I pulled my basket closer and took a whiff. It didn't smell bad at all.

Greg rolled up the sleeves of his gray shirt, then poured himself a beer from the tap. He tipped the glass to his lips in a manner meant to show off his biceps. "Tell me what's going on, ladies?"

"Going on?" I took a bite of my burger, feeling the warm juices trickle over my tongue. "What do you mean?"

"I mean, I haven't seen either of you in fifteen years or more, and now you show up here?" He set his beer on the counter. "I'm guessing you're not here for the food or the beer."

"Why do you think we're here?" Kim asked.

"Well," he turned her way, "I wish it was because you had a sudden craving for me."

Kim pulled a face.

Tuffnall continued. "But I'm guessing it's because you want information."

"And what kind of information might that be?" pressed Kim.

I wiped a paper napkin across my lips. "Let's stop pretending," I said to Kim. Turning to Greg, I said, "You know why I'm here. I heard that Mason Livingston was in here the other night."

Greg grinned. "And you want to know what he was talking about?"

I pursed my lips. "Yes," I admitted. "I do."

Greg folded his arms across his chest. "It's going to cost you."

"What exactly did you have in mind?" I wasn't sure I wanted to know.

"A date."

"What?" Kim spat beer and dropped her mug.

Greg cursed. He snatched a towel from under the counter and wiped up the spill. "One date. That's all I want." He handed Kim a fresh mug of beer.

Kim looked at me. "With which one of us?"

I glared at her. "It doesn't matter which one!" I kicked Kim in the shin. "We both have boyfriends. We are *not* going out with you."

"Okay . . ." Greg grabbed a fry from Kim's basket and ran it over his lower lip before biting into it and swallowing. "How about just a kiss then?" He turned on me and puckered up. "Let's start with you, Amy."

I jerked back and fell off my stool.

Greg threw back his head and laughed. The barmaid, Martha, was laughing, too.

I clung to the barstool with one hand, while Kim assisted me up with the other. "You are a jerk," I said, blushing and straightening my clothes. I resettled myself at the bar.

"Man, you always were a real stick in the mud," Greg remarked, "you know that?"

I frowned. "That's not true at all."

He rolled his eyes. "You were never any fun in high school, and you're no fun now."

"Listen, Greg," I began. "We came in here because a friend of mine was killed the other day. I'd like to know why, and I'd like to know who did it. Are you going to tell me what you know or not?

"Because if you're not, I'm going to stop forcing myself to swallow this horrible piece of shoe leather you pass off as a cheeseburger and leave!"

Greg laughed again. "You are a hoot, Amy." He banged his fist against the bar. "A hoot! Get it?" He pointed his finger at me. "You own a bird store? Hoot?" He shook his head in disgust and turned to Kim. "You need a new sidekick, Kimmy. This one is dragging you down."

"That's it." I pulled out my wallet and threw down a credit card. "Tell me what I owe you so we can get out of here!"

"Tuff!" hollered Martha from the other end of the bar where she was in conversation with a pair of truckers who looked fresh off the road. "You stop giving those two ladies a hard time and answer their questions!"

Greg looked at Martha sheepishly. "Yes, dear."

Kim bobbed her head. "Dear?"

"He's my idiot husband!" Martha barked.

I looked at Greg Tuffnall from under a new light. "You're married."

"Yes, ma'am." He was beaming. "Going on seven years." He held up three fingers. "Got three kids. Two of 'em are stepkids," he said, leaning closer, "but I love 'em all the same."

I felt my heart rate dropping down to something in the normal range.

Kim chuckled and sank her teeth into her burger. "Boy, you really had Amy going there, Greg," she said as she chewed.

"You knew?" I gaped at her. "You were in on this?"

"No, I didn't know."

I studied her face for signs of confabulation and came up empty. That didn't mean she wasn't fibbing; it only meant I was terrible at determining such things. "Fine. Can we get back to the point of this little visit, Greg?" I demanded.

"Okay, so you want to know about this Mason guy."

"Yes. Lance Jennings told me that you told him that the professor was in here the other night."

"That guy was a professor?" Greg seemed genuinely surprised.

"Yes, now spill," I insisted.

"Like I told Lance, Mason came in here with some blonde."

"Describe her."

Greg rubbed his chin. "Tall, for a girl. Platinum blonde. A real looker." He shot a nervous look at Martha, but she hadn't heard or had chosen not to.

"That sounds like Violet Wilcox," I said. "She works for the radio station."

"Did you hear what they talked about?" Kim asked.

"Sure, they were sitting right here at the bar."

"And?" I said. "What did they talk about?"

"This and that." Greg sipped his beer. "She was asking him all kinds of questions."

"Such as?"

"She wanted to know where he got his ideas for his books. He didn't seem to want to talk about it. Then she was asking him some personal stuff. Like was he married and all."

"Did they seem . . ." I wondered how to phrase it. "Intimate?"

"You mean like lovers?"

I nodded.

"I did get the feeling that she was coming on to him. You know, laying into him a bit."

That was interesting. "How long did they stay? Did they leave to-gether?"

"The woman left after about forty minutes. She split the minute Duvall showed up."

"Frank Duvall?" I asked.

"Yep. Frank comes in now and again for a drink. Especially after he's made a delivery.

"Your pal and Frank took a seat at the booth over there." Greg pointed to the back corner. "So don't ask me what they were talking about."

I swiveled my head toward the now empty booth. "So the two of them took a booth in the corner, and Wilcox left." I drummed my fingers against the bar. What did it mean, if anything?

"Yep. Of course, it wasn't just the two of them. When the lady showed up, she joined them."

"What lady? Was it Rose Smith?"

Greg furrowed his brow. "Who?"

I described the bookshop owner. "She owns Bookarama in town."

"I don't read a whole lot of books," Greg remarked. "But the woman you described doesn't sound like the one that was in here. That one had short hair and glasses."

"Cara Siskin," I said.

"Who was that again?" Kim asked. She had finished her burger and was twisting the remaining French fry in her fingers.

"The publicist Mason was working with."

I pushed my hands through my hair in frustration. "Okay. So Mason comes here with Violet Wilcox. Then what? He leaves with Cara Siskin?" She hadn't denied that the two of them were sleeping together. So she could have spent the night with Mason. I had to have been wrong about Rose and Mason's budding relationship.

Greg shook his head. "Your friend, Mason, left alone. That woman and Frank, they stayed a while though." He turned to his wife. "Ain't that right, Martha?"

"Tuff's right, ladies. I served them myself."

"Do you have any idea what they were talking about?" It seemed odd to me that the farmer and the publicist would have had anything in common that would have kept them in the bar together after Mason had gone. Wasn't Mason the common thread?

"No idea." Martha joined us at the bar. "Every time I went to the table to refill their drinks, the whole lot of them shut up. Whatever it was, it wasn't a friendly conversation."

"They were arguing?" I asked.

"Working in a bar you get pretty good at reading body language, and from the way those three bodies were behaving, I'd guess it wasn't exactly a lovefest." She nudged her husband. "Did you tell them how Mason came in again the very day he was murdered, Tuff?"

"No, I didn't get to that."

"When was this?" I asked.

"Around lunch," Greg explained. "Not that he ate anything."

"No," agreed Martha, "but he sure did drink, didn't he, Tuff?"

Greg nodded. "That he did."

"Was he alone?" asked Kim. "Or were the others with him?"

"He was as alone as a lonesome whippoorwill," Greg replied.

17

There had been nothing more to learn at Truckee's Road Stop. I dropped Kim off at her house and called it a night. The next morning, as I was unlocking the door to Birds & Bees, I spotted Chief Jerry Kennedy heading toward the store by way of Ruby's Diner.

"Good morning, Jerry." I held open the door, and he stepped past me in his crisp brown uniform.

"Coffee on?"

I rolled my eyes. "Not yet. Didn't you have your fill at the diner?"

He scowled in reply.

"Fine. I'll start a pot."

Jerry followed me to the kitchen in the rear of the store. "You were supposed to come see me. Since you didn't, I figured I might as well come see you."

Right, and get a free cup of coffee and a handful of peanuts, I thought as I scooped fresh coffee grounds into the filter tray. "Sorry. I've been busy."

Jerry tipped back his cap. "We found a strong laxative in Mason Livingston's stomach."

I acted surprised because I didn't want to get Anita in trouble. "Did it kill him?"

Jerry looked at me like I was crazy. "Jeez, Amy. You saw the guy. He was stabbed to death with a pair of scissors."

"Right. I simply thought that maybe somebody really wanted him dead."

"And?"

"And poisoned him, then stabbed him. Where did the scissors come from, by the way?"

"That I can tell you. Rose Smith says she kept them in a small jar at the register along with some pens and pencils. It's one of the few things she has been willing to explain." He hitched up his belt and opened my mini-fridge. "No pastries?"

"Sorry, like I said, I've been busy. Mom's bringing something down later if you want to stick around." Sure, it was peanut-flavored suet, but I'd let Jerry discover that for himself. I grabbed two mugs from the cabinet and set them on the counter beside the coffee maker. "Is it or isn't it possible that Mason was poisoned first?"

"Oh, he was poisoned all right, but according to the medical examiner, it would never have killed him." Jerry tittered. "It would have made him mighty uncomfortable, however."

I could only imagine. "In other words, Mason didn't take the laxative himself?"

"Nope. It's highly unlikely anyway. There was no sign of any capsules or pills. The man had three things in his gut: laxative, wine, and chocolates."

That didn't sound like a very pleasant combination. "Before you ask, I have no idea how the bisacodyl got in those chocolate-covered cherries I gave him."

Jerry narrowed his eyes at me. "How did you know it was bisacodyl, Simms?"

"Well, I—" The coffee pot beeped. "Oh, look. The coffee's done." I poured us each a cup. "Cream and sugar, right?

I held out the sugar bowl, and Jerry reluctantly spooned some into his cup. "Did you analyze the wine?"

"The laxative wasn't in the wine. It was in your lousy chocolates."

"I wouldn't let Otelia Newsome hear you call her chocolates lousy," I joked.

Jerry didn't think I was funny. "There were several more uneaten chocolates containing that drug in that box of yours."

"Wow." I didn't know what else to say. "I didn't put it there, Jerry."

"I didn't figure you did." He seemed reluctant to admit it. "So who did?"

"You mean who else handled the chocolates?" I gave it some thought. "Esther bought them. Surely you don't suspect her."

Jerry pulled a face. "Of course, not. That old lady's harmless."

I wasn't so sure I'd agree with Jerry's characterizing Esther as "harmless," but I didn't think she would poison anybody's chocolates. Steal them while they weren't looking? Yes. Poison them? No. "The chocolates sat here in the store until the night of the signing."

"Where exactly?"

I told him to follow me to the front of the store. I pointed. "On a shelf under the sales counter. As far as I know, they remained there until I carried them to the book signing and handed them to Mason personally."

"So anybody could have had access to them here." Jerry sipped his coffee thoughtfully.

"I suppose. It's not like we're always watching the front. Sometimes we have to go assist customers. And if one of us is alone in the store . . ." I shrugged.

"Somebody coming in could have laced the chocolates."

"I guess so." Though it seemed unlikely. "What about at Bookarama? Couldn't they have been tampered with there?"

"Not impossible, but I don't see how there was time or opportunity."

I didn't either. "There were close to fifty people milling around before and after the signing. That means plenty of people could conceivably have done it."

"And plenty of people who could have caught them doing it."

He was right. "Have you talked to Mason's publicist, Cara Siskin? Or Frank Duvall?"

Jerry set his mug on the counter and sauntered over to the seed bins—a move I had been expecting. He thrust a hand into the shelled peanut bin and shoveled a generous handful of them into his mouth. "We talked to everybody and came up empty. The only one who seems to have had it in for your professor pal is Amber Smith."

"What about the scissors? There must have been fingerprints."

"Either the killer wore gloves," Jerry mumbled through a mouthful of peanut mash, "or they wiped them clean afterwards."

"Gloves?" I frowned. "Did you search the bookstore and their living quarters?"

Jerry looked at me as if I'd just asked the dumbest question imaginable. I supposed it was. "Yes, Simms, we searched the whole damn house. And we came up empty. No gloves, laxatives, no signed confession with a carefully worded explanation for why one of them murdered your friend.

"But trust me. I don't care how smart a lawyer Amber's mom got for her—she's guilty and I'm going to prove it."

"Has she admitted to egging Mason's trailer?"

Jerry shook his head. "Sooner or later I'll find a witness who saw her do it though. She admits she was camping down by Ruby Lake. Add that to her on tape buying the eggs at the market that very night and you don't need a calculator to get your answer."

"She didn't do it, Jerry."

"She had a class several years back with your friend."

"So did I and thousands of others. It doesn't make us all suspects," I said, reflecting on what Derek had remarked. "Did she pass his class?"

Jerry drew in a long breath. "To tell the truth, she dropped out after the first week or so. Switched to a communications course. Dropped out of school a bit after that."

"Good grief, Jerry. That means she probably didn't have five minutes' interaction with the guy. Those classes are huge."

"Yeah, well," Jerry hemmed and hawed. "I still say she did it and her mother's covering for her. I ought to nail her, too."

"Come on, Jerry. Even if Rose is covering for Amber, can you blame her?"

Jerry's face said that he could. "Maybe the guy wanted a cut of the book sales, and they wouldn't give it to him."

"He's the book's author. He was going to get a cut of the book sales anyway."

"It's just a theory." Jerry was pouting.

"Amber did not kill Mason," I repeated. She might have egged his trailer though, and I had no hunches why. It was the wrong time of year for Halloween tricks, and pummeling the trailer with two dozen eggs was no idle prank. Somebody had been seriously annoyed.

"If Amber didn't kill Livingston, then tell me who did."

I thought a moment as I grabbed a big bag of shelled peanuts and topped off the bin. I liked to start each day with everything just so, and Jerry, as usual, was messing with my sense of order. "Mister Duvall was trying to get Mason involved in some scheme of his."

"What sort of scheme?"

"Duvall wanted the professor to endorse a new plant cultivar he claimed to have developed."

Jerry appeared amused. He bounced the remaining peanuts up

and down in his hands, oblivious to the ones spilling to my clean floor. "And you think maybe they had a falling out and Duvall stuck a pair of scissors in Livingston's neck all because of a flower?"

"He was there, Jerry. At Bookarama. He had the opportunity." I bent and began picking peanuts off the hardwood.

Jerry shook his head. "Hummingbirds and flowers. If it wasn't for a dead body with a pair of shears in his neck, I'd say this whole case was absurd. You know, I even found a flower in his suitcase."

I raised my brow as I looked up at Jerry. "Whose suitcase?"

"Livingston's. I've got it down at the station. Not much in there besides some warm clothes, socks, and dirty underwear. And some flower swathed in some sort of foam and plastic wrap."

I stood and dumped the peanuts I'd retrieved in the trash can near the cash register. That had to be the ratty suitcase I'd seen resting beside Jerry's desk the other day. "Can you describe the flower?"

"Describe it? It was a flower for crying out loud, Simms." He snorted and grabbed a refill on the peanuts. I'd have to top off the bin again once he'd finished marauding. "You know what a flower looks like."

I could see that Jerry was no gardening enthusiast. "Can I see it?"

Jerry gave it some thought. "Fine. I don't see what harm it can do. If you want to take a look at it, help yourself." He leveled a finger at me. "But the flower and the suitcase don't leave the police station.

"I'll leave word that you can take a look." He rolled his eyes. "For what it's worth." He threw open the front door, then turned to me and said, "And if you can think of any other way, any plausible way, that those chocolate-covered cherries got turned into laxatives, you let me know ASAP!"

"What's so important about them? You said it yourself, Mason was killed by stabbing."

"Yeah, that he was," said Jerry. "But maybe our killer poisoned him a little first. Weakened him before finishing him off." He tipped his hat. "At least that's another theory of mine."

Though I'd never admit it to his face, it was a pretty good theory.

"What about Violet Wilcox?"

"What about her?"

"Have you looked into her background? Did you interview her? Ask her where she was at the time of Mason's murder?"

Jerry's hand went to the gun at his hip. "Let me tell you something—that Violet Wilcox is a pain in the butt. Interview her? Heck, I tried, but interviewing her is like wrestling a greased pig. For every question I asked her, she drilled me with twelve more."

"Lance told me she was ambitious," I replied, grinning at the image of the strong-willed woman giving Jerry a run for his money.

"Ambitious?" snorted Jerry. "She's a b—" He held his tongue as two women maneuvered past him and into the store. "Lovely morning, isn't it ladies?"

After they passed, he urged me closer. "What is it now, Jerry?"

"Did you get a chance to talk to Amy Harlan about that discount?"

The corner of my mouth went down. "Yes, I asked her."

"And?"

"And she promised you and Sandra a thirty percent discount." I left off that little bit about me needing to avoid Derek. Personally, I didn't think Amy Harlan would have the guts to tell Jerry and his wife no to the discount when they showed up expecting it. I smiled at the thought of watching her squirm and lose thirty percent of her profit.

"You're all right, Simms."

I took that as Jerry's way of saying thank you.

18

As Jerry swaggered back to his squad car parked in the lot of Ruby's Diner, I tended to my customers. The women expressed an interest in the hummingbird feeders they had been admiring on the lawn and porch before coming in.

"We read about that awful murder of the man who wrote the book on hummingbirds," said the younger of the two women. "Do you carry it? I'd love to get a copy."

"I'm afraid not. Bookarama downtown carries it, but they're closed for the time being."

"Such a shame," said her companion. "Imagine the story we could tell our friends back home if we returned from our vacation from the very town where there was a murder."

"And with a book written by the murder victim!" agreed her friend.

They bought two hanging hummingbird feeders and some prepared hummingbird food, so I held my tongue until after they'd gone.

"What a pair," I said to my mother as I helped her set up a display of her homemade suet cakes.

"Pair of what?" Kim asked, coming in from the back and tying on her apron.

I explained about the women who'd come in asking about Mason's book.

"That's sick," agreed Kim. She picked up one of Mom's suet cakes and inspected it. "Barbara's Bird Bars. Cool." She set the cake back in the stack with the others in their place of honor between the cash register and the credit card scanner. "I'll bet we sell a million of them."

"Please." Mom threw her hands in the air. "I can only make a couple dozen at a time. And even that takes hours."

"You've got to think big, Barbara," Kim said. "I can see it now." She waved her hand in front of her face. "We need a factory."

Mom looked befuddled. "A factory?"

"Sure. A small one at first, but who knows?" Kim tapped her fingers against her chin. "Who do we know that's good distributor, Amy?"

"Sorry," I said, removing my apron and hanging it on the hook on the wall. "My shift is over. I'll leave the two of you to your empire building."

Mom smiled. "Say hi to Derek for me."

"How did you know I was going to see Derek?"

"He called the apartment. He said you weren't answering your cell phone but that you had phoned him earlier wanting to talk. I told him you'd call him back as soon as you could."

"Rats. I do want to talk to him." I was sorry I'd missed him. "I must have been with a customer or talking to Jerry." I pulled my cell phone from my pocket. Sure enough, the ringer was off, and Derek had called.

"Jerry was here?" Kim said. "What did he want?"

"Besides free coffee? He asked me if I could explain how the chocolate-covered cherries got laced with a potent laxative."

"What did you tell him?" inquired Mom.

"I told him the truth. I have no idea," I answered. "Did Derek say where he would be for me to call him, Mom?"

"He said he would be in the office all day."

"Great." Mom had guessed right. That was where I had been intending to go.

"Are you going to mention you-know-what when you see him?"

"You don't have to be coy, Kim. I told Mom all about it."

Kim turned to my mother. "You know that Derek's ex told your daughter to stay away from him?"

Mom nodded. "I do think you might mention it, Amy. If you want an honest relationship with a person, it should be open and frank. I'm not saying you have to throw his ex under the bus or say anything nasty about her, but be truthful."

"I don't know, Mom." Cara Siskin's words came back to me. "I've heard that the truth can be overrated."

Before Mom could argue with that statement, I begged off. I ran upstairs to change out of my store clothes and into a comfortable pair of shorts and a fresh shirt that didn't display the name of my store.

When I arrived at Harlan and Harlan, the reception area was blissfully unoccupied, and I discovered Derek eating a bag lunch at his desk.

Seated across from him was his ex-wife.

So much for bliss.

"Amy!" Derek pushed back his chair and stood. "Mrs. Edmunds didn't tell me you were here."

"Reception was empty. She must have stepped out." I wouldn't shed any tears if she'd abandoned her post for good. I glanced at Amy the Ex, looking svelte and barracuda-ish in a slinky gold dress that exposed miles of gym-toned thigh.

"Ms. Simms." Amy the Ex laced her fingers around a tall paper cup from a local tea emporium and stood. "Thank you for lunch, Derek. We'll talk again soon." She nodded at me and went out the door, leaving a trail of her signature perfume in her wake.

"Was I interrupting something?"

"Of course not." Derek motioned to the chair his ex had recently occupied. "Have a seat."

I opted for the chair beside it. "Mom said you called this morning. I'm sorry I missed you."

"Me too. Same for yesterday. What happened to you?" He gathered up his sandwich wrapper and used napkin, dropped them into the paper bag, and let the bag fall to the wastebasket with a thud. "I thought we were going to ask Dad about his business dealings with Mason?"

I squirmed and crossed my legs. "Something came up." That something being my ugly interaction with his ex-wife and her outlandish ultimatum.

Derek looked surprised. "Something more important than finding out everything you can about Mason's past and his murder?" He grinned. "That doesn't sound like you." He tilted a large cup of tea with a red-and-white straw in it my way. "Care for some?"

"No, thanks."

"Listen, about my ex-wife. We weren't really having lunch together. She had some business issues to go over, so I thought it best we handle it here. In the office."

"Did I say anything?"

"No," he replied slowly. "Not exactly. But you do seem a bit on edge." His eyes went to my bouncing leg.

I forced myself to stop. "Sorry. Did you find out anything from Ben? Was he willing to tell you what Mason consulted him about, or is there some sort of lawyer-client privilege that prevents him?"

Derek shook his head. "No, nothing like that. And it doesn't matter."

"What do you mean?"

"It means the two never spoke."

"No?"

"No. I asked Dad yesterday. He received a call from Mason Livingston, all right. But it went to his voicemail. Mason asked to see him on a legal matter. He didn't say what the legal matter was, and before Dad could get back to him—"

"He was dead."

"Yep." Derek sipped his tea, then extended the cup toward me once more. "Are you sure you don't want some?"

I leaned over and took a drink. It was green tea with mint. "Thanks. This is really good."

"I've asked Dad to see what he can find out."

"Do you really think it will be possible, now that Mason's gone, that he can learn anything?"

"He's put in a call to some attorney in Houston."

"The one that Mason had been on the phone with right before he was stabbed?"

"Yes." Derek swirled the ice around in his cup. "He should be hearing back today."

"That's great. Will you let me know if you uncover anything? Anything at all?"

Derek agreed. "So," he came around the desk and massaged my shoulders from behind, "are we good here?"

"Mmm," I moaned. "Very good."

He leaned over and kissed me softly on the lips. I decided that two could play that game.

When we came up for air, I said, "Derek, I have something to tell you."

"You don't have to tell me. I know."

"You do?"

"Amy, my Amy said...that is . . ."

"I know who you mean," I interjected. "Tell me what she said."

"She said she told you that if you wanted Chief Kennedy to get a discount on some dress from her shop, then, in exchange, you'd have to agree to stay away from me." His laughter filled the office.

"What's so funny?"

"Are you kidding?" Seeing the look of annoyance on my face, he continued. "I mean, come on. You know she was kidding, right?"

"I do?"

"Sure." He took my hands. "It was a joke, Amy. Nothing but a harmless joke."

"Harmless!" I pulled my hands free. "In the first place, I don't see anything funny about it. So don't even get me started on harmless. You do realize your ex-wife hates me, don't you?"

Derek shook his head. "She doesn't hate you. I admit, I don't see her inviting you to lunch at the country club anytime soon, but she does not hate you."

"I wouldn't be so sure about that."

Derek's phone rang, and he picked up the receiver. "Tell her I'll be right with her." He replaced the receiver. "Sorry. Business calls. That was Mrs. Edmunds. My one-thirty is here."

He planted a kiss on my nose. "Can we continue this later? Say, over dinner?" Before I could reply, he added, "And by *this*, I mean this," he said, kissing me hard on the lips.

I felt a shiver up my spine. "I think that could be arranged."

"Good. Let's go out to eat. You choose the place. Pick you up at seven?"

"You're too nice. You know that?"

"Is that a yes?"

I placed my hand behind his neck and pulled his lips to mine. "You figure it out."

Derek offered to walk me out, but I left him to attend to his client and departed through the rear. It was closer to where I'd parked the van, and the fact that I got to avoid the icy Mrs. Edmunds was icing on the cake.

I skirted around the building to Bookarama, curious to see if they'd reopened, but the store appeared quiet. I peeped in the door. There were no lights on, but it was midday and I could see a woman in a baggy T-shirt walking around inside. I banged on the glass. "Rose? Is that you?"

The woman stopped moving. As she turned in my direction, I saw that it was Amber. A bulging black trash bag hung from her left hand. She eyed me curiously.

"It's me, Amy!" I called through the glass. "How are you? Can we talk?"

She glanced upward, then motioned for me to go around to the rear.

I hurried around, cutting through the alley between the barber shop and the hardware store. Amber came out the service entrance of Bookarama lugging the trash.

"Hello, Amy. I'll just be a minute." She dragged the black bag to the dumpster and tossed it inside.

I waited for her in the shade cast by the awning over the rear entrance.

"Is everything okay?" Amber wiped her hands against her blue jeans.

"That's what I wanted to ask you. We haven't spoken since the morning you came by the apartment." I glanced at the upstairs windows. "How are you and your mother holding up?"

"Fine." Amber smiled wanly. "Considering."

"Can we talk inside for a minute, Amber?"

I could sense her hesitation. She twisted a silver ring on her finger round and round before saying, "I-I suppose. Mama's resting though. Come on in, but we'll have to be quiet."

I followed the young woman inside. The space was cold and filled with books. I'd never been in the back of the bookstore before. "Wow. You've got quite an inventory."

"Most of these are used. We buy and sell. Mom tends to get carried away," explained Amber. "I'm not sure we'll ever sell half of these. People come in selling, and Mama doesn't have the heart to say no. You'd be surprised what poor shape some of the books are in when she accepts them."

"Actually, I remember seeing a pile of paperbacks by the front door the other day. All their covers had been torn off."

Amber grinned. "See what I mean?" She took a seat on a small, threadbare stool near a bookshelf and offered me a wobbly office chair that was missing one of its arms.

"Amber, did you egg Mason's trailer?"

The young woman's lower lip trembled. "Yes."

"Why?"

She was silent a moment, playing with her ring. "Because I saw him before the signing. He was back here with Mama. He was trying to kiss her."

"Oh. I see."

"I thought it was disgusting." She looked into my eyes. "It turns out I was wrong about the whole thing. Mom told me later that she liked him."

I couldn't help smiling. "I saw Mason and Rose together at Brewer's. They did seem to be getting along rather nicely."

"I felt so stupid. It's been a long time since Mama's had somebody in her life. I overreacted. But I didn't kill him."

Tears had begun to fall. "I mean," she rubbed her nose with the back of her hand, "I know it was stupid, egging his trailer and all." She took a deep breath. "But I felt I had to do something."

I smiled. "Did you tell Chief Kennedy that?"

"Yeah. He thinks I killed Professor Livingston."

"Well, I don't." I clasped my hands on my knees. "And I don't think your mother did either."

"She didn't."

"I know. She was talking to a friend of mine at the time. Why do you think said she killed him?"

Amber smiled sadly. "She told me she thought I did it."

"Why would she think that?"

"When she came down and found him dead, she jumped to conclusions. She couldn't imagine who else might have done it. I mean, we are the only people living here."

"But there were dozens of others here that night," I replied. "Do you think I could talk to her?"

"Mama? I don't think now is a good time. I don't want to disturb her. She's been having trouble sleeping."

I nodded commiseratively. "I can imagine. Perhaps another time."

"I'll ask her. I promise." She rose and pulled a paper cone from a steel sleeve attached to the side of a five-gallon water cooler, filled it from the jug, then drank.

"You know, with all these shelves and nooks and crannies, it wouldn't be hard for a person to hide in the store."

Amber turned her head slowly, looking thoughtful. "I guess so."

"Who else was here in the bookstore that night who might have had the opportunity to kill him?"

Amber shook her head in frustration. "You were here, Amy. And after what you just said, I think just about anybody could have murdered the professor."

"You didn't notice anyone in particular hanging around, waiting for Mason maybe?"

"No. I left as soon as the signing was over."

"That's right, you went to the lake."

"Yeah."

I rose. I didn't want to intrude on Amber any longer than necessary. "Derek told me your mother has hired a lawyer."

Amber nodded. "Mama said it was for our own protection." She wrung her hands. "I do hope this is all over soon."

"I hope so, too. If there's anything you can think of that will help Chief Kennedy solve the case, you shouldn't hesitate to tell him. Trust me, he wants the real killer as much as we all do."

"I will."

I walked to the back door. "Will you be opening Bookarama back up soon?"

"I hope so. Business is so-so at best, and this should be the busiest time of year for us. I'm hoping Mama agrees to open back up."

"What's stopping her? The police?"

"No, they've said they're done here. No, Mama doesn't want nosy reporters and lookie-loos poking around."

"I don't blame her. I've been getting a few of those myself."

Amber shook herself. "I think they're morbid."

"I agree. Please tell your mother I said hello and give her my wishes."

Amber opened the door. "I will."

I tapped the door handle. "And you should keep this door locked during the day. There's been a string of break-ins."

"Really? I hadn't heard." She fingered the lock. "I'll try to remember that."

I stepped out into the sun.

"You know," Amber said, "speaking of reporters before . . ."

"Yes?"

"I saw Ms. Wilcox arguing with Mister Duvall and the professor's publicist yesterday. I don't remember her name."

"Cara Siskin."

"That was her name." She grinned at the memory. "She was really badgering them."

"You mean Ms. Wilcox was badgering Mister Duvall and Ms. Siskin?"

"That's right."

"Where was this?"

"Outside the professor's trailer."

"When were you there?"

She dropped her eyes to the ground. "I felt sort of bad about what I did to the professor's birdhouse. I was thinking of maybe trying to clean it up." She shrugged. "Not that I suppose it matters now that he's dead."

"Could you hear what they were arguing about?"

"No. I rode my bike over to the campground and held back when I saw them standing beside the professor's trailer. I don't think they saw me, and I was too far away to hear anything." She twirled a finger through her hair. "Why? Do you think it's important?"

"At this point, with a murderer loose in Ruby Lake, I'd say everything is important."

Amber tilted her head. "I think I hear Mama coming down. I should get inside."

Amber closed the door behind me, and I heard the sound of the lock being set. Smart girl.

I gave it a minute, then made a beeline for the dumpster.

19

While dumpster diving wasn't my favorite sport, I'd make an exception in this case. I knew I was grasping at straws, but I had an itch and I needed to scratch it.

I wanted to know what was in that bulging bag of trash that Amber had just tossed. I believed she and her mother were innocent. "But just in case," I mumbled before taking a look around to make sure the coast was clear and somebody didn't see me jump in the dumpster.

I held my breath and climbed up and in. The commercial-sized trash bin was piled high with various bags and loose odds and ends of assorted refuse.

And it all reeked to high heaven.

Fortunately, if there was a fortunate side to standing knee-deep in a smelly dumpster, I had no trouble finding Amber's recently deposited trash bag. I ripped off the tie and pulled open the top, wishing I'd brought gloves.

Dirty paper towels, paper plates, an assortment of mail and catalogs, scraps of lettuce, broccoli, and chicken bones. And that was just the stuff I could recognize.

Half-gagging I hauled myself out of the dumpster and brushed myself off as best I could. My little dumpster dive had been a waste of time. I'd come up empty-handed.

And I was glad I had. Nothing I'd found inside could in any possible way have implicated them in Mason's murder.

If they were innocent, there was a cold-blooded killer loose. The question I had to answer was who.

I still had plenty of time before I had to go home and get ready for my date with Derek. I decided to spend it doing something I'd been meaning to do ever since the murder, or at least since the name Violet Wilcox kept popping up—and that was pay a visit to her.

The radio station was located well out of town. It had been around since the fifties, though it had been idle probably more often than it had been active. Operating an independent AM station in the Town of Ruby Lake had rarely been profitable.

I popped in the soundtrack to *Man of La Mancha* as I drove. As much as I loved the musical, the film version with Peter O'Toole and Sophia Loren was my favorite. Maybe I'd talk to Ms. Wilcox about airing a Broadway show tunes program. She'd have at least one listener in town.

As "Little Bird, Little Bird" played through the speakers, I eased on the brakes when a white flatbed truck pulled out in front of me and onto the state highway from behind a stand of thick bushes. It was a Duvall's Flower Farm vehicle, and Frank Duvall was at the wheel.

I waved as he passed but he ignored me or didn't recognize me. Cara Siskin was in the passenger seat beside him.

It was a small world and seemed to be getting smaller by the day.

The big billboard at the side of the road read: AM Ruby. I lifted my foot from the gas pedal. There was little traffic on this stretch of highway, so I stopped for a moment before turning in.

A squat cinder block building painted yellow sat just off the road. The wide gravel-and-dirt parking lot held a black van with some electronic gizmos sticking from its roof and the name AM RUBY emblazoned on its side in bright red and yellow. The van had Texas plates and was even more dilapidated than my own van.

Tall radio towers stood beside the building, and a large satellite TV dish was perched atop the building's flat roof. Pine trees surrounded the building on three sides.

I pulled up to the front door and climbed out. I pushed the buzzer at the windowless door. A monitor hanging under the eave sparked to life, and Violet Wilcox's face appeared. "Hi, this is Violet."

"Hi, Violet. I don't know if you remember me, Amy Simms? From Birds and Bees?"

"I'm on the air right now. Please call the station and leave a message. I'll get back to you as soon as I can."

"Oh, but this will only take a minute."

"Sorry," Violet waved. "Gotta go!"

The screen went blank. I considered pressing the buzzer again but didn't want to get her mad at me. She'd never speak with me then.

I heard a loud noise behind me and turned. Violet Wilcox, dressed in blue jeans and a black AM Ruby V-neck shirt, had thrown open the side door of the van and was climbing out. I glanced at the monitor, then back at her.

She had her hands full and didn't notice me for a second. "Oh, it's you," she exclaimed, finally laying eyes on me as she set down her box of well-coiled cables. "What are you doing here?"

"I was hoping to have a word with you. I thought you were on the air?" I pointed helplessly to the monitor overhead.

"I don't like anybody to know when I'm not around. We've had a few things stolen. Broadcasting equipment isn't cheap, let me tell you. And when you're in a campestral setting like this, miles from the nearest house, it's easy pickings for burglars."

"I see." I had no idea what *campestral* meant but wasn't going to give her the satisfaction of knowing. I'd look it up on my smartphone once I was out of there.

She picked up her box off the ground and walked toward me. "My god, woman!" Violet Wilcox fanned her hand madly in front of her nose. "You smell like a landfill on a hot summer's day!"

I felt my face go red. "Sorry." I'd noticed the smell while I drove but had assumed it was my old van having one of those days. "I was—" I shut my mouth. How could I explain to this woman that I'd been dumpster diving and why?

"Never mind," she said punching some numbers on the keypad at the door. "I don't want to know."

She went inside the building and, though she hadn't invited me to follow, I did.

"So what do you want anyway?" Violet Wilcox asked. She set the box down on an office chair at the entrance. The desk in the vestibule seemed more like a holding area for junk than somebody's workspace.

The windows that looked out onto the parking lot in front had been blacked out.

"I heard you had been looking into Professor Livingston's background and hoping to have him as a guest on your show."

"What about it?" Wilcox grabbed an open box of station logoed T-shirts and foam rubber soda can sleeves and carried them out to the van. I tagged after her. "I'm kind of in a hurry here. I'm setting up for a promo outside Lakeside Market. I'm doing an oldies show and giving away some freebies to the customers."

"Sounds fun." I stepped aside as she returned once more to the station. "Lance Jennings had some interesting accusations to make against the professor. I was wondering if you'd heard anything untoward."

Violet's laughter was filled with scorn. "That snot? I dug up dirt Lance Jennings could only dream of," Violet boasted.

"Such as?"

"Such as it's none of your business. Listen to my radio show."

"Did Mason agree to an interview?"

She pulled a face as she stuffed CDs into a handbag the size of a small country. "Not on the record. But that's okay. I think I've got enough material to go on."

"He's dead. Is it really worth soiling his reputation?"

"I'm trying to make a living here, Amy. News sells. Dirt sells."

"He was a good man."

"Tell that to the people he ripped off." She snorted. "Tell that to his ex-wife!"

"A friend of mine saw you with Mason at Truckee's Road Stop."

"Good for them." She pushed past me. "If there's nothing else?" She held the door open.

"Was that Frank Duvall I saw leaving a few minutes ago?"

Violet locked eyes with me. "He's thinking of running some ads on AM Ruby. I gave him a rate card, and we discussed some options."

I wondered what those options were and what all they might have involved. "And Cara Siskin?"

Her smile was anything but friendly. "My, you are observant, aren't you?"

I ignored the barb. "What were the three of you arguing about outside Mason's trailer yesterday?"

"Birds and bees," Violet quipped. She pulled me out the door and set the alarm code before closing it. "Speaking of which, if you ever want to advertise that bird store of yours, give me a call. If not," she marched to the van, her back to me, "*do* be a stranger."

Determined not to let the station owner get the best of me, I shouted after her, "How well did you know Mason in Texas, Ms. Wilcox?"

She spun on me, and I saw venom in her gaze. "What are you talking about?"

I nodded toward the rear of the van. "I noticed your license plate. You're from Texas."

She threw open the passenger side door and dropped her bag on the seat before replying. "Why are you so concerned about who killed Mason Livingston?"

I was taken aback. "Because he was my friend. And because he didn't deserve to die."

Violet's brow flew up. "Didn't he?" She stomped around the front of the van, climbed in on the driver's side, started the engine, and drove off toward town.

20

"And that's all she had to say?" Derek tore off a slice of bread and soaked it in olive oil.

I had finished recounting my conversation with Violet Wilcox. We had opted for dinner at the Lake House restaurant. Located waterside at the marina, it was the most romantic restaurant in town. Thank goodness I'd gotten home in time to take a long shower and wash the stink out of my hair.

The outside deck was open this time of year. and we had a table at the rail with a view of the lake, park, and campground. The roof of Professor Livingston's crazy birdhouse on wheels stood out among the sea of tents, camper vans, and motor homes. "The man was unique."

"What?" Derek had dressed casually in light brown trousers and a soft white shirt. I had pulled my favorite green dress from the back of my closet. I'd owned it since college.

I pointed toward the roof of Mason's trailer.

"Oh, yeah. Your friend Mason was certainly one of a kind."

"But was he a good kind?"

"How do you mean?"

"I've been thinking about what Violet said. Why would she make a remark suggesting that he deserved to die?"

Derek leaned back in his seat. "She was probably just spouting off. She doesn't sound like the most pleasant or sympathetic woman I've ever met."

"I suppose." I tapped the edge of my salad bowl. "Did I tell you that Amber Smith admitted to egging the professor's trailer?"

"No. I had heard about the incident, but I didn't know that." His countenance darkened. "Some people around here think Mister Mulligan did it."

"Why would they think that?"

Derek shrugged as the waiter set our plates in front of us. "The thing was egged." Derek squeezed a lemon wedge over his shrimp. I had ordered the bass.

"And Pack's an egg farmer. Well," I said, folding my napkin over my lap, "you won't have to worry about them thinking that now. As I said, Amber has admitted it now, though she had denied it to the police earlier.

"I hope the Smiths' lawyer advises the young lady that she shouldn't go lying to the police. It doesn't help their case. More wine?"

"Please." I held up my glass while Derek poured. "I feel so sorry for the two of them. I think that Rose is too embarrassed about the whole thing, what with everybody thinking that Amber committed murder."

"You've got to try these." Derek grabbed a spoon and dropped several shrimp on the edge of my dinner plate. "Cara Siskin is the only person in the vicinity with a clear connection to Mason. Plus, you said they had a relationship."

"Physical, at least."

"Maybe too physical," Derek quipped. "I wonder if Ms. Siskin has a volatile temper."

I gave the idea some thought. "I could see her as the hot-headed type." I played with my fish before taking a bite. "Personally, Frank Duvall is at the top of my list. He'd contacted Mason before Mason's arrival in Ruby Lake and had been trying to get his endorsement for that flower he developed."

"He'd been at the book signing and the Birds and Brews get-together," added Derek.

"And, according to Greg Tuffnall—"

"Who?"

I explained how Tuffnall ran Truckee's Road Stop out by the interstate.

"Why did you go see him?"

"Lance told me that Mason was seen there the day before the murder with Violet."

"So you wanted to question this Tuffnall guy yourself." Derek grinned. "What did you find out?"

"That Mason had been in Truckee's Bar, first with Violet, then Frank Duvall. You know what else Amber told me today?"

"What?"

"If Amber is to be believed, and I've no reason to think she'd lie to me, she saw Frank arguing with Cara Siskin and Violet Wilcox outside Mason's trailer *after* the murder."

"Interesting," admitted Derek, "but it gets us no closer to figuring out who really killed Mason."

I looked out across the lake. The stars were out now, their faint light reflecting off the quiet water. "If the real killer isn't caught, they might never open Bookarama back up."

"It wouldn't surprise me if Rose and Amber left Ruby Lake for good," Derek suggested.

"That would be a terrible shame. I hope it doesn't come to that."

After dinner, we walked arm in arm to Birds & Bees. It was a pleasant evening. We had strolled to the Lake House from my house. Derek's car was parked out front.

Paul Anderson waved to us from the outdoor patio of Brewer's Biergarten. "Come on over for a beer, guys!" He waved to us.

"Sorry," Derek said. "I can't tonight."

Paul waved again and turned back to his customers. I noticed Violet Wilcox and Cara Siskin at the outside bar. "Are you sure you can't come up?"

"Sorry. Dad and I have a court case down in Charlotte starting tomorrow. We'll be gone several days."

"I'll miss you, but good luck."

"Thanks. We're hitting the road at seven, so I have to make it an early night." He kissed me. "Try to stay out of trouble while I'm gone?"

"Don't worry." I ran my fingers through his hair. "All I want is a good night's sleep."

We lingered in each other's arms until Derek finally broke away. "I'll call you tomorrow," Derek said, climbing behind the wheel of his car.

I watched his tail lights recede, then started up the front steps. A strong hand grabbed me from behind a shrub and yanked me around. "Frank!"

Frank teetered in the flowerbed. He was in his faded dungarees with a white T-shirt underneath. He smelled like he'd been drinking. "I want a word with you, Amy."

I pulled at Frank's hand clenched around my upper arm. "Let go of me, Frank!"

He relented but fixed his bloodshot eyes on me. "What's your problem, Amy?"

"At the moment," I couldn't help saying, "it's you." I stumbled back and hit the side of the porch, banging my hip bone.

"Why are you following me around? Why are you harping on and on about the professor's death?"

"Because," I said, struggling to regain my footing in the dark, "I'd like to find out who killed him and why." I looked at him carefully, his face a mask of shadows under the moonlight. "Was it you, Frank? I know all about how you wanted Mason to help you promote some flower of yours that's supposed to be some sort of magnet for hummingbirds."

Frank's jaw tightened. "Who told you that?"

I smirked. "Everybody's talking, Frank. Everybody. I also saw the letter you wrote to Mason urging him to go into business with you. Why did you lie to me about it?"

"I didn't lie to you about anything." Frank's voice was hard and deep. "What I do is none of your business." He slammed the side of his fist against the porch rail. "I've sunk all the money I've got into my business, and this new flower is going to make me rich." He jammed a finger at my nose. "Don't you go messing this up for me."

"Was that the problem, Frank?" I swatted his finger away. "Was Mason going to mess things up for you? Was that why you stuck a pair of scissors in his neck?"

Frank loomed over me. I hadn't been paying attention and had let him get too close once more. His strong, thick fingers latched onto my wrist. "Stay out of my business, Amy. Isn't one murder in town enough for you?"

I swallowed hard. My eyes teared up from the pain of Frank's grip on my arm, his nails digging into my flesh. "Please, Frank, let go."

"Are you going to stop your interfering?" I smelled whiskey on his breath.

"Frank," I said, struggling to remain calm and wishing Derek would suddenly return, "if you do not let go of my arm right now, I am going to scream loud enough for all of Ruby Lake to hear."

Frank dug his nails in deeper. "I've gone too far, Amy. I owe too much. This flower is my last chance."

"This is your last chance, Frank. I'm counting to three." I closed my eyes for a second, then began. "One...two . . ."

The front door opened with a creak and an accompanying tinkle of tiny bells. "What's going on out here?"

Frank released his hold on me. We both whirled around. My mother stood on the porch. "Amy? Frank?" She stepped to the edge of the porch and looked down at us, a questioning look in her eyes. "What are you two doing down there?"

I trained my eyes on Frank. "Mister Duvall and I were talking, Mom."

"Talking?" Mom fixed her eyes on Frank. He teetered unsteadily under the weight of her stare. "It's late, Amy. Frank, go home."

The flower farmer thrust his hands in the side pockets of his dungarees and dipped his head. "You should tell your daughter to stick to birds, Barbara." Frank ran his fingers along his unshaven chin. "If she knows what's good for her, she'll mind her own business."

"If you know what's good for you," my mother said evenly but firmly, "you'll get off our property." She folded her arms over her chest. "Before I telephone the police."

I massaged my throbbing arm. "And don't ever lay a hand on me again."

Frank spat, then trounced off through the flowerbeds, mangling and trampling my beautiful flowers left and right with his heavy boots. There'd be a mess to clean up in the morning.

Mom came down the steps. "Come inside, Amy." She planted her hands on my back and guided me through the door. She locked it behind us, her eyes on Frank as he slunk away.

Mom insisted we drink some chamomile tea, and she prepared it herself. I brought the honey jar to the table with a spoon. Mom poured the tea, then sat.

"Thanks, Mom." I smiled at her. "For the tea. And for rescuing me."

"Young lady, you know you're in trouble if you need the likes of me rescuing you!" She picked up her mug and sipped. "But you know I'll always try." She set down her cup. "I could hear Frank from the upstairs window. What was that all about?"

"I'm not sure, to tell the truth." I massaged my throbbing temples. "He was drunk, and I don't know if he was warning me not to look into Mason's murder or not to interfere with his plans to bring that flower of his to market."

Mom shook her head. "I've never known the Duvalls well, but I've never heard anyone say anything about them that would have led me to believe that Frank Duvall was a thug or, worse, a killer."

I told Mom how Amber had admitted to me that she had egged the professor's birdhouse. "All because she mistook his advances towards Rose."

"Some girls take longer to grow up than others," Mom replied. She opened her mouth to speak, then closed it.

"What is it, Mom?"

"You don't mind that I've been seeing Ben, do you, Amy?"

"Of course not." I patted her hand. "I'm happy for you."

"That's good. I wouldn't want you egging my bedroom." Mom finished her glass and took it to the sink. "I'm off to bed. Are you coming?"

"In a minute," I said, running my finger in the circle of the mug's handle. "I have some thinking to do."

21

All my thinking had gotten me nowhere. I'd gone to bed after one in the morning, listening to the owls hooting in the distance, their calls reminding me of the goofy sound of Mason's pickup truck horn the day he had arrived in Ruby Lake. I had crawled out of bed at six, unable to get an hour's solid rest. Whatever was going on with Frank Duvall, I was determined to get to the bottom of it.

I didn't relish the thought of another restless night or another wrestling match with the man in my shrubs. I showered, grabbed a fresh store shirt and a pair of shorts, and dressed as quietly as possible. I scribbled a note to my mother that I was going down to the farmers market and should be back in time to open Birds & Bees.

I left the note in front of the coffee maker and slipped out the door, being sure to lock it behind me.

The farmers market opens at seven in the morning, seven days a week, and runs from early spring through late fall. It's been a town fixture for as long as anyone could remember. It was a place you could shop for practically anything and meet practically everyone. A place for buying, selling, and gossiping.

The sun was bright, but the air was cool and the streets calm. I found a spot close to the vendor tents on the square and parked the van. It was closer to seven thirty by the time I arrived on the scene, but several sellers were still in the process of setting up their wares for the day, unloading trucks or vans and arranging goods in their tents.

In the distance, several stalls down from the Duvall's Flower Farm tent, I saw Packard Mulligan. Derek had told me Pack offered his eggs at the market, so seeing him was no surprise. Pack was rolling up the front flap of his tent and securing the corners. An orange-feathered hen bustled nervously in and out of his feet.

Maybe I'd go say hi to Pack after talking to Frank. First things first. It was time for Frank to come clean and in front of witnesses where I'd be safe and he'd be less prone to doing anything stupid.

Besides, I wanted to clear the air. Like Mom said, he wasn't a bad guy. Circumstances may have been getting the better of him, but hopefully we could bury the hatchet, let bygones be bygones—at least agree to stay out of each the other's way and not pounce unexpectedly on one another from behind dark shrubs.

I ambled slowly along the walk leading to the farmers market, enjoying the weather, wishing I had more days that I could spend just like this. It really was all about the simple pleasures in life. I made a note of a silversmith's stall. She had some pretty things, rings and bracelets, that I wanted to come back and get a closer look at another time.

As I approached, I could see that the Duvall's Flower Farm tent was not open for business yet. The front and side flaps, designed to protect merchandise from weather and theft, were still tied down. From what I'd heard, that wasn't like Frank.

"Frank? Are you in there?" Several eyes watched me from surrounding stalls, including a local organic vegetable stand owned by a cute couple who sipped coffees and were speaking with a young woman holding an empty mesh shopping bag. "Frank? It's me, Amy Simms. We need to talk."

He didn't answer. I maneuvered around to the side of the tent. Frank's vehicle sat at the curb. There were several open boxes in the flatbed with flowers of reds, whites, and yellows protruding from within. "Frank?" I couldn't see him at the truck either.

A rugged young man in floppy shorts and a tank top rolled a handcart toward me, and I stepped aside to give him room. "Have you seen Frank Duvall?"

"I saw him a while ago," the young man replied, holding the cart one-handed. "We pulled in at about the same time."

"What time was that?"

"About quarter till six. He's around here someplace. Always is. Frank never misses a chance to sell something."

I scratched the top of my head. "Maybe he went for coffee, you think?" There was a stand here at the farmers market, plus the Coffee and Tea House on the square kept early hours.

"I doubt it. Frank always brings his own. Coffee and an egg sandwich and apple. Like clockwork. Comes in early, sets up, eats, then opens up." The kid laughed revealing a gap between his two front teeth. "That guy is as cheap as they come." With that, he continued on his way, hauling a half dozen boxes of lettuce heads to the opposite end of the market.

I was about to give up, then remembered the unusual flower I'd seen in Frank's stall the other day. He hadn't seemed to like my showing an interest in it. With Frank nowhere to be seen, now was my chance to take a closer look at it. Could it be that it was the special flower he'd been hoping to capitalize on?

The canvas tenting was heavier than I had expected. Using two hands, I was able to lift the material high enough that if I bent over low enough, I could crawl under. Light filtered in through the cracks in the tent. It was anything but weatherproof.

"Frank?" Just my luck he'd be standing here and our confrontation from the night before would start all over again. Satisfied that he wasn't around, at least long enough for me to take a look at his stock, I sidled past the outer table and moved into the middle of the tent.

"Frank!"

Frank Duvall lay stretched out in the center of the space, surrounded on three sides by his display tables, wearing pretty much what he'd worn the day before and the day before that. The man was no slave to fashion.

His arms were stretched out overhead, and he was on his stomach on the matted earth and grass. An open thermos bottle was lying on its side, its contents spilled out in a small brown puddle.

Frank Duvall's eyes were closed. Was he passed out drunk from the night before? There was a smear of dirt on his cheek. I knelt beside him, my bare knee dipping in the cold coffee. "Frank?" I nudged his shoulder. "Frank, wake up."

He failed to respond. Worriedly, I placed a trembling hand to his neck and felt nothing but near lifeless flesh.

I gasped. "Frank!"

I scrambled to my feet and crawled quickly out the front of the tent. The two young organic grocers were arranging yellow summer squash on a wooden display stand. "Hurry!" I waved. "Call an ambulance!"

Within minutes, the ambulance and the town's biggest fire truck had arrived. Three EMTs had raised the tent flap, hustled in, and laid Duvall on a portable stretcher.

I had been shoved off to the side with the rest of the early shoppers and sellers. We congregated in a ring across the way, held back by Officer Larry Reynolds, who was the first policeman on the scene.

Chief Kennedy arrived in a blaze of sirens and smoking tires. Jerry hopped out of the driver's side of the squad car, and Officer Dan Sutton extracted himself from the opposite side. "Wait a minute!" the chief called gruffly as he jogged up, one hand holding the gun on his belt.

The two EMTs holding the stretcher shifted the unmoving body of Frank Duvall. His clothing was soiled with vomit.

"What have we got here?" Chief Kennedy pulled up close and examined Duvall.

Frank Duvall's face was a dirty, contorted mess.

"He's in bad shape," remarked the third EMT, a stethoscope to Frank's chest. "I don't know if he'll make it. We're rushing him to the ER."

Chief Kennedy stepped aside. "Go! Go!"

"What do you think, Chief?" Dan tipped his cap farther back on his head. "Heart attack? Stroke?"

Jerry chewed his lip. "Maybe." He eyed the retreating EMTs, then passed his gaze over the gathered crowd with unveiled annoyance. "Anybody see anything? Hear anything?"

"Could be food poisoning," suggested the husband of the organic grocer.

His wife agreed. "He looked fine when we saw him earlier."

There were a lot of mutterings but nothing else of any use. Several people said they had seen Frank pull up in the predawn hours and start unloading.

Chief Kennedy turned back to his men. "Let's take a look around ourselves."

"What are we looking for?" Officer Sutton inquired.

"If I knew that, I'd tell you to look for it," snapped Jerry.

Reynolds and Sutton looked at one another before complying.

They moved idly about the stall, stopping to examine the flowers and kicking at the ground with their feet.

Officer Reynolds opened a brown paper bag and withdrew a sandwich wrapped in aluminum foil and a green apple. "If it was something he ate, it wasn't this." Both were untouched.

Chief Kennedy stepped over to the thermos and nudged it with his toe. He leaned over and sniffed. Over his shoulder he yelled for Officer Sutton to bring an evidence bag from the squad car.

He focused his gaze on the man who'd suggested food poisoning, then said, "Careful how you handle this." He pointed to Officer Reynolds. "Keep everybody away for now. And get your camera."

"Yes, sir. I've got it in my car." Reynolds made a beeline to his vehicle and returned with his fancy camera.

Chief Kennedy's eyes played over the crowd. "Who was the last person to see Mister Duvall? Anybody have any idea?"

Two hands pointed in my direction—it was the young couple selling organic produce—and that's when Jerry spotted me standing near the support pole of the tent opposite. I reddened and slowly raised my hand. "I guess that would be me." I stepped forward through the throng.

"Lord have mercy," Jerry said, shaking his head forlornly. "What did I do to deserve this?" He slowly raised his arm and, using his forefinger, motioned for me to come closer.

"Good morning, Chief." I rarely called him chief but figured today was worth an exception.

"You were the last one to speak to Duvall?"

"I found him." I pointed to the puddle on the ground. "Lying there. I never spoke to him. He was like that when I came in."

"And just what were you doing here this early in the morning?"

"I came to see Frank."

"Do you mind telling me why?"

"We had a little disagreement last night. I came to clear the air."

Jerry looked at the captivated crowd, then locked his steely eyes on me. "And you didn't speak with him at all?"

"I told you. I never got the chance."

Jerry tipped back his cap with his forefinger. "Yeah." He turned to the onlookers. "Okay, folks, nothing more to see here. I suggest you all go about your business."

"What about me?" I made the mistake of asking.
"If I have any questions, I'll call you."
I nodded.
He pointed to the road. "Now go."
I went.

22

"Morning, Amy." Kim looked up lazily from a glossy women's magazine she had been leafing through at the sales counter. Apparently business was off to a slow start.

"Hi. Sorry I'm late. I meant to be back in time to open up."

"No problem. Barbara called and asked me to do it when you didn't show." Her face showed concern. "She told me what happened with Frank Duvall last night and how you left a note saying you were going down to the market to talk to him about it."

"That was the plan." I turned and gazed out the window to the spot where Frank had accosted me just last night. I had told him to never do it again, and now he never would.

"Though if I were you," Kim snapped the gum in her mouth, "I'd have sent the cops to do my talking. How did it go?"

"It didn't."

Kim perked up. "How do you mean?"

"I mean that when I got there, Frank was lying on the ground."

Kim set her magazine aside and came around from behind the counter. "What do you mean, lying on the ground?"

"I mean like lying stretched out on the ground not moving, not talking, and looking like he was on the threshold of death's door." I blinked at her. "For a minute, I thought he *was* dead."

Kim gasped. "Is it serious? What was it? A heart attack? Stroke?"

"Funny, Dan asked the very same thing."

"Dan was there?"

I nodded. "I don't know what happened to Frank. I'd say it's very serious. Someone in the crowd suggested it might have been food poisoning."

"I had that once," remarked Kim. "I felt like I wanted to die."

I remembered nursing her through it. She hadn't been a pretty sight. "Mom did say once that he had heart problems, so that could be it." But I couldn't stop thinking about the fallen thermos and mentioned it to Kim.

"What are you suggesting, bad coffee? Spoiled cream?"

"Sounds farfetched, doesn't it?"

"I'll say."

"They took Frank to the hospital," I explained. "I need coffee." Kim followed me to the back where I poured us each a fresh cup of strong black coffee. I had a sudden aversion to milk.

Kim took a seat in one of the rockers, and I copied her move.

"I can't help thinking this has something to do with Mason's murder." I rocked slowly, careful not to spill.

"Don't you think you're getting carried away now? Frank could have had a heart attack or be having trouble with his blood pressure." She wiped a lipstick smear from the side of her mug. "Or food poisoning like somebody suggested."

"You could be right, I suppose." Duvall certainly seemed to be under a lot of stress of late. "But I don't think heart attack victims vomit all over themselves."

Kim made a face of disgust. "That leads us back to food poisoning."

I reluctantly agreed. "It just seems like too much a coincidence. Mason gets killed, he had a relationship with Frank, though I have no idea how deep it ran. Mason, Frank, Violet, and Cara all seem to be tangled up in something." I bit down on the inside of my cheek. "Now Frank is in the hospital himself."

I shot Kim a sideways glance. "What does it all mean?"

"You're asking the wrong person," replied Kim.

"I guess Frank will tell us what happened when he recovers."

"Maybe we should go see him? When are visiting hours?"

"I don't even know if he's conscious yet, but that's not a bad idea. Assuming seeing me doesn't upset him. I've already got Jerry upset with me. That's enough for one day."

"Why you?"

"I'm the one who found Frank," I replied stonily.

"Again?"

I glared at her.

"Sorry," she said quickly. "I just meant that you have bad luck that way."

"Frank and I had our differences, but I hope he gets better soon." I yawned, still feeling the effects of my lack of rest. "In the meantime, we'll see what the doctors find out."

"I have a friend who's a nurse. I'll send her a text and see if she knows anything."

"Thanks." I changed the subject. "Is Mom around?" I could see by the gaps in the counter display that at least a half a dozen of her homemade Barbara's Bird Bars had been purchased.

"She took the bus downtown to do a little shopping." Kim sipped, her eyes on the front door. "Speaking of police...." She played with the sapphire ring on her left finger. "Let me ask you something."

"Yes?"

"What do you think of Dan?"

"Dan Sutton?" Kim nodded, and I continued, knowing I had to tread lightly. "He seems like a good guy. Why do you ask? How do *you* feel about him?"

"That's just it," Kim said, clearly bothered. "I'm not sure how I feel about the man."

I rose and topped off our coffees. "There's nothing wrong with that. In fact, it's only natural. You two haven't known each other, at least on a personal level, for a very long time."

Kim set her mug on the floor and leaned closer. "Why did he invite me to Jerry and Sandra's wedding then?"

"Dan invited you to the Kennedys' vow renewal?" That was news of sorts.

Kim bobbed her head up and down. "What should I do? What should I say?" She clasped her hands tightly together. "The ceremony is months away—what should I tell him? I don't know if I can make that kind of a commitment!"

I chuckled. "Slow down, Kim. Dan's not asking you to marry him. He's merely asking you to be his date at his boss's ceremony." I made an effort to show more interest. "Has he ever been married?"

"No. He's had some fairly serious relationships, but he's never taken the plunge."

I wrinkled my nose. "Why do people say that? It sounds like you're jumping off a cliff."

Kim snickered. "I'll bet some people feel exactly like that."

"I hope I don't feel that way if and when the time comes. What about family?"

"What about them?"

"Have you met Dan's parents? As I recall, they live in town."

"They do, and no, I haven't."

"And he hasn't met your mother?"

"You know she's still in Florida."

"If you ask me, and you did," I quipped, "I'd say the two of you are still getting comfortable with one another." I patted her leg. "Relax. Go with the flow."

Kim snorted. "Is that what you and Derek are doing? Going with the flow?" Before I could reply, she asked, "By the way, what did he say when you told him what his ex-wife said? You did tell him, didn't you?"

"As a matter of fact, I did mention it to him. Not that I needed to."

"Huh?"

"He said that she had already told him herself and that it was all a big joke."

"Not a very funny one." Kim scratched her ankle.

"I agree."

"That woman is evil with a capital E."

I agreed with that, too, and said so. "Are we good here? I want to go out and check on the hummingbird feeders."

"Fine," Kim relented. "I guess it's hummingbirds before girl-friends."

"You know you'll always be number one in my book." I winked at her. "At least one notch above hummingbirds. Blue jays on the other hand . . ." I tipped my open hands like a pair of scales.

"Very funny. You know, nothing you said explains why Dan asked me to the wedding or helps me to know what sort of answer to give him."

"Because he doesn't want to go stag?" I cocked my eyebrow. "As for your answer, just say yes. And have a good time and save me a piece of cake."

Kim frowned at me. "You're no help at all."

"Sorry," I replied automatically. "I guess I have other, more im-portant, things on my mind." I rose at the sound of the front door opening. "Have you heard a word I've said about Frank Duvall being in serious condition and having to be raced to the hospital?"

Kim picked up her mug and hurried to catch up with me. "Every word, and I hope he's okay. Shall we take him some flowers?"

"Do you really think a flower farmer needs more flowers?"

Kim followed me step for step. "Chocolates, maybe?"

"Like chocolate-covered cherries?"

"That sounds nice." Kim stopped, suddenly remembering the box of spiked chocolates that Mason had ingested. "Oh."

"Oh is right."

After taking care of our customers, we stepped out front, and I checked the level of each hummingbird feeder. "I'd say they're good for another day." I'd rinse them and refill the sugar water tomorrow. A ruby-throated hummingbird buzzed past the side of my head, and I turned toward the sound. A flashy, late-model red convertible sped past the store heading up Lake Shore Drive. "Wasn't that Cara Siskin and Violet Wilcox?"

"I don't know," answered Kim. "I wasn't looking. Why?"

"I saw the two of them drinking at the *biergarten* last night. It was right around the time that Frank jumped me from those shrubs." I pointed to the spot where we'd tussled. I made a mental note to ask Cousin Riley to trim them down to waist height, thus preventing any further ambushes.

I untied my apron and handed it to Kim. "Do you mind watching the store?"

Kim grinned. "Do I have a choice?"

"No," I said, returning the smile. She followed me inside while I retrieved my keys and purse. "What time does Esther get in?"

"She's playing bingo at Rolling Acres. She said she'd be in around one or two."

"Esther's playing bingo at the senior center?"

Kim shrugged. "So she says."

"I wonder if she's thinking about moving." No more secret cats, no more forbidden cigarettes. No more walking around the store during business hours in a ratty bathrobe and slippers.

"Your guess is as good as mine, but I wouldn't go getting your hopes up."

"You're probably right, but a girl can dream, can't she?"

I warned Kim to lock the back door after me and climbed in the Kia. Mason had told me that Cara Siskin was staying at a motel. In a town the size of ours, that had to mean the Ruby Lake Motor Inn. There were few other options, and the motor inn was the biggest and closest to the campground.

The Ruby Lake Motor Inn was only a mile or so away, and as I swung into the parking lot on the street side, I saw the AM Ruby van pulling away.

The L-shaped inn had been built in the fifties with rooms running the longer length and the office and a small diner occupying the shorter line of the L. Several rustic cabins with stone fireplaces and kitchenettes had been constructed behind the motel. The giant ruby-red neon sign on thirty-foot-tall steel posts in the parking lot proclaimed that there were no vacancies.

Standing beside the red convertible, the publicist swiveled her eyes at me as I inched into a tight space between a behemoth of a 4x4 and a station wagon.

I climbed out of my minivan, and she turned on her heel and headed for her room. I ran and caught up with her as she slid the key-card into the lock on her door.

"Wasn't that Violet Wilcox from the radio station I saw leaving?"

"So what if it was?" Cara Siskin pushed into her room.

I followed her unbidden. "Wow, it's freezing in here." I rubbed my arms for warmth.

"Then leave." She wiped her damp brow. "It's plenty hot outside."

I noticed a nearly packed suitcase open on the nearer of the two beds in the small room. "Is that what you're doing, leaving?"

She turned on me and ripped off her glasses. "Is that any of your business at all?" The room smelled of the same cologne I'd caught a whiff of in Mason's camper.

I chose to ignore the question, considering the answer was no. "Have you heard? Frank Duvall is in the hospital."

She grinned smugly. "As a matter of fact, I did. Ms. Wilcox and I just came from the hospital."

That took me by surprise. "How is Frank? Did you speak with him?"

"No." She flopped down beside her suitcase on the bed and toyed with her clothing. "We were told he isn't conscious yet."

"Why did you want to see him? Does it have anything to do with the business he had with Mason?" I moved toward the bathroom, looking for what, I didn't know—anything amiss, anything that might clue me in to the professor's killer.

"And what business would that be?" She eyed me warily.

"I know Frank wanted Mason to partner up with him in promoting a cultivar of some flower he was working on."

Cara crossed her legs and propped herself up with her hands against the mattress. "Mason mentioned something like that. I admit, I was curious about it. I thought if there was anything I could do in memory of dear Mason . . ." She let her voice trail off.

I'd seen better acting in elementary school plays. "And Violet Wilcox? I saw you with her at Brewer's last night. Did you know Frank accosted me outside Birds and Bees around that same time?"

"I had no idea. Why would he do that?"

"I was hoping you could tell me."

"Ask him yourself," she quipped, "when he recovers."

"I plan to do just that. When I spoke with him last night, he was too drunk to be coherent. Had he been drinking with you and Ms. Wilcox?"

"No. I never saw him at all last night."

"It seems odd to me that you and Violet Wilcox would keep getting seen together."

"What are you saying?"

"Only that I heard you were together at Truckee's Bar and again last night. And today."

"She's new to town, and I'm a stranger in town. We had drinks. It's better than drinking alone."

"Was Wilcox interested in the flower or Mason?"

"Both, I suppose. She's interested in anything newsworthy. The woman's always looking for stories to build up her listenership. I believe the station isn't quite profitable yet." The telephone on the bedside table rang, and Cara chose to ignore it.

"Aren't you going to get that?"

She looked at the phone. "It's probably the front desk. I asked them for more towels. Speaking of which," she rose, "I was about to shower."

I nodded and walked slowly to the door. "Will you be leaving soon?"

"As soon as my business is complete."

"Mason's dead. The book tour is over. Isn't your publisher expecting you back in the office?"

"Of course." The publicist eyed me provocatively and began unbuttoning her blouse. "I'm hoping to attend Mason's funeral first."

"Do you think Frank Duvall murdered Mason?"

"What possible reason could he have? Besides, you said it yourself, he needed Mason alive. Do you really think I'd be visiting Mister Duvall in the hospital if he had?" came her frosty retort.

The truth was, I had no idea. And with everybody going around saying how much they needed Mason alive, why was he dead?

"Any more questions?" As her hands tugged at her skirt, I ran for the door. The woman freaked me out. I heard her laughter follow me out the door.

23

The following morning I woke to the sound of banging on my door. I threw on a robe and answered. Mom's bedroom door was closed. "Who's there?" I called through the apartment door as I cinched my robe tight around my waist.

"It's me, Paul."

I pulled open the door and yawned. "What are you doing here?" One of the many problems with having live-in tenants was their ability to bang on your door at all hours of the day and night.

"Esther told me you wanted to ask me something."

I yawned and brought my fist to my mouth. "Excuse me. I need coffee." I motioned for him to step inside. "I did mention to Esther last night that I wanted to ask you about Cara Siskin and Violet Wilcox."

"I know who Violet is."

"I'm sure you do," I quipped, remembering how he'd been drooling over the station reporter the night of our monthly Birds and Brews meeting.

"But who's Cara Siskin?"

"You saw her. She was with Mason the night he spoke to our group."

"Oh, yeah." Paul bobbed his head. "Kind of mousy, short hair?" He was dressed for jogging in a pair of red running shorts, a white T-shirt, and colorful, fancy sneakers.

"That's the one."

"What about them?"

I scooped coffee into the filter basket, filled the carafe with water, and prayed for coffee soon. "They were in your *biergarten* drinking together the other night."

"Good." He grabbed a powdered doughnut from a bag on the counter and bit in. "I'm always happy for the business."

"Did you happen to hear what they were talking about?"

He shook his head, raining powder sugar from his lips to the floor. "I can't say that I did. I said hello to Violet, but she pretty much gave me the cold shoulder."

"You poor boy." I grabbed a couple of mugs.

"None for me, thanks." He patted his belly. "I don't like to run on a full stomach." He grabbed another mini doughnut from the open bag and held it lightly with two fingers. "Are we done here?" He glanced at his fancy watch. Apparently I was cutting into his jogging time.

"One more thing. Did you see Frank Duvall with them?"

Paul furrowed his brow. "The farmer guy? Always wears dungarees?"

I nodded.

"Yeah, I think he was with them. He didn't stay long though. Speaking of which, I'm out of here."

"Busy day?"

He grinned enigmatically. "You might say I've got a big idea brewing."

I rolled my eyes in response to the lame pun and showed Paul the door. He had left a trail of powdered sugar in his wake.

I grabbed the broom and dustpan and was sweeping up when my mother joined me. "Good morning, Mom." I set the broom and dustpan back in the coat closet and planted a firm kiss on her cheek. "Coffee?"

"Thanks, dear." Mom grabbed the bag of mini doughnuts and dropped it on the kitchen table. "I see you found the doughnuts I brought home from the market."

"Paul found them." I rinsed my hands in the sink and dried them on the dish towel. "I'm in charge of cleaning up his mess."

Mom laughed and accepted the coffee mug I handed her.

"Got any plans today?"

"Nothing special."

I sat across from her and smiled. "How about whipping up another batch of your famous Barbara's Bird Bars?"

She cocked her head in my direction as she reached for a doughnut. Mom knows she should lay off the sweets but finds treats like doughnuts irresistible. "Are you serious?"

"Of course I'm serious." I reached into the bag and pulled out two for myself. I found them quite irresistible myself and wanted to get my share before they were all gone. "We only had four bars left at the end of the day yesterday."

I bit a doughnut in half and swallowed, washing it down with coffee. "I think you've got a hit on your hands."

Mom chuckled. "Please, you're almost as bad as Kim." Mom swept a pile of powdered sugar from the kitchen table into her palm. "Did you know she spent at least an hour yesterday afternoon researching commercial kitchens?"

I laughed. "That sounds like Kim. Speaking of which—" I glanced at the kitchen clock. "I suppose I should go to work for a change."

"Couldn't hurt once in a while," joked my mother. She stood and twisted the bag shut and sealed it with a twist tie. "And I'll see what I can do about baking a fresh batch of bars." She frowned. "I might need a trip to the store though. I'm not sure I have everything I need."

I grabbed my purse at the door. "I can give you a lift later, if you like?"

"That's okay. I'll call Anita or Ben."

"Ben's out of town with Derek."

"That's right. I'd almost forgotten. No matter. If Anita can't go, I'll ride the bus."

"The bus?"

"I enjoy it," Mom said. "I meet the most interesting people that way."

"Okay," I replied, opening the apartment door, "but if you change your mind, let me know."

I headed downstairs and found Kim had already opened the doors. A customer was idling spinning a carousel holding bird-related greeting cards.

I picked up my binoculars from behind the counter and went to the front window to see how the birding day was shaping up. Several hummingbirds flitted from feeder to feeder, a cardinal ate leisurely from my pole feeder, two towhees pecked at the grass, and a pigeon was weaving in and out of traffic looking for scraps. So far, so good.

"You're not going to like this."

I turned, binoculars still pressed to my eyes, bringing Kim in big and sharp.

She hung up the phone behind the sales counter and glanced at our sole customer.

"What won't I like?"

Kim's face was ashen. "That was my friend from the hospital." She frowned. "Will you stop looking at me through those?" She kept her voice low and motioned for me to come closer.

"What's happened?" I lowered my glasses, crossed the distance between us, and leaned over the counter. "Has Frank Duvall taken a turn for the worse?"

Kim pulled a hand through her ponytail. "You could say that." She repeated the process. "He's dead."

I dropped the binoculars. "Darn!"

I picked up the binocs and inspected them carefully. They didn't appear to have been damaged. The frames and lenses seemed to have survived intact.

Frank Duvall, on the other hand, hadn't survived at all.

I arrived early at the police station, wanting to stay in Jerry's good graces—it was quarter till twelve, which was tons early in my book. I had been summoned by Chief Kennedy to come make a more detailed statement regarding what I had or hadn't seen and done the day that I had discovered Duvall's comatose body at the farmers market.

I waved to Officer Reynolds.

Dan Sutton was nowhere to be found. Too bad. Kim had made me pinkie swear not to say a word to him about our conversation, but I had been hoping to quiz him about their relationship in general terms—try to get a sense of his feelings for my best friend. It would have to wait.

Anita sat at her desk in the corner, talking to someone on the telephone. Judging by her body language, it was nothing urgent in nature.

To my surprise, Jerry was speaking with Cara Siskin. He took a quick look at me over her shoulder but continued talking to the publicist who nodded from time to time. She wore a white dress and red flats. A strand of rose-colored pearls hung around her pale neck.

When she turned to leave, she arched her finely shaped right eyebrow at me by way of greeting but remained mum. Speaking of mums, she was wearing that flowery perfume of hers again.

Jerry motioned to me. "Come on back, Simms."

I wiggled my fingers Anita's way and mouthed a hello before taking a seat across from the chief.

I craned my neck and watched Cara Siskin as she headed for daylight. "What did she want?"

"She didn't want anything. I wanted her statement."

"You think she was somehow involved in Frank Duvall's death?"

"What do you know about Duvall's death?" The chief pointed a finger at me. "How did you even know he was dead?"

There was no sense in lying. I had nothing to hide, at least, in regard to my knowledge of Frank's passing. "One of Kim's friends works at the hospital. She mentioned it to Kim."

Jerry frowned as he said, "And Kim mentioned it to you. This town is full of blabbermouths."

I shrugged. He wasn't wrong.

Jerry shuffled some papers from his chair to his desk. "Bloody mess around here." He glared at the officer across the room like it was his fault, then sat. He glanced at the sheet on top of the pile. "Mason Livingston's body was flown back to Texas this morning for burial."

"I'm happy to hear that. He must have some family to handle matters, see that he gets a decent ceremony."

"A couple of cousins in Dallas."

"Have you learned anything about Mason's past that might have led to his death?"

"Not particularly."

"Did you know he was going through a messy divorce?" At least that was the unsubstantiated gossip I'd been fed.

Jerry rolled his eyes. "Texas to North Carolina is a long ways to go to stick a pair of scissors in a man's neck."

"In other words, you've come up empty."

Jerry smiled enigmatically. "I didn't say that."

"Oh?"

"Let's just say I'm looking into some things." He paused and smiled with evident satisfaction. "And things are going my way."

"Care to elaborate?"

Jerry laced his fingers and studied me. "There is the divorce, sure, but there's some other stuff, too. Other people." His eyes were a wall of secrets. "Did you know that your professor friend has been accused of plagiarism?"

I admitted I did. "Nothing was proven. And I think it poor form to speak ill of a dead man."

"Okay, but there are some other matters, too," Jerry said testily.

"Such as?"

"I'm not at liberty to say." Jerry's jaw worked back and forth. "I also found some sealed records. I'm trying to get a court order."

I pinched my eyebrows. This was real news. "That sounds serious."

"We'll see, I hope." He leaned in. "It's got to do with some minor stuff. That much I know for certain." He reached into a lower drawer and pulled out a form. "Let's fill out your statement concerning yesterday morning. I've got a lot going on here."

"Fine, but before I do, did you know that Violet Wilcox from AM Ruby is from Texas?"

"So is the former president," replied Jerry, tapping his finger against the form. "Shall I put out an APB on him?"

"It couldn't hurt," I muttered. I took a look at the form, snatched a pen from his desk, and began filling it in.

"There's really not much to tell, you know," I said, glancing at the chief as I gathered my thoughts. "What do you need my statement for anyway? People get sick all the time, even in public. It may not be pretty, but so it goes. Mister Duvall was already on the ground of his stall when I got there." I scratched the inside of my elbow. "It's not like he was murdered or anything.

"No?" Jerry looked like the cat that had swallowed the canary. "I wouldn't be so sure about that."

My eyes grew wide. "Do they know what killed him?"

"Duvall was intentionally poisoned," Jerry explained. "And it was in the coffee he drank."

"Are you sure? Isn't there any chance that it could have been accidental food poisoning?"

"Reasonably certain. Based on what the lab and doctors have told us so far, this wasn't the kind of poison you'd get from eating any of your basic foods. And Duvall hadn't eaten anything, not even the food he'd brought with him to the market."

I nodded. I remembered the uneaten breakfast sandwich and apple. "So it was definitely the coffee."

Jerry nodded. "It seems somebody laced it, all right. We'll know for sure soon enough."

"Wouldn't he have noticed that the taste was off?"

"Alice, his wife, says he liked his coffee strong and sickly sweet. There's a good chance he noticed nothing amiss." Jerry paused meaningfully. "Until it was too late, that is. I'm told it's a nasty way to go. Painful, vomiting, diarrhea, cramps."

I recalled how bad Frank had looked lying there. "What was it exactly? What did the killer use? Rat poison?"

He frowned. "I'm not at liberty to say."

"Fine. Tell me this, Jerry. If it wasn't an accident, somebody poisoned him on purpose. Why would somebody do that?"

"Well, we know it wasn't for money. He had ten grand in his pocket."

I whistled. That was a lot of birdseed.

"As for the who . . ." He left the sentence hanging in the air like a tantalizing grub baiting a bluebird.

"Yes?"

He only grinned and changed gears. "I hear that you and Duvall got into a bit of a shouting match two nights ago."

"Who told you that?" I knew Mom would never have snitched.

"Some witnesses at the *biergarten* next door heard arguing. One of them saw you and Frank outside Birds and Bees."

"Frank was shouting. I was trying to get him to leave me alone." I stiffened. "You think I poisoned Frank?"

"Relax, Simms. I don't think you'd poison Frank—or anybody else for that matter." He paused and chuckled softly. "You might just henpeck them to death though."

I fumed but kept my lips shut.

Jerry pointed to the paper. "Now write."

I wrote.

As I did, Jerry continued the third degree. "Did you notice anyone in particular around the farmers' market yesterday morning?"

"Do you mean anybody who shouldn't have been there? That sort of thing?" I was still seething from his comments.

"Sure," he said slowly. "Or somebody lingering around Frank's stall."

I froze, pen in hand, and looked at Jerry. "What are you asking, Jerry? If I saw somebody poison Frank?"

Jerry sucked in his gut, then let it back out. There was only so much pressure one torso could take. He ignored my question and asked, "Did you happen to notice Mister Mulligan?"

"Pack Mulligan?" I pulled a face. "Yes, I saw him. I saw lots of folks, men and women. Even a few children. I saw some pretty jewelry, too. Oh, and I talked to a kid delivering lettuce."

Jerry nodded. "Yeah, I already got his statement. He mentioned that the two of you talked." Jerry watched me closely as he added, "He also happened to see you pull up one side of Duvall's tent and sneak inside."

"I wasn't sneaking!"

"You weren't exactly sashaying in the front entrance for all the world to see."

I slammed the pen on his desk, leaving an ink mark that I hoped he wouldn't notice. "The stall wasn't open yet."

"Then maybe you shouldn't have gone poking around inside." He glared at the fresh blue stain on his desk, wet his thumb, and attempted to wipe it out. No such luck.

"If I hadn't, Duvall could have died right there!"

We stared at each other for a minute. Jerry broke the silence. "Where was Mister Mulligan when you saw him?"

"You mean the night Mason was murdered?"

Jerry creased his brow. "Excuse me? We're talking about the morning you found Frank."

"Of course we are. That's what I meant." I could feel my face turn bright red.

Jerry stilled my writing hand. "Out with it, Simms. I know that face. You saw Pack Mulligan at Bookarama the night Livingston was killed. Isn't that right?"

I swallowed hard and let out my breath. There was no use lying any longer. "Yes."

"Aha!"

"But he wasn't in the store," I said loudly and quickly. "He-he was outside the store. And all he did was ask me or tell me or—no, I think he asked me if somebody was dead."

There was a long, scary silence as Chief Kennedy gave me the evil eye for about a million years before spitting out, "Why didn't you tell me this straight away?"

"I forgot!" I pulled my hand free. "That's all. I forgot." I rubbed my fingers. "Besides, I didn't think it was important." Pack Mulligan seemed scary at the time but so harmless in retrospect.

"You didn't think it was important?" Jerry was half out of his chair now. "A man was murdered, had a pair of scissors stuck in his throat, and you didn't think seeing a man outside the scene of the murder was important?"

If my face was red, Jerry's was redder.

"Now, Jerry," called Anita from her corner, "you mind your blood pressure."

He opened his mouth to reply to Anita, then clamped it shut again, having apparently thought better of it. Judging by the look on her face, he'd made the right choice.

His fists opened and closed like twin pistons. After another moment, the chief fell back into his chair. "Ms. Simms," he said in a forced calm, "we will amend your statement regarding the night of Mason Livingston's murder some other time.

"Right now," he pressed his thumb into the desk, "please, tell me exactly where you saw Packard Mulligan . . ." Apparently the calm could only last so long because he was practically shouting when he added, "the morning Duvall was poisoned!"

I was about to say something sarcastic but realized I had no good reason to except that I was mad. Besides, Anita was shaking her head at me in warning. From the corner of my eye, I saw Officer Reynolds doing the same.

I said evenly, "Chief Kennedy, I saw Mister Mulligan, Pack Mulligan, setting up his egg stand."

Jerry steepled his fingers and pressed them to his lips several times, in and out, in and out. "Which is only a few tents down from the Duvall tent," Jerry said.

Numerous other merchants' stalls were as closer or closer. It was a bustling farmers market. "Why all the questions about Pack Mulligan?"

"Let's just say I've taken a sudden interest in his whereabouts and activities at the time in question. More so since you say you saw him outside Bookarama the other night."

"So you don't suspect the Smiths anymore?"

"I suspect the daughter's got a screw loose." He tapped a finger against his skull. "I told her if she ever eggs anybody's house in this town again, birdhouse or otherwise, I'd lock her up for thirty days. I think she got the message."

"I'm sure she did. Personally, I'm not convinced Pack Mulligan is guilty of anything." I folded my arms over my chest defiantly. Something about Jerry always made me want to defy him. "Except being different," I quipped, remembering Karl Vogel's remarks.

"We'll see about that."

"What about Mason's laptop? Did you find anything of use on it?"

"Not a darn thing. And believe me, we went all through that computer."

"Mason, Violet Wilcox and Cara Siskin were seen talking at Truckee's the other day. Frank, too."

"There's no law against socializing, Simms. I can't go arresting people just because they congregate."

"No, but you can investigate them."

"I know how to do my job," huffed Jerry. "I don't need you telling me how to do it. Besides, this case is all but locked up—along with the perpetrator, I might add."

Jerry was full of bluster, but whatever cards he was holding, he was confident in how the hand was going to play out.

"Can I have my books back?"

"What books?"

"My copies of *Hummingbirds and Their Habits*. The ones you confiscated the night of Mason's murder."

"Oh, those." He waved a hand dismissively.

"You said they were evidence. If this case is all but locked up as you think, you won't mind releasing them." The book would be my last physical reminder of Mason and our friendship. Whatever he'd written on the dedication page for me would be among his last thoughts.

"As a matter of fact, I don't need them anymore. That's why I gave them back to Rose Smith."

"Oh," I said, taken aback. "Great." I was about to slink away when a deep voice I was certain I knew but shouldn't have been hearing just then called Officer Reynolds by name.

"Good afternoon, counselor," Reynolds replied casually.

I turned. "Derek!"

24

Derek stood at the station entrance in a pin-striped charcoal suit, a cranberry red tie, and shiny black shoes. "What are you doing here?" I rose to greet him. "You said you were going to Charlotte."

Derek shifted his black leather briefcase to his left hand and gave me a quick one-armed hug. "I was. I did. Dad's handling the case solo now." He swiveled toward Chief Kennedy. "Hello, Chief. I got here as soon as I could. Though I'm not sure what use I can be. I'm not a criminal attorney."

"Good afternoon, Mister Harlan. That's up to you and your client to sort out. All I know is that he wanted to talk to you, and there's no reason he shouldn't. I wouldn't want folks getting the wrong idea and thinking we're railroading anybody around here."

I had no idea what either of them was talking about.

Jerry glanced at his watch. "You made good time. I hope you weren't speeding," he joked, inappropriate as it was at the moment.

"Now would I do a thing like that? No, I kept it under ninety the whole time." Derek glanced up the hall toward the holding cells and interview room. "How are you holding up, Amy?"

"Fine. Does your asking me mean that you heard about Frank Duvall?"

Derek said yes. "I was informed that he expired in the early hours this morning," he said soberly. "I also heard you found him unconscious at the farmers market." He squeezed my shoulder. "I'm going to want to hear all about it later." He turned his attention back to Jerry. "Now, I'd like to speak to my client, Chief."

"Sure, Mister Harlan." Jerry pulled himself up from his desk and grabbed a folder from a hanging file on the wall behind him next to a hokey picture of himself being sworn into office. "We've been expecting you." He hitched up his trousers. "He's waiting in the interview room. Follow me."

"Derek?" I watched both men in confusion. "What on earth is going on?"

His lips grazed my cheek. "Like I said, we'll talk later. It sounds like we both have a lot to share. I've got to go. I'll call you."

Jerry stopped at the edge of the hallway leading to the interview room. "Reynolds, see that Simms finishes filling out her statement."

"Yes, sir." Larry's chair skidded against the floor as he jumped to attention.

I sat back down in my chair and resumed writing, though my mind was scattered in a million directions. Derek's sudden arrival seemed to have turned my world upside down.

Nonetheless, I wrote down everything I could remember, which wasn't much. Since it was now out in the open, I even included the part about how Frank had come around late the other night and practically threatened me with bodily harm if I didn't leave him alone and mind my own business in the matter of Mason Livingston's murder.

After I'd finished and Jerry and Derek still hadn't returned, I twisted around and said to Officer Reynolds, "What's this all about?"

"All I know is that after talking to the chief, Mister Mulligan asked to talk to Mister Harlan," Reynolds answered. "I reckon your boyfriend is representing Mister Mulligan in this, too."

"Pack?" I leaned sideways, trying to catch a glimpse of the action in the interview room. No luck. The door was shut. "What happened, Larry?"

Larry looked nervously toward the cells in back. "I'm afraid it's not my place to say."

I made a face at him but let it go. I was sure he didn't want to get in trouble with his boss. I pointed to the battered suitcase beside Jerry's desk. "Can I take a look inside? Jerry told me it would be okay if I checked out the flower."

Reynolds grinned and tapped a pencil against his desk. "Yeah, he said before that you might ask and to let you." He waved his hand. "Go ahead. Only the chief said you have to be careful not to damage anything."

I raised my hand. "You have my word."

He turned back to whatever he was doing at his desk. Apparently I wasn't very important.

I knelt on the floor and unlatched the suitcase. Jerry hadn't been lying—rumpled clothing, socks, underwear, and there in the middle, nestled among it all, was a plastic-wrapped flower with water-absorbent foam around the stalk. I lifted it gently. "It looks like a cardinal flower on steroids."

"What's that?" I hadn't noticed Reynolds come up from behind. He leaned over my shoulder.

I waved the flower in the air. "Does Chief Kennedy believe that this is the flower that Frank Duvall was trying to get Mason to endorse?"

Larry shrugged. "Beats me. A flower's a flower, right?"

"It's pretty, but it doesn't look like anything special, you think?" I sniffed the flower but smelled nothing through the plastic wrap. I waved it at him. "Give it a whiff. Tell me what you think."

"Careful with that." Reynolds grabbed my hand. "I don't smell a thing. Should I?"

Officer Reynolds was as hopeless as Jerry. I laid the flower back in the suitcase and shut it. It certainly could have been the cultivar I'd been hearing so much about. The cardinal flower was very attractive to hummingbirds. Duvall could have developed an even more potent variety. If it was the flower in question, what was it doing in Mason's suitcase? Had Duvall given it to him? Was it a sample? Proof that the plant existed?

Using Jerry's desk as a crutch, I lifted myself up and dusted myself off. As much as I hated to think it, I was acutely aware that there was another reason that the flower could have been in Mason's suitcase.

He could have stolen it, and Duvall wanted it back.

That would explain the falling out the two men had apparently had.

It was also a really good motive for murder...

"I have a hunch it was Frank Duvall who murdered Mason," I said as Derek and I shared drinks later in the courtyard of Brewer's Biergarten. It was only a few days ago that the professor had been entertaining us here with his stories. Now he was gone. How long would it take me to not dwell on such thoughts?

"Are you forgetting," Derek said, "that the man you think had the strongest motive for killing Mason Livingston is now lying in the morgue himself?"

"That does sort of throw a monkey wrench into my theory. I was just so sure." I frowned and stirred my mango margarita. "Especially after the way he came after me that night. If you had seen the anger, the fear in his eyes . . ."

"I wish I had been there," Derek practically growled, mashing his right fist into his left hand. "He'd never try a thing like that again."

It made me feel good to know that Derek wanted to protect me, though it hadn't been necessary. "Are *you* forgetting? Frank won't be bothering anyone ever again."

Derek sighed. "So what are we missing?"

I ran through everything in my mind and came up blank. "Maybe Duvall had a partner?"

"Care to elaborate?"

"I wish I could." I picked up the menu. I had a sudden craving for something sweet. Or fatty. Better yet, both. "This is so frustrating."

"Believe me," said Derek, his hands wrapped around his beer, "I'd like nothing better than to have the perfect suspect all wrapped up to hand over to the police."

"Unfortunately, it sounds like the police already think they have that." I brought my glass to my lips and drank slowly, enjoying the salty sweetness.

"Yeah. Several witnesses saw Mister Mulligan carrying Duvall's thermos."

"That's pretty incriminating."

"Agreed, but it's also circumstantial."

"How does Pack explain it?"

Derek spread his hands out on the table. "He said he found the thermos on the ground near Duvall's truck. He recognized it as belonging to Frank. He took it to the market every morning."

"That makes sense."

"Yes, and Pack told me and the police that he figured that Frank dropped it while he was unloading his truck. He picked it up and carried it over to Duvall's tent. Duvall was nowhere to be seen, so he left it on one of the tables next to Frank's brown-bag breakfast."

"And he didn't see Frank after that?"

Derek shook his head. "Only with the rest of you once the police and EMTs showed up."

"Pack only did what seems natural, but it doesn't look good for him, does it?"

"Not a bit. And given their history . . ."

"Whose history?"

"The Duvalls and the Mulligans. They're neighbors, you know, but from the way I've heard tell, they aren't all that neighborly. In fact, the two families don't seem to have ever gotten along much."

"You're right. Now that you say that, their farms are adjacent. I don't know why I hadn't thought of that before."

"There's no reason you should have."

"I'm sorry I let slip about seeing Pack outside Bookarama the night of Mason's murder, Derek. I've only made things worse for him."

"Don't worry about it. It's the truth, and the truth has to come out. Besides," he said, patting my hand across the table, "if you'll remember, even before all this, I suggested that you tell Chief Kennedy about it."

"Did Pack say what he was doing in that part of town that night?"

"Even worse. Pack admits to being at Bookarama that night."

"Did he say why?"

Derek shrugged. "It's a bookstore. He said he went for books."

It was hard to argue with that. "What about the ten thousand dollars that was found on Duvall when he was poisoned?"

"I heard about that from the chief. He questioned Pack about it, and so did I. Pack denies knowing anything about the money."

"And if Pack did know Frank had the money on him and Pack was up to no good, wouldn't he have taken it?"

"That's an excellent point."

"Do you think he did it?"

"Do I think Pack poisoned Frank Duvall and stuck a pair of scissors in Mason Livingston's neck?"

"Do you?"

Derek drummed the table a moment. "No."

"Neither do I."

"But Chief Kennedy does. In fact, he's convinced of it."

"Why would Pack murder Mason? He didn't even know him. There's no connection."

"No, but there is with Frank Duvall. The two men were constantly feuding," explained Derek. "Border disputes, noise complaints, arguing about each other's dogs, chickens, you name it."

"I had no idea."

"Did you know Frank Duvall is one of the witnesses who claimed to see Pack Mulligan in the vicinity of some of the break-ins we've been experiencing?"

I shook my head no.

"Chief Kennedy thinks Pack might have killed Mason hoping to frame Duvall for the murder."

"That's crazy!"

Derek continued. "When that didn't happen, the chief says, Pack may have decided to get rid of Duvall for good."

"This whole thing is a nightmare." I tugged at my hair. Little could I have known that my former professor coming to town for a book signing could lead to murder and mayhem. "What happens next?" The waitress came by, and I ordered a slice of chocolate-orange cheesecake.

"Would you care for anything, sir?" she inquired of Derek.

"He's sharing with me," I replied for him.

Derek looked at the young waitress. "Like the lady said."

She left to place our order.

I grinned at Derek. "I need comfort, but if I eat an entire slice, I won't be comfortable in my pants."

"Oh?" He wriggled his brow. "Would you be more comfortable *out* of them?"

I felt my mouth go dry and my forehead pink. Fortunately the waitress arrived quickly with my dessert. "Thanks," I gulped. I slid the plate to the middle of the table and handed Derek a fork. "Dig in."

We ate in companionable silence. When the slice had all but disappeared but for the graham cracker outer crust, I said, "Go ahead." I leaned back. "You finish it."

"Are you sure?" I nodded, and Derek polished it off without having to be told twice.

"What happens next?" I said, downing the remains of my margarita and switching to ice water.

"You mean for Mister Mulligan?"

"Yeah."

"I'm glad you asked."

"Oh?"

Derek ran his napkin across his lips and tucked it under the edge of the dessert plate. "First, I've arranged for him to consult with a criminal attorney from Raleigh, a buddy of mine. He's excellent."

"That's nice of you."

"I've also begun the bail process."

"Do you think he'll manage to get released?"

"I'm pretty confident. Did you know Mister Mulligan, Pack, has never been out of the county?"

"Wow."

"I think we can convince a judge that he's no flight risk."

"I hope so."

"Of course," Derek said, raising his empty mug, the universal sign for a refill, which our waitress was quick to do.

After she'd gone away, Derek went on. "As I was saying, Pack also has his business to run. He can't do that if he's in jail."

"Right, the egg farm."

"He needs somebody to take care of all those chickens."

I pressed my finger into the crumbs on the plate and licked. "Right, the chickens."

"I told him we'd do it."

"Sure, we'll do it." I locked eyes with Derek. "Wait. What?"

25

"Derek!" I exclaimed. "I don't know a thing about chickens!" "Chicken seed, birdseed, it's all the same, right? How hard can it be?"

I goggled my eyes at him. "It can be very hard. I watch birds. From a distance mostly. I don't raise chickens." I planted my elbows on the table, regretting that I hadn't ordered a second margarita. "And I don't sell chicken feed."

"Don't worry," Derek said lightly. "I'll give you a hand."

I turned up the corner of my lip. "You'd better. How many chickens are we talking about?"

"Not many." Derek called for the check and laid his credit card on the table. "Two or three hundred."

"Two or three hundred!"

"It's only for a day or two," he said with a chuckle.

"A day or two?"

The waitress ran Derek's card, and he returned it to his wallet before signing the receipt.

"One day." He held up a finger. "Two tops. Pack will be out on bail by then."

"If he's not," I warned, rising from the table, "beware." I grabbed my purse. "Because somebody's going to have to come bail me out for murdering you!" I said with a wink and a grin as we made our way out of Brewer's.

Derek walked me next door to Birds & Bees. Mom and Esther were rocking on the front porch. I noticed that Cousin Riley had trimmed the bush Frank Duvall had hidden behind down to about waist height.

"Good evening, ladies." Derek waved to them.

"Care for some lemonade?" Mom asked.

Derek patted his belly. "Thanks, but I'm filled to the brim. Another time."

Conscious of Mom and Esther's eyes on us, I gave Derek a hug. "Good night, Derek."

"Good night?" He looked taken aback. "How about a movie? Your choice."

I shook my head. "Sorry. It's been a long day. I'm exhausted and really need some rest."

He pouted. "Are you sure?"

"Sorry," I said, planting a kiss on his nose. "You're cute. But we have to be up with the chickens remember?"

Derek groaned. "Right. Pick you up at five?"

"I'll meet you there. I have some errands to run afterward." I was planning on making the rounds of some of the retirement centers where we had set up birdfeeders for our Seeds for Seniors program.

"Okay. When I get back to my apartment, I'll email you the instruction sheet for the chickens in case you want to study up on them."

"Instructions?"

"Yes, Mister Mulligan was quite specific as to what needs to be done."

"Why do I get the feeling I'm going to regret this?"

He grinned. "Think of this as your good deed for the day."

"Can I at least get a dozen free eggs out of this?"

"I'm sure Mister Mulligan won't mind one bit."

We kissed once more, and Derek climbed into his Civic. He rolled down the passenger side window and beckoned me. "If you're there before me, Pack says there's a spare key in the bucket of the wishing well."

Before I could begin to form a reply, Derek drove off, leaving me alone with Esther and Mom.

The following morning, having gamely set my alarm for four thirty, I dressed in blue jeans and a budgie-green Birds & Bees shirt. We'd just gotten the new shirts in, and I loved them. The bright green reminded me of the pet parakeet, Nicky, my mother's mother, Grandma Hopkins, had owned when I was a young girl.

Grandma had explained to me that the pet bird was a male and that one could identify it as such by the blue strip running horizontally at the top of its nose, or cere, as that fleshy lump at the top of a bird's beak is better known by ornithologists and birders.

The budgie or, more properly, budgerigar, had followed Grandma Hopkins around the house incessantly—and she gave him the run of the place, much to Grandpa's chagrin.

Grandpa claimed the broken leg he'd suffered had been due to Nicky camping out on the middle step of the stairs the day he took a tumble.

Of course, Grandma said it was his own fault and that Nicky, if anything, had been trying to save him. Grandpa had replied at the very least that the bird had been gnawing at the stair railings again. The melodious and social parrot did have an unfortunate propensity for gnawing on wood, including the stair rails and living room and bedroom furniture.

Nicky's favorite perch was the kitchen faucet where he was known to catch the afternoon sun on good days. On bad days, he accidentally left bird doo-doo on the living room carpet, and Grandpa chased him around the house while Grandma yelled at them both to grow up.

I grabbed a light jacket, my purse, and keys. There was no time for coffee, but I grabbed one of the remaining mini doughnuts for an energy pick-me-up. That reminded me—I needed to grab the box of cupcakes that my mother had bought late yesterday. Carefully carrying my package, I went downstairs, noticing on the second floor that Esther's light was on. What could she be doing up so early?

The store was dark and quiet. Too spooky for my taste.

I hurried out to the van and placed the cupcakes on the passenger seat. I turned on the sound system and cranked up the soundtrack to *The Lion King*, always a good courage boost. Yawning, I pulled onto Lake Shore Drive, which was blissfully free of traffic, and headed out to Pack Mulligan's farmhouse.

To deal with birds of a whole other feather.

I wasn't used to being up when the stars were still hanging in the sky, but it was a pleasant drive.

I recognized the house from a distance, even though I hadn't seen it since I was a young girl. The Mulligan farmhouse looked pretty much like I remembered it, perhaps a little more rundown.

A sagging chain-link fence wrapped around the yard. I remembered catching my shorts on it once. That was the day Kim and I had tried to sneak under the fence in an effort to peek in the front window and catch a glimpse of Packard and his dead father. We had failed and seen only a room filled with newspapers and books. There hadn't been a soul around.

A broad porch hugged the front of the house. The windows were dark. I pulled into the rutted drive and turned off the engine. There wasn't a soul around now either. There was no sign of Derek's car or the man himself.

Where was he?

To my far right, I made out the hulking shape of a two-story house and several outbuildings. That had to be Frank Duvall's place. When I was finished tending to Pack's chickens, I'd pay a social call on the new widow.

I turned off my headlights and felt the sky fall down upon me. A dark line in the distance marked where the farms ended and the forest began.

I stepped down from the van, feeling suddenly a bit on edge and vulnerable. Perhaps it was my memory of being accosted the other night by Frank Duvall outside Birds & Bees. Perhaps it was just me being silly.

I hurried to the front gate and closed it behind me. With still no sign of Derek, I was glad he'd told me where to find the key. I didn't relish standing outside alone in such a bleak, desolate spot all by myself. A pair of gnarly, sparsely leaved monkey puzzle bushes struggled for life, buttressing the porch steps. There were no other bushes or flowers nearby. Only weeds.

To the left of the path leading to the house sat a fieldstone wishing well. A thick hemp rope disappeared into the hole. Questioning my sanity for agreeing to come feed a potential killer's chickens, I placed my fingers on the handle and pushed. At first, the rusty handle refused my efforts, but after a little more pushing and a few choice words, it loosened.

I turned it quickly in one direction, then realized I was going the wrong way. I reversed direction, and after about half a minute, a stout wooden bucket that had seen better days rose from the black hole.

I locked the handle in place and thrust my hand in the bucket. It only took a second to discover a small house key lying alone at the bottom of the bucket. I removed the key, looked at it under the light of the stars, then scurried to the front door. I unlocked the door and went inside. The smell of hickory hit me. I locked the front door behind me and fumbled for a light switch.

A chandelier sprang to life, revealing a parlor that looked nearly like it had the day all those years ago when Kim and I had sneaked a look. There were more newspapers and more books, but the room was otherwise as I had pictured it in my memory, from the furnishings down to the simple braided rug sitting like an island between two blue sofas straight out of the fifties. There was a wood-burning fireplace at the far end. Judging by the pile of wood beside it, this was the source of the hickory smell.

I pulled out the sheet of paper I'd printed out the night before. It was Derek's email telling me where to find the key to the chicken coop and instructions for feeding and gathering the eggs.

The keys to the chicken house were in the kitchen drawer nearest the back door. I worked my way to the right and turned on the light in the kitchen, a simple room with an old gas stove and a small refrigerator. There was nothing new like a microwave. An old-fashioned coffee urn sat on a folding tray across from a small rectangular table.

I pulled open the drawer nearest the door and found a small glass dish inside that held a key ring containing several keys. "Bingo," I said aloud, mostly because all this quiet was spooking me.

I buttoned up my jacket and went out the back door and down the steps leading to the chicken house. Following a beaten path, I found myself winding between a pair of chinaberry trees. There was a small family plot with several gravestones to my left, and I stopped to take a look. I pulled out my phone and waved its flashlight app over the markers. Each grave was a Mulligan, including one for Tyler Andrew Mulligan, Pack's father.

I couldn't help smiling at how silly and gullible I'd been as a girl. "So much for murdering his father, then embalming him and keeping him on display in the parlor."

I felt a hard, icy hand on my shoulder.

26

I shivered and turned. "Derek!"

"Good morning." His breath came out in clouds.

"You scared me half to death."

"Sorry."

I gave him a loving punch in the arm. "You're late."

"I slept through my alarm." His hair was tousled, and he was unshaven and wearing a pair of navy blue sweatpants and a black Wake Forest University sweat shirt. He'd attended law school at Wake Forest. He took my arm. "You have the key?"

I held the key ring aloft.

"Great, let's get this over with. I've got a full day today."

As we approached the chicken house, the enormity of the thing struck me. "It's bigger than I would have imagined."

"Mister Mulligan said there were a lot of chickens."

I fumbled with the key in the lock while Derek held his phone over it to provide light. "And we're in," I quipped. "I think I remember the note saying the light switch was on the wall right about—" I flipped the switch. "Here," I said rather smugly.

"Wait, don't—"

A long row of bright lights shot to life.

"Turn on the lights," finished Derek.

At least that's what I think he said. The din of the chickens was near deafening because the instant I'd hit the light switch, the chickens had shot to life too.

I clamped my hands over my ears. "What the devil is the matter with them?" I shouted.

Derek laughed. He shook his copy of Pack's instruction in front of my nose. "You were supposed to turn the lights on gradually." He pointed to the wall. "There's a dimmer switch. We were supposed to ease the lights up gently, slowly."

"Oh!" My hand went to the dimmer. "Maybe if I bring the lights down now!"

"Forget it!" Derek shouted, shaking his head. "Too late for that now, I'm afraid." He pulled me outside.

I gladly let him. We closed the door behind us. "What are we going to do?"

"Wait for the birds to calm down a bit," he suggested.

I leaned my back against the door. The sound of the chickens was muffled but not deadened. "Good idea."

"Come on," said Derek.

"Where are we going?" My ears were ringing. I'd never heard such a cackling cacophony in all my life.

"I've got coffee in the car. By the time we finish drinking it, those monsters will hopefully have settled down."

"You are an angel!" I kissed him.

We retreated to his Civic. True to his word, two takeout coffees were in the drink holders on the dash. We sat and drank.

"Have you come up with any brilliant new theories as to who killed Mason or Frank?" I asked, cradling my cup in my hands.

"No, you?"

"Not a one," I was sad to admit. "I might have more ideas if the police weren't so loathe to share information."

Derek chuckled. "Like what?"

"Like where was everybody else the night of Mason's murder?"

"Duvall was supposedly home, if that's who you're wondering about."

"How do you know that?"

"Chief Kennedy mentioned it."

"It must be nice to be a lawyer."

"It is," he replied with a smirk of self-satisfaction. "He also mentioned where Mason's publicist, Lance, Violet Wilcox, and a half dozen others say they were. But the truth is, anybody could have been hiding in that store. It's a warren of shelves."

"In back, too." I described the storage room.

"See what I mean?"

I nodded. "Which leaves us nowhere."

"Well . . ."

"What? What is it?"

He turned to face me head-on. "Mason was murdered, stabbed with a pair of scissors—"

"So?"

Derek laid his hand on my wrist. "So let me finish. Before he was murdered, not much before from what we've learned, he was poisoned. Not enough to kill him but enough to make him ill."

"What's your point?"

"My point is: Who else do we know that was poisoned?"

"Frank Duvall."

Derek nodded, satisfied that he'd made his point. "The same method. Two men were poisoned in a matter of days. What are the odds?"

"Long." I sipped from my cup, deep in thought. "Mason was drugged with that laxative called bisacodyl. It made him sick, but it didn't kill him. We know that." I tapped the dash thoughtfully. "I wonder what poison was used to kill Frank . . ."

"Hold on." Derek dug his phone from the glove box. He tapped the screen, then read, "A toxin called tetranortriterpenoid, according to Chief Kennedy. I made a note of it."

"What the heck is it?"

"Beats me." Derek dropped the phone on the console between us.

It beat me, too. I could see that he wanted to say more but was holding back. "What is it you aren't telling me?"

Derek ran his hand over his unshaven cheek. "Somebody put that laxative in Mason's chocolates."

"That's been established."

"Think about it. That somebody wanted to . . ." Derek shook his head in frustration. "I don't know—annoy him, make him sick?"

"But they didn't want to kill him."

"Who do we know who wanted to annoy the professor or take out their frustrations on him somehow?"

I frowned. "Amber Smith."

Derek nodded once. "I'm afraid so."

We looked at each other in silence. "And you're thinking maybe that if Amber poisoned Mason, then she poisoned Frank Duvall, too."

"I'm afraid so."

"It makes no sense. Why? Besides, she has an alibi for the time of Mason's murder. She was caught on tape on the other side of town buying eggs in Lakeside Market."

"Right. Which, assuming the two murders are connected, leads us back to Pack Mulligan," Derek noted.

"Which leads us back to Pack," I sighed in agreement. The two murders had to be connected somehow.

"That's Duvall Farms over there," I told him, turning my head toward the passenger side window to indicate Frank's farm, which was growing more visible in the dawn light.

"I heard he had a wife," Derek said softly. "I wonder how she's holding up."

"I was going to call on her when we're done here. Pay my respects."

Derek looked at me funny. "I'm not sure she'll appreciate that this early in the morning. And so soon after Frank's death."

I shrugged. "Maybe not. But when Mom heard I was coming out to the Mulligan place to care for his chickens, and knowing that the Duvall farm was next door, she asked me to express our condolences. I promised I would. She even picked up some cupcakes for me to give Mrs. Duvall. They're in my van."

"Cupcakes?" Derek's brow went up in hope. "One would go great with this coffee about now."

"Sorry, widows only."

"Too bad." Turning serious, Derek added, "I barely knew the Duvalls, but give her my condolences, too."

I said I would. "I wonder if Mrs. Duvall has family with her?"

"I hope so. This is the time a person needs it the most."

I nodded. I wouldn't want to be alone at a time like that. "If it looks like no one's up and about, I'll come back later. I don't want to disturb her."

"That would be wise." Derek cupped a hand over mine as he said, "Chief Kennedy spoke with her briefly, but out of respect, he's left her pretty much alone in her time of grief. For now."

"I would like to know what she thinks about Pack having killed her husband."

"That sounds like a question for the police to be asking."

"I suppose." A sudden thought occurred to me. "What if she did it?"

"What?"

"What if Frank's wife poisoned him? If the poison was in the coffee, what better person to have done it than his wife?"

Derek was shaking his head even as I made my argument. "I don't think so. What would be her motive? Frank went into town by himself that morning. Alice Duvall was nowhere near the market."

"Are you sure?"

"That's what Chief Kennedy said. Believe me, I'd love to find somebody to blame for the murders besides Mister Mulligan. Too bad nobody's been willing to confess."

"I have a confession of my own." I was cold, and I was hungry. My stomach growled, and I was starting to lose my resolve concerning the cupcakes in my van. "I'm not sure I'm cut out to be a chicken farmer."

"Me either," Derek replied, smothering yet another yawn. "Thank goodness neither of us has aspirations to be one." Derek set his empty cup back in the drink holder. "Ready? The sooner we tend to the chickens, the sooner we can get back to town."

I downed the rest of my coffee in one gulp. "I'm game if you are."

We returned to the chicken house where, although the chickens had not fallen back into slumber, they were blissfully quieter than they had been twenty minutes before. Maybe they were simply hungry.

Following our written instructions, we had to change out the water in the dish, add a large scoop of chicken feed, and remove the egg.

Times three hundred.

"I saw a pile of egg cartons in a storage room," Derek said. "I'll start carrying them in. You snatch the eggs from these little feathered monsters, and I'll move them to the refrigeration room."

"Deal." The henhouse was a good eighty to a hundred feet long with three rows of chicken-wired cells that were roomier than I expected. The floor of the building was covered in straw.

Somehow I had the feeling that the hens would be less annoyed with a woman removing the eggs than a man. As it turned out, the hens didn't mind me reaching in and stealing their eggs. In fact, I had the impression that most appreciated it.

The eggs had to be placed pointy end down because this was supposed to keep them fresher somehow. I didn't have the strength to even wonder what sort of biology or chemistry or magic made that work.

And except for the one ornery hen that shot past me, jumped to the ground, and led me on a merry ten-minute chase up and down the chicken coop before I could catch her, it all went rather smoothly.

"That's the last of them," I said, brushing my hands against my pants. The miscreant was safely back behind bars or, in this case, chicken wire. "Don't even think about it," I warned the red-feathered fowl as she pecked at the latch.

Derek chuckled. I eyeballed him. Red, brown, and white feathers clung to his cotton sweats. "You look like a chicken."

He sniffed. "You smell like one."

I took a whiff of my jacket. "Indeed I do."

"Let's get out of here."

Once again, I was quick to agree. I locked up behind us and dropped the key ring in my pocket. We washed and rinsed our hands and arms using the hose outside the door with a big blocky yellow bar of soap that had been stuck to the window ledge. "I don't know about you, but I'm exhausted."

"Who knew taking care of chickens and running an egg farm could be so hard?"

"Pack Mulligan for one." I swiveled my head. "Oh!"

"What's wrong?"

"I forgot my dozen eggs." I fished in my pocket for the keys.

"Forget it," said Derek. He reached his hand under his bulky sweatshirt. "My treat."

"What?" I watched as he pulled a carton of eggs out from the folds of his sweat shirt. He handed the carton to me. I opened it. Twelve perfectly lovely ovals. "Care to come by for breakfast? I make a mean omelet."

Derek looked at his watch. "I'll bet. Sorry, but I can't. I'm meeting Pack's attorney first thing at the office, and I don't want to go up smelling—" He stopped and plucked several bits of feather from his sleeves and pants. "Or looking like this."

"Good idea. You get going. We'll cook these little jewels tomorrow. I'll put the coop keys back in the kitchen and lock up."

"Are you sure?"

"I'm sure. Now go."

He kissed me long and hard. "I told Pack we'd leave the house key back in the wishing well bucket."

I promised to return it right where I'd found it. "Now go already." The sooner Pack was released on bail, the better. I did not want a repeat performance of getting up at four thirty and feeding chickens again tomorrow.

I waited till Derek had gone up the long drive to his car and climbed in. He honked his horn twice, then stuck his arm out the window and waved goodbye.

I headed back to the farmhouse, passing once more between the chinaberry trees. I stopped and picked up a berry. Birds loved them. I scooped up a handful and stuck them in my pocket for the birds back home. I knew Pack wouldn't mind.

I returned to the kitchen, where I'd left the lights on. I set the carton of eggs on the counter, pulled the coop key ring from my pocket, opened the drawer, and returned it to the glass dish.

As I pulled out the key ring, a chinaberry fell from my pocket and rolled under the lip of the lower cabinet. I stooped to retrieve the tiny berry. The berries resemble a wrinkled, white marble. Studying the berry in my fingers, I recalled that, although birds loved the fruit, eating too many of them left them seemingly drunken.

What I could not remember was why. I made a mental note to check one of my books when I got back to Birds & Bees; failing any useful information there, I'd check the internet.

Hadn't I read somewhere that the tree was poisonous to cats and dogs?

Could that poison be the tetranortriterpenoid that Derek had mentioned? The two things did seem connected somehow in my brain.

"Which once again leads us back to Pack Mulligan," I muttered in frustration.

I picked up my carton of eggs, shut off the kitchen light, and walked out through the parlor. A tattered paperback novel with its cover missing sat on a wing-backed chair. I picked it up. It was a Western romance novel with a Bookarama sticker on the back.

It seemed that everything led to Pack.

27

At the front of the house, I turned off the shiny chandelier, locked the door and placed the key in the bucket of the wishing well. As I wound the bucket back down into the bowels of the well, I made a couple of wishes myself.

I then returned to my van. I set the eggs carefully on the floor between the front seats and pulled out my cell phone. I couldn't wait until I returned to the store. I wanted information now.

Unfortunately, looking glumly at the bars—or lack of them—on my phone's screen, I realized that information was not to be forthcoming. I returned my phone to my pocket and started the engine.

Backing out of the long drive, I saw a white pickup truck leaving from Duvall's Flower Farm, kicking up dust as it came slowly toward me. That meant the household was awake, up, and moving.

As the pickup passed, I saw a stranger behind the wheel. The back of the truck was loaded with fresh-cut flowers. He was probably heading to the farmers market.

And I was heading for the Duvall house. I pulled up to the long, single-story farmhouse and parked next to an old black Ford sedan. A half-filled tube birdfeeder hung from a lone oak out front. A blue jay and a young wren fought for position, though there was plenty of room for both—a metaphor for the relationship between the Duvalls and the Mulligans if ever there was one.

By contrast with the farm I'd left, the Duvall homestead was well kept. The drive was lined with flowers. I parked on the gravel drive. As I turned off the ignition, exited the van, and started toward the white front door, I wondered, with Frank gone, how much family was left and whether that family would be interested in running the business. I knew next to nothing about Alice, his wife.

I rang the bell.

A sixtyish woman wearing a drab gray dress answered the door. "I'm sorry. We're closed for business. Besides, we deal in wholesale only, except for the farmers' market in town."

"Mrs. Duvall?"

The woman nodded. "That's me, Alice." Her short brown hair was cut simply. She appeared haggard. A stroke of eye shadow heightened the shallow look of her dull blue eyes. She wore a half-apron decorated with peonies.

"I'm Amy Simms from Birds and Bees in town. Your husband came to our last Birds and Brews event."

"My husband is dead. Didn't you hear?" She dabbed at the corner of her left eye with a tissue.

"Yes, of course. That's why I came." I couldn't decide whether she sounded angry, sad, or both.

"What do you want?" She twisted the hem of her apron in both hands.

"I'm so sorry about your husband's death. My mother and I wanted to pay our respects." I peeked past her into the house. Little light shined into the space. The furniture was from the sixties, though well-polished and clean. The beige drapes hung limp, and I noticed dog hair along the edges.

She looked past me. "Your mother? Where is she? I don't see nobody but you." She dabbed her eye once more with the tissue, then thrust it into a pocket in the folds of her skirt.

"Mom couldn't make it."

Mrs. Duvall's lower lip turned down.

"I brought you these." I offered the tray of cupcakes from C is For Cupcakes, a small bakery on the square.

"Thank you." Frank's widow took the plastic tray from my hands and reluctantly stepped aside. "You might as well come on in." She waved me to the sofa and took a seat in a hard rocker near the bay window, setting the cupcakes next to a ball of navy blue yarn and a pair of knitting needles on the table beside her. She squeezed her knees together and clutched her hands in her lap. "Tea?"

"No, thank you."

She pried open the lid of the cupcake container and sniffed.

"There's strawberry with cream cheese frosting, cinnamon-pumpkin, and chocolate," I explained. "I wasn't sure what you liked."

She pulled out a strawberry one and slowly peeled back the wrapper. When she offered me the tray, I went for the cinnamon-pumpkin. I wasn't particularly hungry but wanted to be sociable. "Thanks." I took a bite.

"He was poisoned, you know," Mrs. Duvall said.

"I know. I'm so sorry." I was apologizing a lot, but I didn't know what else to do or say.

A palmetto bug the length of my little finger crawled out from the woodwork. The widow spotted it at the same time I did. She set her half-eaten cupcake on the table and snatched up a knitting needle. She leaned over and deftly skewered the insect before it even knew what hit it.

I held my breath.

Mrs. Duvall rotated the needle in her fingers. "Nasty bugs." She pushed aside the curtain, cranked open the front window with her free hand, and scraped the palmetto bug off into the shrubbery. She closed the window, wiped the knitting needle with a tissue from her pocket, and placed it back on the side table. "I can't stand them."

I did my best to ignore what I'd just seen and erase it from my short-term memory. "Can you tell me more about business your husband had with Professor Livingston?"

Alice Duvall drew herself up. "Frank developed a new plant. We grow flowers, you know. He wanted that professor to go into business with him. I told him it was useless to even try, that he shouldn't waste his time." The knitting needles clicked in her hands. "But Frank loved to dream."

I nodded. What Alice Duvall said jibed with what I'd read in Frank's letter to Mason. And I was pretty certain I'd seen the flower in Mason's suitcase.

Mrs. Duvall continued. "Frank was crossbreeding and doing Lord knows what out in the greenhouse. It was beyond me. But he never stopped. Finally, he told me he'd come up with a new varietal of cardinal flower that the hummingbirds just couldn't get enough of. They fly all around that flower likes bees on honey. He said folks would pay big money for a flower like that."

She stood. "You want to see?"

I jumped to my feet. "I'd love to."

I followed Alice Duvall around the side of the house to the back yard. A long greenhouse stood farther back. If I'd been alone, I would have taken a peek inside.

In the distance was an expanse of flowers of all types. "Over here." She led me along a gravel path to a large circle of bloodred flowers. Dozens of hummingbirds darted all around, as if they'd been drugged.

"It's amazing." I watched in wonder.

"I told you so. Frank named the flower Alice's Hummingbird Heaven."

"That was very sweet."

She planted her hands on her hips. "I don't know what's going to happen to them now." She turned her head, scanning the acres of flowers. "To all of this."

"Won't you continue running Duvall's Flower Farm?"

"Frank was the businessman. I never had a head for it."

My heart went out to her. "Do you have any family, any children who can help? As I came in, I saw a gentleman driving away with flowers in the back of the truck."

"That was a hired hand. He's going to run the stall this morning." Alice Duvall shrugged ever so slightly. She shook her head. "We have a boy. He's moved away to Raleigh. Said he wanted to live in the city. He's coming home this weekend for the funeral."

I'd thought I wanted such a thing once myself—to move away to the big city. Now I was glad I had come back to Ruby Lake. "Will you sell? The flower farm could be quite valuable. You should try to find a buyer."

She eyed me silently for a moment. "I just don't know. This place has been in the family for generations. It's hard to let go."

"Like your neighbors, the Mulligans."

Her eyes narrowed. "What do you know about the Mulligans?"

"Nothing. I mean, only that the Mulligan farm is nearest yours. I used to play with a friend of mine, Mindy Foster. Her parents owned the place on the other side of the Mulligans."

Alice Duvall bobbed her chin. "I remember the Fosters. They've been gone a long time." She plucked at a flower. "Good people."

"Do you believe he murdered the professor, too?"

"Yep."

"Any idea why?"

She waved her finger at me. "Because Pack was jealous. The Mulligans have always been jealous of the Duvalls. Pack knew all about Frank's special flower. He knew we were going to be rich. It's plain and simple," she said. "He was jealous."

"How did Pack hear about it?"

"Frank bragged about it one evening down at the farmers market. If you ask me, he'd had too much to drink. If he hadn't told Pack, he'd still be alive. So would that professor."

"I barely know Pack Mulligan, but I find it hard to believe he could have done such a horrible thing."

"The Mulligans are nasty creatures, all of them that were ever born," she spat. "Pack murdered my Frank." She turned and started up the path. "Come on."

We left the hummingbirds and the flowers behind and walked back to the house. "I hear you were Professor Livingston's friend, Ms. Simms, so you'll pardon me for saying this but he was not a nice man."

She led me into the living room where I'd left my purse. She handed it to me by the strap. "Frank told me the professor demanded fifty percent. Fifty percent rights in the plant my husband spent years developing!" She waved to the front door. "All because he felt his name was worth that much.

"Just a minute. I want to show you something." She turned on her heel and disappeared into the next room. I watched as she snatched up a book from a side table near the mantel. She shoved the book toward me. "Read what it says. You just read what it says. The professor autographed Frank's copy of his silly hummingbird book and made Frank pay for it. Full price, too!"

When she wouldn't stop prodding me with the book, I took it and opened the cover. Mason had written: *To Our Good Fortune.*

I nodded. "I understand how you're feeling, Mrs. Duvall. I'd be upset if my husband died, too."

"Are you married?"

"No, I—"

"Then you don't understand. You can't understand."

"I suppose not. But Mason didn't kill your husband. He was murdered himself."

Mrs. Duvall's face turned hard and ugly. "He may not have done the dirty deed with his own hand, but he's responsible for my Frank's death. Mark my word."

I tried to hand back the book.

184 · J.R. Ripley

"Keep it," she said.

"Supposing Pack Mulligan didn't poison your husband, who do you think might have done it, Mrs. Duvall?"

"He did it," the woman said with no doubt in her mind.

"But if he didn't?"

She frowned at me as if the very idea of someone other than Pack murdering her husband was distasteful. "Then it had to be one of that professor's friends, of course. Who else would want Frank dead?"

"Such as?"

"Such as that woman who was with him when he came to the house."

"Mason came here?"

"The day before he died. Him and Frank had a business meeting. My husband didn't like it that he brought that woman with him."

"What woman? Rose Smith from the bookstore?"

Mrs. Duvall looked at me like I was crazy. "Of course not. Why would he bring her? No, he brought that woman who said she worked for him doing publicity."

"Cara Siskin?"

"That sounds about right. Frank wasn't happy. That flower was supposed to be a secret." She shook her head side to side. "The professor shouldn't have told anyone else about it. He gave his word."

"Ms. Siskin saw the flower, too?"

"Of course, she did. The woman isn't blind, you know."

"How did she react?"

"What do you mean?"

"Did she seem, I don't know, excited or especially interested in the flower?"

Mrs. Duvall looked at me with a pained expression. "I wouldn't know. I wasn't there. The four of them were out in the greenhouse."

"Wait." I counted silently on my fingers. "You just said the four of them, but if it was Frank, Mason, and Cara, that's three."

"The other woman was there, too." She sounded fed up with my questions.

"What other woman?"

"That floozy from the radio station."

"Violet Wilcox?"

"If you say so. I don't like the way she looks or behaves."

"What was she doing here? Did she come with Mason or Cara?"

"She came in a black van."

"And you didn't hear what they talked about? Frank didn't tell you afterward?"

"Like I said, my husband handled the business. I was fixing lunch, which is what I'm fixing to do now." The widow shooed me to the door and slammed it in my face.

Lunch? It was far too early to be fixing anybody's lunch. I'd been given the heave-ho.

But there was one more thing I wanted to know. "What about the ten thousand dollars that was found in Frank's dungarees the morning he was poisoned?" I shouted through the thick front door.

I started to step down from the porch, thinking she had chosen to ignore me, when I heard the door being thrown open behind me. I turned around.

Mrs. Duvall faced me. "I'm going to tell you what I told the police. I don't know where Frank got that money, and I don't know what he was doing walking around with it." She narrowed her eyes. "But I'll tell you this—that money is mine, sure as there's a sun in the sky. That money is mine."

She slammed the door once more.

28

"You just missed Greg Tuffnall." Esther looked up from the crossword puzzle she was filling in at the sales counter. "You know he's married, right?"

I ignored whatever it was she was trying to intimate. "Tuff was here? What did he want?"

"He telephoned. Said you should call him right back. He said it was urgent."

"If it's so urgent, why didn't he call me on my cell?"

"Maybe he doesn't have your number."

"You could have given it to him."

Esther blinked at me. "You want me to start giving strange men your cell phone number?"

I didn't have to think long. "No. Definitely not."

"I thought not." Esther picked up her pencil and started filling in squares. "He wants you to call him back." She pushed a slip of paper to the end of the counter. "I wrote Truckee's number down."

"Okay, thanks." I picked up the paper and slid behind the counter. I dialed Truckee's from the store phone. I cupped my hand over the receiver as the phone at Truckee's rang and said, "Don't you have anything to do, Esther?"

Esther didn't even bother to look at me. "Nope."

I heard somebody pick up on the other end. "Hello, Tuff?"

"This is Martha."

"Hello, Martha. It's Amy Simms from Birds and Bees." I rubbed the edge of the paper across my chin. "I had a message that Tuff called?"

"That's right. He's kind of busy right now in the kitchen. One of the line cooks didn't show up, and it's breakfast rush. Truckers like to hit the road early.

"But he said to tell you that Violet Wilcox from the radio station and that other woman who was working with your professor friend are here."

"They are?" I couldn't keep the excitement from my voice.

"Yep. I can see them myself at a table not twelve feet away."

It wouldn't take me long to drive to Truckee's. "Do you think they'll be there long?"

"They only just now got their waters and haven't even ordered their meals. If you hurry, you can catch them."

"Thanks, Martha. And tell Tuff thanks, too." She said she would.

"I have to go out, Esther."

"So I hear." Esther stuck her pencil behind her ear. "You leaving me in charge?"

"I guess so." I hadn't seen Mom around. That left Esther.

Esther nodded. "It seems to me what with everything I have to do around here and all these responsibilities, I ought to be assistant manager by now."

I was taken aback. "Assistant manager? I'm not sure we need an assistant manager." I didn't have that large a staff. Plus, Esther had only been working at Birds & Bees for a very short time.

"I'll need my own key, too."

I could see that Esther was only going to hear what she wanted at the moment, and I had somewhere to be. "I'll give it some thought." I headed through the back to my van. "We'll talk later!"

I drove as quickly as I dared to Truckee's Road Stop. I snagged a spot close to the restaurant, and killed the engine, and marched inside. Sure enough, Cara Siskin and Violet Wilcox occupied a table near the center of the room. A third woman sat at the table with them. Her back was to me. Martha hadn't mentioned anything about a third woman.

I headed straight for the group, pausing only to wave to Martha.

"Good morning."

The third woman turned her head. "You? Are you following me?" It was Alice Duvall. A short stack of pancakes rested on a plate in front of her.

"So much for being in a hurry to fix your lunch, I see. Going to breakfast first makes much more sense this time of day." I pulled up a chair. "So what are we talking about?"

I looked at each woman in turn. Each woman gave me an ugly look. "What? Am I interrupting something?"

"This is a private business meeting, Ms. Simms," Cara Siskin snapped. She shoved a plate of eggs across the table. It banged against her water glass, sloshing ice water over the tabletop. "I, we would all appreciate it if you'd leave." She clutched her butter knife so hard her fingers were turning white.

I started to smile. "Which one of you murdered Mason?" I turned to Cara. "Was it you?" I looked across the table. "Or was it you, Ms. Wilcox?"

Violet made a face. "You're crazy. Why would any of us kill Livingston?" She must have been watching her weight. She had nothing but a small bowl of oatmeal with strawberry slices.

Alice Duvall had thus far remained mum, choosing to sip a cup of hot tea rather than join the conversation. Finally, she spoke. "Nobody here killed anybody, Ms. Simms. Like I told you before, Pack Mulligan killed Mason, and he killed my Frank. If I thought anybody at this table was a murderer, do you think I'd be here?"

I stared hard at Alice Duvall. She might be a lot of things, but I didn't think she'd be the type to intentionally consort with a murderer, especially since whoever had murdered Mason had very likely been responsible for her husband's death as well. By all accounts, she had loved Frank.

"Did either of you give Frank the ten thousand dollars that was found on him?" I asked, turning to Cara Siskin and Violet Wilcox.

"Where would I get ten grand?" huffed Violet. "The station barely pays its bills as it is."

"Well, I certainly didn't." Cara wiped her brow with a paper napkin. "Now, if you wouldn't mind?" She motioned toward the door with her hand. "We are trying to conduct our business here."

I noticed she had dropped the butter knife, and I couldn't help feeling relieved. I pushed back my chair but kept my butt planted. "What kind of business exactly? What do a flower farmer, a radio station owner, and a book publicist have in common?"

The three women looked at one another. Cara and Violet shrugged simultaneously, but it was Violet who spoke. "If you must know, the three of us are trying to figure out a way to proceed with Alice's Hummingbird Heaven."

"The flower Frank developed?"

"That's right," Cara said. "Just because Frank and Mason are dead doesn't mean we shouldn't proceed. I have a lot of contacts in the business. Violet runs a radio station and has a lot of promotion and marketing ideas." She played with a corner of toast on her plate. "As do I."

"And Alice here owns the flower."

Alice nodded. "Frank wouldn't have wanted me to give up. He had big plans. I think, with Ms. Siskin and Ms. Wilcox's help, that we might just be able to make Frank proud."

I closed my eyes and sighed before standing. "I'm sorry for interrupting." I patted Alice Duvall's shoulder. "Once again, I am so sorry for your loss."

I left the diner in a daze, my thoughts more muddled than ever.

I thought I had been close to solving two murders and had reached a dead end.

I returned to Birds & Bees. After putting the eggs away, I spotted Mom stepping off the public bus across the street. I ran over to help her, and we crossed back to the Birds & Bees side of the street together.

"Buy anything interesting?"

Mom pulled a colorful silk scarf from a small bag. "This. It was on sale."

I ran my fingers along the soft fabric. "It's beautiful. I'm surprised the shops were open this early."

"It was a lovely little boutique operating out of a tent at the farmers market. You should visit it sometime. The woman running it has some very nice things."

"I'll do that." I still wanted to check out that jewelry dealer.

"I stopped at Bookarama while I was in town."

"You did?"

"Yes. The store wasn't open, but I ran into Rose shopping for produce at the farmers' market. She looked so wan. The poor dear."

"You talked to her?"

"Yes, we had a little chat."

"That's great. I've been worried about them."

"She did admit that she felt like everybody's eyes were on her. It made her uncomfortable."

"Was Amber there, too?"

"No, Rose said Amber was off on some errands." We climbed the porch steps and sat in the rockers. I saw Esther inside helping a couple of ladies but figured she had things covered. If she needed assistance, she knew where to find us. Kim wouldn't be in until afternoon. "I ran into Derek, too. He was returning from Jessamine's Kitchen across the square."

"Was he able to get all the feathers out of his clothing?"

Mom laughed softly. "He told me all about the two of you dealing with the eggs this morning."

I couldn't help laughing. "At least I got a dozen fresh eggs for my trouble." I explained that I'd put them in the fridge. "I hope Pack gets released soon. I don't see myself making a habit of caring for chickens."

Mom reach across and patted my leg. "You won't have to worry about that. Derek said Pack has been released."

"He has?"

Mom nodded.

"Wow, that was fast."

"Derek and that other lawyer from Raleigh were able to get the judge to release him on bail. Derek says all the evidence the police have is circumstantial at best." Mom placed her scarf carefully back in the shopping bag. "Did you see Alice Duvall?"

"Yes. I gave her your condolences. And the cupcakes."

"I hope she's holding up all right."

"She's shaken up, but I think she'll be okay." I stood. "That reminds me."

"What is it?"

"I need to check something. I'll be right back."

Mom nodded, and I ran inside and hurried up to the apartment. I grabbed my laptop from the bedroom and returned to the front porch. I sat down and booted up.

"What are you up to?"

"I saw a pair of chinaberry trees out at Pack's farm this morning. Birds love the berries, but I seem to remember they are poisonous to people."

"They most certainly are," said Mom. "Your grandmother had one in her yard. Don't you remember?"

I said I didn't, but it must have been buried somewhere deep in my subconscious.

"As a girl, she always warned me not to eat the fruit. Very dangerous, she said." Mom slipped off her shoes and massaged her feet. "She used to give Nicky a berry or two. She said any more and he'd be hammered."

I keyed in "chinaberry tree" as my mother reminisced. "You're right. It says here that the fruit is poisonous, even deadly, to humans." I sucked in a breath. "And it contains tetranortriterpenes." I tripped over the syllables. It was a mouthful. No pun intended.

"What's that?"

"That," I said, folding the cover down on the laptop, "is the poison that killed Frank Duvall."

Mom pushed her brows together. "And you say you found a tree like that at Pack Mulligan's house?"

"Two of them." I held up two fingers.

Mom rocked back and forth. "That's not going to look good for him."

"No. It's not." I settled the laptop on the small wrought iron table between us. "I wonder where Pack is now. Do you suppose he's home, or is he with Derek and his other lawyer?"

"Derek said he had to go back to Charlotte to assist Ben with that case they're handling. I'm not certain where the other attorney is at the moment. He could be halfway to Raleigh."

Mom ran a hand through her hair. "Derek said Amber had picked Pack up from jail and offered to give him a lift. I'm sure he wants to get back to his chickens."

"Amber? Doesn't that seem strange to you?"

"I don't know. Should it?"

I thought hard. Something wasn't adding up.

"Speaking of Amber." Mom folded her hands in her lap. "There's something else that I learned. Actually, it concerns your friend, Professor Livingston, too."

I looked at my mother. She looked so serious. "What is it?"

"You aren't going to like it."

"Mom," I replied, struggling to maintain my patience. "I already don't like it. Spit it out. I can take it." Nonetheless, I mentally braced myself.

"Derek told me that the police have found a link between Amber and Professor Livingston."

"You mean that she once took a class with him for like two seconds?" I waved a hand dismissively. "I know all about that."

"Did you know that there have been allegations made that Professor Livingston made untoward advances toward some of his students?"

I bristled. "I don't believe it." I knew Mason liked the ladies, but I couldn't picture him as a sleaze.

"It's true," Mom said. "He'd been facing similar charges in Texas."

My sigh carried across the yard. "I hate to believe it is even possible." First I'd heard allegations of the professor resorting to plagiarism, then I'd heard murmurings that he was having trouble in Texas, a messy divorce and other problems. Jerry had hinted at something to that effect himself. Who else had told me about Mason's obscure troubles in Texas? Had it been Violet Wilcox, Cara Siskin, or both?

I watched two hummingbirds fight for sole possession of one of my hanging hummingbird feeders. There were at least four other feeders sitting birdless, yet they insisted on fighting over the one. "But it would explain Amber's actions toward him, wouldn't it? Putting laxatives in his chocolates . . ."

"Egging his birdhouse camper." Mom slipped her shoes back over her feet. "It would explain why Amber dropped out of his class so quickly."

"Yes. But does it make her a murderer?" She dropped out of college soon after and was living above her mother's bookstore. Had she grown bitter? Would she commit murder? And how?

"I can't see how. She was at the lake," Mom said.

"True, she has an alibi...of sorts. The cameras at the Lakeside Market could be wrong. Their internal clocks could be off. It wouldn't need to be by much in order to have given Amber time to thrust a pair of scissors in Mason's neck."

"You might mention that to the police. They may not have considered that. I hate to think of Amber as a killer though, Amy. She's so sweet."

I rocked faster and faster as thought after thought raced through my mind like hummingbirds zipping through air. I felt like all of the pieces were there. I just wasn't putting them together right.

Until suddenly, everything became clear.

Sort of.

I jumped to my feet. The rocking chair clattered against the house.

"Amy! What's gotten into you? You look like you've just been stung by a bee!"

I grinned. "A *mason* bee maybe."

I rushed for the door.

"Where are you going?" shouted Mom.

"I think I know who the killer is!"

I threw open the door.

"But where are you going?"

I spun around to address her. "To the bookstore. I need to check something first!"

"But—"

"Tell Jerry!"

29

I couldn't wait for Mom to finish. I had a feeling that Pack Mulligan might be in danger—maybe of being poisoned like Frank Duvall, the man he was accused of poisoning.

I was certain that somebody was trying to set him up for two murders: Frank Duvall and Mason Livingston.

And if I was right, I'd have the answer to who very shortly.

I raced through Birds & Bees, paying no mind to Esther and our nonplussed customers, cut through the storeroom to my van out back, started the engine, and sped toward the town square.

Knowing Derek and Ben were out of town, I parked in Derek's reserved space behind Harlan and Harlan and hoofed it to Bookarama. The store was dark except for the outside light spilling in. I tried the door. It was locked.

I rapped on the glass with my knuckles. After several moments, a light went on toward the rear, and a shape appeared in the hallway. It was Rose Smith.

I waved. "Hi, Rose!" I called through the glass separating us. "I heard you were open."

Rose approached, dressed in dark slacks and a loose white top. She turned the thumb lock from the inside. "We are. But not this early. I was just bringing some books in from the back."

"Do you mind if I come in?"

"I guess not. What's up?"

I entered, and she relocked the door behind us. "Is Amber around?" The bookstore had been put back in order. All the folding chairs and the signing table had been put away or returned to their usual places. Everything was neatly arranged.

"Amber?" Rose blinked at me.

"Yes, I'd like to talk to her, Rose."

"She's fragile. I think it would be best to leave her alone, Amy."

"Of course." I smiled warmly. "I understand. Actually, the real reason I came was to pick up my books."

"Your books?"

"Yes, you remember. The books Derek bought, three copies of *Hummingbirds and Their Habits*. Jerry, Chief Kennedy, said he gave them back to you."

Rose was silent a moment as her eyes scanned the store. "Yes. I put them behind the counter." She blinked at me. "I'll get them for you."

"Thanks. You don't mind if I take a look around the shelves while you do, do you?"

"Go right ahead."

I turned down the romance aisle. "I imagine you heard that Packard Mulligan was arrested on suspicion of murder for the death of Frank Duvall."

"Yes," Rose called from the other end of the store. "I heard that."

"The police also think he murdered Professor Livingston." I grabbed a new paperback. A darkly tanned hunk holding a lariat in his fingers graced the cover. I idly flipped the pages.

"That's terrible."

I glanced at Rose from across the store. There were several rows of shelves between us. "Why did you tell me you had done it? I thought you'd gone mad!" I smiled.

Rose shook her head. "I thought it was Amber. It was stupid of me. I realize that."

"I understand. You love her. You wanted to protect her."

"Yes, I did."

"Frank's widow, Alice, thinks Pack killed the professor to keep Frank Duvall from going into business with him. Plus, Pack and Frank had been feuding with each other for years."

Rose stroked her chin. "I didn't know that. I don't know Pack very well. He's a simple man." She stepped out from behind the counter carrying my three copies of Mason's book. She set them on top of a book display near the front door. "Has Pack said why?"

"Why he murdered two men?" I replaced the paperback and chose another. This cover featured a shirtless motorcycle rider, also tan. He gripped the handlebars and stared at me menacingly with his bulging biceps and hard abs. "As far as I know, he hasn't admitted to anything."

I stood on tiptoes and looked across the store. "Are you sure Amber hasn't come in?"

"I'm sure."

"I was told she was giving Pack a ride home."

"Now that you mention it, I believe she did."

"How did she know?"

"Know what?"

"That he needed a ride home?"

"He called her on her cell and asked for a ride back to his farm."

"So they were friends?"

"I wouldn't say that. She's house-sat for him a few times to earn a few extra dollars."

I was reminded of the Western romance novel I'd found at Pack's house. The cover of the book had been torn off. I read the first few pages of the novel in my hand and felt myself blushing. I quickly put it back on the shelf.

Rose picked up my books and brought them to me. "Here are your books. I hate to kick you out, but I really should be getting the store ready, and I do have new books to unpack and shelve."

"Thanks." I took the books from her. I noted the Bookarama stickers on back showing they'd been purchased. Rose moved away, and I followed her to the front of the store.

She slipped behind the counter and opened the cash register. "Is there something else?"

I set all three books down on the display table and opened the top one, carefully flipping thought the first few pages while Rose arranged money in the till. The first pages of the top book were blank. "That's funny."

"What?"

I slid that book to the bottom and tried books two and three. They were also blank except for the words on the printed page. None of the books had been signed. I slowly turned in Rose's direction. She stood stiffly at the register.

I felt my heart racing.

"What's funny, Amy?"

My throat and lips were dry. I ran my tongue over my lower lip. "It *was* you," I whispered. "You killed Mason . . ." I felt my blood pounding inside my ears.

Ruth chuckled as she stepped out from behind the register. "Why are you so surprised, Amy? I told you from the start that I had."

She stepped closer. She held a gun in her right hand.

30

"How did you figure it out?" There was an ugly smile on Rose's face as she trained the gun on me.

"It was a lot of little things, but they began to add up." I risked a look toward the storeroom. "Did you and Amber conspire?" It would have made sense. "Between the two of you, you could have pulled off both murders.

"While the police were looking for one killer, there could have been two in reality."

My fingers groped for the hummingbird book. It wasn't bulletproof, but it was a hefty hardcover. It might not make a great weapon, but it was the only thing near to hand.

"Leave Amber out of this. She had nothing to do with Mason's murder. Or Frank's." Her eyes locked onto my hand. "Leave the book alone."

I pulled my hand away.

"Amber was a victim herself."

"Of Professor Livingston's advances?"

"That's right. That man ruined her life. She was a young girl. He tried to take advantage of her. I'll never forget the night she called from school to tell me how that man had nearly defiled her."

Rose glanced out the front window. There was no one around. Even if there had been, I didn't know if I would have risked shouting for help.

"Can you blame her for egging his stupid birdhouse trailer or putting some of my laxatives in his chocolates?" Rose asked. "Believe you me, I'd have done a lot worse than that!" And she had.

Rose swiped at the corner of her eye where a tear had formed. "He ruined her life. Amber dropped out of college after that and never went back." She waved the gun in my face. "She was going to be a nurse! She was going to have a life!" Rose's free arm flailed in the air. "Not be stuck in this little town with me, running a crummy bookstore. Barely paying our bills. Barely making ends meet."

She pulled in a jagged breath. "That man deserved to die. Do you know Mason didn't even remember Amber?" She sniffed. "The lousy scumbag didn't even remember my daughter. Didn't remember her face, her name, or what he'd done to her!" Rose began pacing, though never taking her eyes off me.

"How many other young girls must he have done something similar to that he couldn't even remember them all? Huh? Answer me that!"

I had no answer. At least not a good one. And I wasn't sure how stable Rose was at that moment. "But you invited Mason here! Why?"

Rose glared at me defiantly but made no reply. She didn't need to. I knew why. To murder him. "What about Frank Duvall? Did he deserve to die?"

Rose frowned. "He was blackmailing me. Frank was another scumbag. He was wandering around in back of the store that night. I thought everybody was gone.

"It turns out he saw the whole thing. He said if I didn't pay him off, he'd turn me in," she spat, clearly as disgusted with Frank as she was with Mason, probably all men. "He was desperate for money. His farm's been on the verge of bankruptcy for months. So I paid him." She grinned wickedly. "And then I killed him."

"So it was you who gave him the ten thousand dollars?"

"Yes. And I would have gotten it back if you hadn't shown up. You cost me a lot of money, Amy."

"You saw me at the farmers market?"

Rose nodded.

"And you had access to the Mulligan place through Amber. You knew where to get the chinaberries that you used to poison him." I ever so slowly inched away, only to find myself backed up to the display table. "What I didn't get was how you managed to stab Mason when you were video chatting with John Moytoy at the time. It took me a long time to put that together."

She raised a questioning brow, as if calling my bluff, so I continued. "I figured it out after remembering the setup down at AM Ruby."

"The radio station?"

I nodded. "Ms. Wilcox has a prerecorded message set up to play when someone rings the bell and she doesn't want visitors to know she's out of the station. She said it's to prevent thefts."

"She's a clever girl," quipped Rose.

"And you were at the station. You recorded several commercials at AM Ruby for Mason's upcoming book signing here at Bookarama. You would have seen that very setup.

"Then when I saw that Mason had not autographed these books," I turned slightly and risked tapping the cover of the top book with my forefinger, "I knew it had to be you."

"How?" When I hesitated to answer, she jabbed the gun toward me.

"John told me that when he was video chatting with you, you mentioned that Mason had signed the books." I couldn't help smiling. "At the time you made your recording, you assumed Mason would have autographed the books to us. But he hadn't. And you killed him before he had the chance."

"Not bad."

"It also means that you planned the whole thing in advance, Rose. You killed him in cold blood." A premeditated murder. Why was I goading her?

"I remember John saying how he could hardly get a word in edgewise. I'm sure you planned it that way. The more you talked and the less you let him talk, the better your chances of getting away with a prerecorded talk."

"John's not much of a talker."

She was right. John would always be content to listen. "All you had to do was keep talking, maybe let him nod and say yes now and again, and then plow on. It wouldn't be so hard to do. The entire conversation was only a matter of minutes."

"A matter of minutes during which you stabbed Mason in the neck." I pointed at the empty space on the floor between the door and the counter. "I figured something else out, too. Unlike Frank Duvall, whom you didn't know was here, you intended for Pack to be here so he could be blamed for Mason's death."

She eyed me with curiosity. "What gave me away?"

I kept talking, wondering where Jerry was. Had Mom called Jerry like I'd told her? "It was the books that were right there on the floor." I pointed at the empty spot once again. "There was a pile of books right there with their covers torn off. I saw another like it at Pack's house."

She shrugged. "I gave Pack free books. I rip the covers off to get credit for the books from the publishers for the units I don't sell. I'm supposed to throw the books out, destroy them. But I didn't see anything wrong with giving a few to Pack now and again."

Rose Smith had a twisted sense of morality.

"I promised him some that night. Told him to meet me here at ten."

"Right at the exact time you intended to stab Mason while having your fake video chat with John."

"Pack was late, but I couldn't postpone. Then you showed up unexpectedly. I dumped those books by the door, hoping they would be traced back to Pack. If he'd shown up on time like he was supposed to, I'd have been sure to get his fingerprints on them."

"And the police would peg him for Mason's murder."

"A murder that occurred while I was upstairs in my apartment chatting with John." She smiled. "As you said, I had everything planned."

"Except for Frank coming out of the backroom afterward and blackmailing you." I dodged for the door, but Rose stepped in my path and I froze.

"Nice try, Amy. But don't try it again." She angled the revolver so I could see the chamber. "This thing is loaded."

It was. I gulped, my heart in my mouth. "I have to admit, you were clever."

"You're clever, too." She smiled evilly. "Too clever. Let's go." She motioned with the gun muzzle.

"Where are we going?" I was sweating profusely. My hand clung to my purse strap. If only she'd look away long enough for me to get to my phone.

"Just walk until I tell you to stop."

I did as I was told. "I saw Pack afterward. Outside the bookstore. I think he saw the whole thing, too. He saw you stab Mason."

"Maybe."

"Are you planning to kill him, too?"

"What for? Who's going to believe him over me? Nobody, that's who. Besides, he's already Chief Kennedy's prime suspect. It's no coincidence that Frank's thermos ended up in Pack's path."

"You planted it?" We had reached the back storeroom, piled high with books on shelves and in open boxes.

"Frank and I had arranged to meet before the market opened. I gave him his money." She turned on the light.

"Then, when he started unloading his truck, I removed his thermos and slipped in a little something special."

I turned to face Rose. "The chinaberry poison."

"That's right. Then I saw Pack pull up. It was the perfect opportunity to get rid of two problems at once. Everybody at the market recognized Frank's beat-up red plaid thermos. And he'd written his name on it with a black marker—as if anybody else would want the filthy thing.

"When Pack turned to unload his eggs, I laid the thermos in his path. It wasn't long after that he picked it up and took it to Frank's stall."

"Bookarama is only steps from the farmers market. And you're a regular there. Nobody would think twice about seeing you."

Rose skirted around me toward the back door. "Don't move!" she instructed as I twisted my neck to follow her movements.

"What happens next?" I strained my ears for sounds of an approaching police siren but heard nothing.

"I shoot you, of course."

"Rose, this isn't going to work."

"I think it will. There have been a number of burglaries around town. I believe you said so yourself. What with that and the murder in my store, I was nervous. I heard someone at the back door. I yelled for them to get out. When they didn't, I fired." A wicked and determined look crossed her face. "I'm a pretty good shot. And I do have a license."

She motioned for me to take a couple of steps back. "It will be a tragic accident."

"Rose, you don't have to do this. You can turn yourself in. Tell the court what you told me about what Mason did to Amber. I'm sure they'll be lenient—"

"Enough, Amy!" Rose moved back toward the short hall that connected the storage area with the store. As she did, I ran for the stacks. Maybe I could dodge a literal bullet or two while hoping the police would be there soon.

As I dove behind the nearest shelf of books, a shot rang out and ricocheted against the cement block wall. Another followed. Rose screamed in frustration. The third shot had been more direct, and I heard it impact the books.

Through a crack between the books, I saw Rose running toward me, the gun extended, ready to fire again. The back door flew open. A blur in blue denim and khaki pants burst in.

A shot went off. I heard a yowl of pain as Rose fought off her attacker. I saw his fist drive into the top of her head. I yanked a wood shelf free, scrambled from around the teetering shelf, and slammed the board down across her back.

Rose slumped to the ground. The board fell at my feet, and I swiped at my blurry eyes. As my vision cleared, I saw Pack Mulligan standing there, clutching his left arm. It was bloodied. He stooped and picked up Rose's pistol with his good hand. He passed the gun to me, then settled down on the floor with his back to the wall.

"This would be a good time to call the police," he said, his voice weak and hoarse.

I nodded and reached for my purse. Only then I realized that I'd dropped it somewhere in the confusion. I stepped over Rose's inert body and ran to the front of the store.

I set the gun down on the counter and picked up the phone beside the register. As I did, I saw a Ruby Lake squad car lurch to a stop outside. Dan Sutton was behind the wheel.

I set the phone down and unlocked the door to let him in.

I held up my hand to stop him as he began to surge past me. "Rose is back there. I'll get an ambulance."

"Ambulance?" Dan tipped his cap, looking confused. "Your mom called the station wanting to talk to the chief. I told her he wasn't around. She said you'd gone to Bookarama and insisted I come. What's going on here?"

"Rose killed Mason Livingston." I felt myself getting lightheaded. Events were catching up with me.

"For real?" Officer Sutton appeared unsure if he should believe me. I couldn't blame him.

"For real. She poisoned Frank Duvall, too." I pointed. "She's back there."

"Why the ambulance? Is she hurt?"

"Not too bad, I think. But Pack's been shot."

"Pack Mulligan?"

204 • J.R. Ripley

I nodded as I picked up the phone. I said into the receiver, "Did you get all that, Anita?"

"Yep. Hang in there, Amy. The ambulance is on its way along with reinforcements."

"Thanks." I hung up the phone and returned to the storeroom. Rose hadn't moved. Neither had Pack.

"You okay?" I asked, watching as Dan ministered to Pack's wounded arm.

Pack nodded. His eyes were watery, and I could see that he was in intense pain. "Yeah. I'm okay." He winced as Dan applied a tourniquet to his upper arm.

"Sorry," apologized Dan. "Don't worry, Mister Mulligan, a few days in the hospital and you'll be good as new."

He looked at the officer in anguish. "Who's gonna take care of the chickens?"

I winced. I was afraid I knew the answer to that question. Oh well, at least my supply of free farm-fresh eggs wouldn't be drying up anytime soon.

The ambulance arrived shortly thereafter and carried Pack away. Dan had roused Rose, who glared at us like a mad ostrich but refused to speak.

Dan cuffed her and led her out to Officer Reynolds's squad car, which had parked in the rear.

"Hey, Dan!" I called. "Before you go, I have one question."

"Yeah?"

"Why did you ask Kim to go to Jerry's vow renewal?"

He looked at me like I was stupid or something. "Because I don't want to go alone. Duh."

I squeezed my eyes shut. I knew that.

Duh.

"Tell her that!" I yelled to Dan as he slammed the door on Rose and motioned for Reynolds to haul her off to the town jail.

31

I finished filling Kim and my mother in on what had happened at Bookarama yesterday. My mother had heard it all before, but most of it was new to Kim, who had been busy showing clients house rentals all day and never came in for her shift at the store—it wasn't the first time and wouldn't be the last.

"Pack is still in the hospital. The bullet went clear through his biceps." Rose Smith and her daughter were in jail—Rose for murder and Amber for being an accomplice, though it was unclear if the charges against Amber would stick. Rose insisted that Amber hadn't known that she planned to lure Mason to town to murder him. She thought the plan was merely to humiliate him in some fashion—like trying to make him violently ill during the signing.

Kim winced when I mentioned Pack's injury. "It hurts just to think about it." She rubbed her left arm.

"Not to mention that might have been you, young lady," scolded my mother.

"Believe me, I know." I'd come close to dead-duck status and wouldn't soon forget it.

"Are you saying Pack knew the entire time that Rose was responsible for Mason's murder?"

"He's admitting everything, singing like a proverbial canary. I feel sorry for him. He said he saw Rose stab Mason and got confused. He also didn't want to turn her in because she had been so nice to him over the years. Plus, Amber had talked to him afterward and begged him not to say anything."

"Why would he agree to a crazy thing like that?" Kim asked.

"Because Amber told him what Mason had tried to do to her."

"Oh . . ." Kim folded her hands in her lap.

206 · *J.R. Ripley*

"I promised I'd go see him at the hospital this afternoon. You two want to come?" Both agreed. Mom suggested we bring flowers. I suggested we didn't.

"Pack has a cousin who's coming over from Morganton to take care of his chicken farm," I said.

"Fortunate for the chickens," quipped Kim. I'd told her about the misadventures Derek and I had had with chicken farming.

"And my beauty rest," I added.

"Do you think Mason was really guilty of plagiarism and accosting all those women?" Kim wanted to know.

"As much as I hate to believe it . . ." I left the rest of my words go unspoken. I really did hate to think of the man I had once admired as behaving in the ways that were coming to light after his death. "As for Cara Siskin and Violet Wilcox, it seems the two of them are guilty of nothing more than greed."

"No crime there," Kim replied.

"I guess not." I had my eye on a hummingbird that had alighted on the slender branch of a maple. "I honestly hope Frank's widow makes out all right."

"Me too." Mom rocked slowly. "Have you heard yet whether Pack will be charged with anything?"

"Jerry's yelling that Pack was withholding evidence, but Derek seems to think he'll be willing to let Pack off."

"I hope so," Mom replied.

"Me too. He did save my life."

"And Jerry had accused the young man of murder." Mom tsk-tsked. "I bet Pack was frightened."

"He was innocent of the burglaries, too," I said.

"Yes," Mom replied, "Anita told me the owner of Grace's B and B found a lot of merchandise in one of her guest rooms, stashed in the closet. She got suspicious and phoned the police. The two young men staying in the room admitted to the crimes."

"What I want to know," cut in Kim, "is where was Rose's daughter the entire time she was trying to shoot you?"

"Amber? She dropped Pack off at his place, then went to the lake to think, she says.

"Pack loaded up his van with eggs and headed straight to the farmers market. But he wanted to appeal to Rose once more to turn herself in." I clamped my hands over my knees. "I think holding the information in was eating him up inside."

"So he storms in and saves the day." Kim fiddled with her cell phone. She was expecting a call from a client.

"Pretty much. Pack said he heard us yelling inside, then heard the shots and figured I was in trouble." I bit my lower lip, remembering the risk I'd taken. "He knew what Rose was capable of. He'd seen evidence of that with his own eyes."

"To think," Mom muttered, "I'd been talking to Rose just that morning. I had no idea that a couple of hours later she'd be trying to shoot my daughter."

"Incredible," said Kim, nodding. "Unbelievable."

"I heard it all yesterday, and I still can't believe it," said Mom.

"Believe it," I said. "And you," I added, pointing to my best friend, "you need to call Dan and tell him yes."

"Yes what?"

"That you'll go to Jerry's vow renewal ceremony. Don't make the poor man ask you again, and don't make him go alone."

Kim opened her mouth to sass me, when out of the corner of my eye, I saw a humungous shape being pulled slowly up Lake Shore Drive by a truck that I knew well. Too well.

"Hey! I'm not done with you!" Kim hollered at me.

I waved her off, jumped off the front porch, and ran to the street. My shoulder slammed into a hummingbird feeder, and it crashed to the ground, splashing sugar water all over the lawn and walkway. I'd pick it up later. Kim followed me to the street.

"What's *that* doing here?" I was staring at Mason Livingston's giant birdhouse on wheels, his former home away from home. Paul and Derek climbed out of Paul's pickup. Derek had rushed back to town the moment he'd learned what had happened.

"Isn't it great?" Paul was beaming as he slapped me on the back. "I bought it off Livingston's estate. You wouldn't believe how cheap I got it."

"Yes. I would." I took a step closer. "But what is it doing *here*?"

"I got a variance." He readjusted a plastic peony in one of the trailer's window boxes nearest the sidewalk.

"A variance?" I scratched my head.

"Yeah, I'm on the town planning commission. You remember."

"I do now. But you still haven't answered my question, Paul. What is it doing here?" In front of my place of business. This was just too much déjà vu. Paul and I had met when he'd begun parking a dilapidated camper on this very spot.

"I thought it would make a great promotional tool." He pulled his cell phone from the front pocket of his blue jeans and snapped a quick picture of the birdhouse.

"For promoting what? Giant red birdhouses to sell to the tourists?"

"Very funny, Amy. For promoting you and me." Paul threw his arms out. "Birds," he said, pointing first to Birds & Bees. Then, moving his arm over to his place, he added, "and brews. Birds and Brews."

"No offense to the recently departed Mason Livingston, but it looks more like a giant funhouse." That was Kim.

"I don't know," Derek interjected. "It does have a certain kitsch factor, Amy."

"It was a dead man's last home," I retorted.

"Yeah," agreed Paul. "But he didn't die *inside* it."

I shook my head. Surely the two of them had gone crazy. It was up to me to be the voice of reason. "And the town told you that you could just leave it sitting here on the street all the time?"

Paul shook his head. "No, don't worry. We'll only park out here on Birds and Brews days. From six till ten in the evening. That's the best the town would do. Believe me, I fought for more."

"I'd have fought for less."

Derek chuckled. He was dressed casually in cargo shorts and a black T-shirt.

I leveled my eyes at him. "I hadn't intended the comment as a joke."

"I've always thought it was kind of cute." Kim ran a hand along its side.

"Don't worry, Amy," Paul assured me. "The rest of the time we'll park the trailer out back behind our shops." He stroked the side of the birdhouse lovingly. "And the insurance on her is a lot less than you'd think."

What was it with men and things on wheels that so infatuated them? And why did they think of them as feminine? And how much money for insurance were we talking exactly?

And why was he saying "we"?

"I'm thinking of using it to sell beer, too. It will be a Brewer's

Biergarten on wheels. I can set it up at fairs and carnivals, street fes-
tivals."

"I have to admit, that's not a bad idea, Paul." If anything, it would
keep Paul Anderson and the trailer far from my sight.

"I knew you'd like it." He looked past me to Derek. "Didn't I tell
you she'd like it?"

"That you did." Derek's eyes went from Paul to me and back
again. "But you forgot to tell her the best part."

My left brow went up. "There's a best part?"

"Oh, yeah. I almost forgot." Paul rubbed his hands together like
he was trying to start a fire. "It's half yours."

"Oh, no, it's not." I folded my arms firmly across my chest.

Kim snorted and covered her mouth with her hand.

"Sure it is." Paul pulled a receipt from his pocket. "I've got the receipt right here. See?"

"I am not paying one nickel for a share of this thing." I ignored
Derek as he laughed behind me.

"You don't have to. Barbara already gave me your share of the
money." He turned to my mother who had joined us curbside and had
an impish grin on her face. "Surprise!"

My arms fell to my sides, and my eyes went to the legal-looking
paper Paul held open before me. Sure enough, I owned one-half of a
giant red birdhouse. I wouldn't have been surprised if Derek had
drafted the document himself.

"My mother gave you money for this thing?"

"Yeah, a check from your Birds and Bees business account. I've
already deposited it in the bank. Your mom says she's thinking of
selling those Barbara's Bird Bars of hers out of the trailer, too. Right,
Mrs. Simms?"

"I was thinking it might not be a bad idea." Mom cast a hesitant
look my way.

"I think that's a great idea, Mrs. Simms!" Paul rubbed his hands
together. "You can sell your suet cakes out one window while I sell
beer out the other."

"Did you know about this?" I asked Kim.

Kim threw her hands in the air. "Not a word."

I wheeled on Derek. "What about you? Are you going to be offering legal advice from the back step?"

Derek hooted. "Not a bad idea!"

A black SUV lurched to a stop behind the giant birdhouse, one wheel hopped the curb. Lance Jennings from the *Ruby Lake Weekender* was behind the wheel. He cut the engine, climbed out, brushed himself off, and rushed over. A fancy camera dangled from his hand. "Hi, sorry I'm late."

"No problem," said Paul.

"Hello, Lance. What are you doing here?" I asked. He'd already been by yesterday afternoon for an interview with me about the murder and what had happened at Bookarama. "I've told you everything I know."

Lance turned my way. He was dressed in khakis and a navy polo shirt. "Hi, Amy. I'm not here for you. I'm here for this." He pointed to the trailer.

Paul came between us. "I asked Lance to come by and take a picture of the trailer for the newspaper ad we're going to run."

"Newspaper ad?" I goggled at them both.

Lance bobbed his head as he began snapping photos, circling the giant birdhouse like it was an ostrich and he was on a photo safari in Africa. "There's going to be a story, too."

Paul explained. "Lance is going to give us a write-up on the christening of the new Birds and Brewsmobile." His eyes twinkled with delight.

"Birds and Brewsmobile?" My mouth hung open.

"Birds and Brewsmobile." The beginnings of a smile passed Derek's lips. "I like it, Paul." He avoided looking at me.

"It does have a certain ring to it," added Mom, looking happy.

I kept my opinion to myself. How could I rain on her parade?

"Come on!" Esther stuck her head out of the truck's driver side window and blew the horn.

Hoo-hoo-hoo-hoo!

Where had she come from? "Aren't you supposed to be minding the store?"

She ignored me and tooted the horn a second time.

I shook my head. "Some assistant manager," I muttered.

Hoo-hoo-hoo-hoo!

Oh, brother.

Esther locked her hands around the steering wheel. "Let's test her out!"

I scurried over to her door. "Do you even have a driver's license, Esther?"

Esther pulled a face. "Sure, I've had it since sixty-seven."

"Was that the year when you were issued the license or your age at the time?"

Esther thought a moment before saying rather uncertainly as she blinked at me through her failing eyes, "Both?"

I yanked at the door handle. "Scoot over, I'm driving."

With luck, by the time I maneuvered this behemoth across town to the hospital, it would be visiting hours.

Please turn the page for an exciting sneak peek of

J.R. Ripley's next Bird Lover's mystery

CHICKADEE CHICKADEE BANG BANG

coming soon!

1

"It says here," read Kim, "that the black-capped chickadee is slightly larger and a tad brighter than the Carolina chickadee." She had her nose in a well-worn copy of one of my birding field guides.

"What good does that do us?" whispered Otelia, hovering nearby like a baby jay. "We have nothing to compare it to." She cinched her light sweater tighter. A light, cool breeze had kicked up.

Sally Potts snapped her chewing gum, and the little bird jumped to a farther branch. It was late September and leaves were beginning to fall from the trees, but there were still plenty of yellow-orange leaves on the maple to obscure our bird.

"Shh." I pressed a finger to my lips. The bird in question was the chickadee singing in the tree overhead, but I wasn't sure yet which species it belonged to. "Go ahead and read some more, Kim," I suggested softly.

"Umm."

I watched for a moment as Kim's eyes scanned the page, then lifted my binoculars and trained them once more on the small chickadee.

Chickadee-dee-dee! The bird extended its neck and shook itself briskly after singing its signature song—a sure sign that we were spooking it.

John Moytoy, a Ruby Lake librarian, lowered his binoculars and rubbed the bridge of his nose where his eyeglasses hit. "The Cherokee called it *tsikilili* because of the sound it makes." John is well versed in the Cherokee heritage, being of Cherokee descent himself. He has jet black hair and is cherubic in body and spirit. He'd been letting his hair grow out, and it was now long enough that he sported a ponytail.

"Thanks, John," I said. "Like many other animals, numerous birds are commonly named for the sounds they produce such as cuckoos and bobolinks."

"And whip-poor-wills, right?" That was Tiffany LaChance. Tiff works as waitress at Ruby's Diner. She's a buxom blonde, who is very easy on the eyes. Hers are green. She was a few years older than me but had already been married and had a child. She had been wedded to Robert LaChance, but I didn't hold it against her because they were divorced now. Robert and I have had our differences. Tiffany and her eleven-year-old son lived in a condo by the lake.

"Good example," I whispered. Tiff wasn't one of my regulars, so it was especially nice to see her join us.

Kim cleared her throat. "It also says that the black-capped chickadee has a larger area of white behind their, um, aur-auriculars." Kim paused and shot me a questioning look. She's a long-legged, blue-eyed blonde who can eat any amount of food and get away with it, as evidenced by the tight jeans hugging her hips. Life really wasn't fair.

"That's right," I said. "Go on." Kim and I were both in our mid-thirties. The blue eyes were practically all we had in common physically. On a good day, I was a tad heavier than her—a tad being measured in five-pound increments—but I also had an inch on her heightwise. While Kim often goaded me to dye my hair blond like hers, I was sticking with the chestnut brown I'd been born with.

Kim took a sip from her water bottle, then read a little more. "The Carolina chickadee's auriculars are more grayish." She closed the book and looked up into the maple.

"What the heck is an auricular?" Karl scratched the side of his head and pushed his thick black-rimmed eyeglasses back up his nose for the hundredth time since our in-town bird walk had begun. He owned an ancient pair of binoculars that he'd had since his younger days. The weight of them strapped around his neck threatened to bring him to his knees.

"The area around the ears," I replied. "That's the name for the feathers that cover their ears."

The four-inch gray, white, and black bird hopped to yet a higher branch. The black-capped chickadee and the Carolina chickadee share a territory, and their markings are quite similar, making them difficult to differentiate. The fact that they sometimes interbred made it near impossible to distinguish such birds with the naked eye.

"Like a covert?" Floyd asked.

"Exactly." I smiled. "In fact, they are also called coverts because they protect the ears."

Floyd had once told me that in his younger days he had been a duck hunter, so I wasn't surprised to see that he was familiar with the coverts that hunters often used in the field. I was glad he'd given up shooting ducks—not only for the ducks' sake. Floyd's eyesight wasn't the best. He occasionally mistook branches and even rocks for birds.

"So what do we think? Black-capped or Carolina?"

"I vote black-capped," answered Kim. She stuck her water bottle back in its holder attached to her waist belt.

"I vote Carolina," countered Sally Potts. Sally's a slender woman with red hair and sharp green eyes.

"I vote lunch," came Steve Dykstra's reply. Steve was also new to our group. He'd come into the store once or twice for birdseed, and when he saw the sign on the chalkboard announcing our next walk, he had asked to sign up. Steve had been mentioning lunch ever since we'd met up after breakfast.

"I'm thinking Carolina myself," I said, studying the little bird closely and ignoring the digressions that always seemed to pop up on these walks.

"Look at that beauty." Karl whistled. "White with teal accents."

"Where?" I turned and followed the line of his binoculars. "I don't see anything."

There was too much traffic. My little birding group and I were on a birding-in-the-city walk and had stopped at the Town of Ruby Lake's spacious town square to observe the large variety of birds that could normally be found there.

People who weren't into birding didn't realize how many interesting species lived in an urban setting—though *urban* was generous when describing our modest town nestled among the Carolina foothills.

I moved my binoculars back and forth. Could Karl have possibly seen a blue-winged teal? The ducks were rare to this part of western North Carolina, but it wouldn't be impossible to see one—especially with the lake being so near. And with the fall, we would get our share of migrators.

"Right there!" Karl said loudly. "Heading east. You can see its rear end!"

"I can't see anything," complained Otelia Newsome, a fiftyish brunette with a beehive hairdo. She owns a local chocolate shop that I'm drawn to like a bee to nectar.

"Me either." That was Kim.

I refocused my binoculars on an elm across the road.

Karl lowered his glasses. "It's gone now. Turned the corner. What do you think, Floyd?" asked Karl. "Was that a fifty-seven Chevy or maybe a Pontiac?"

I lowered my glasses and gaped at Karl. "What?"

"That was no Star Chief," Floyd said, lowering his own glasses and wiping the eye pieces with the corner of his shirt—something I'd warned him a hundred times would only scratch them. "Didn't you see those taillights? Definitely a fifty-seven Chevy Bel Air. Man, what a beauty."

"You guys were looking at a car?" I shook my finger at Floyd and Karl. "We're supposed to be bird-watching."

"Yeah, but not just any car, Amy," explained Karl. "That was a fifty-seven Bel Air."

The corner of my lip turned down. "So I heard. Can we get back to bird-watching now, do you suppose?" I asked with a smile.

Karl nodded sheepishly.

Floyd nudged Karl and said in a stage whisper, "That car's not from around here. I'll bet it's in town for the car show."

The car show in question was part of an upcoming annual event. Among the myriad special events the Town of Ruby Lake helps organize, each fall we host the Ruby Lake Fall Festival. It's held the first weekend after the fall equinox. The fall festival features a number of popular events, including a classic-car-and-tractor show and a baking competition. The local residents enjoy it, the tourists come from miles around, and the merchants love what it does for their bottom lines.

I was hoping it might do the same for mine, though I wasn't sure I could count on an uptick in my bird store traffic from fans of classic automobiles and farm equipment or even baking. But you never know, so I was participating like most every other business owner in town. Kim had suggested we bake up a couple dozen mock four and twenty blackbird pies. But considering we ran a shop catering to birders, it seemed a bit tasteless to me. No pun intended.

We did intend to have an outdoor presence along with dozens of other street vendors; we'd be selling my mom's surprise hit, Barbara's Bird Bars, along with other food and bird-watching and feeding products.

To my surprise, the Birds & Brewsmobile that I had found myself a reluctant partner in, thanks to the machinations of my mother and the business owner next door, could prove to be a winner. We were planning on setting up the trailer, which had been built to look like a giant red birdhouse, along one of the streets surrounding the town square.

That former camping trailer still gave me the heebie-jeebies, considering that it had once belonged to a friend of mine who'd met an untimely end. Buying it had not been my idea. That idea had been my mother and Paul Anderson's doing. Now I was stuck with it and doing my best to make the most of the situation—and bury the unpleasant associated memories.

Paul Anderson, my neighbor and now business partner, had taken care of the business permits. Cousin Riley had remodeled the interior of the trailer, which had once served as my friend's home away from home, into a proper mobile storefront for Birds & Bees and Paul's business, Brewer's Biergarten. We'd even sprung for a fancy solar-lighted sign reading: Birds & Brewsmobile, which Cousin Riley had affixed to the roof.

"I'm pooped," said Steve. In his early fifties, Steve was one of the youngest of our group. He was tan and fit with coppery hair swept back dramatically. His eyes were painted bunting blue. Having come dressed in white slacks and a raspberry red sweater, however, he might have been having a negative impact on our bird sightings.

Birds are visual creatures and communicate a lot with color. Red and white are danger signals to birds as they are to other animals. Warning signs of trouble, like the flash of a bird's white tail feathers or a scared deer's white tail. The best way to see birds or any other wildlife in a natural setting was to blend in. That meant wearing neutral colors.

Steve was a friend of Otelia Newsome. He works as a mechanic at Nesmith's, the gas station on the edge of town. The next closest stations were out along the highway. I didn't know him well, having only a nodding acquaintance from seeing him around the gas station when pumping gas.

"I'm starved." Otelia looked meaningfully across the town square, her eyes on Jessamine's Kitchen, our planned lunch stop. She'd come with Steve.

I looked at my watch. It was a little early, but I could see that my flock's attention was beginning to stray. "Fine. Let's eat. Besides, if we dine now, we can beat the lunch crowd."

Normally, I liked to start my bird walks early in the morning. That was the best time to spot birds as they busied themselves in search of breakfast, but in an effort to appease the group, we'd picked a mid-morning start with lunch afterward. I had reconnoitered the proposed walk the day before and was confident we'd see plenty of birds.

We had, despite the time of day and Steve Dykstra's clothing choices.

Using my mobile phone, I snapped a quick photo of the chickadee in the tree for later inspection.

We cut across the town square with Steve and Otelia leading the way. Tiffany waved to Aaron Maddley, who was working out of his stall at the farmers market. Their relationship seemed to be developing into something beyond casual dating. Good for them.

Aaron, dressed in blue jeans and a gray T-shirt, was selling farm-fresh arugula, lettuce, radishes, and other fall vegetables under his tent. Besides being good at working the earth, Aaron was good with his hands. He provided me with handmade bluebird houses and other nesting boxes for the store.

"Go on without me," Tiffany said with a big smile on her face. "I'll catch up in a minute."

I smiled back. "Okay. Say hi to Aaron for me."

My relationship with Aaron was still a bit strained. He was having a hard time letting go of the accusations I'd once wrongly leveled at him. When we'd first met, there may have been some chemistry between us. But that shipped had sailed. I was happy for him and Tiffany. I was even happier for me and Derek Harlan, the handsome and steady man I'd been getting closer to since returning to Ruby Lake to open Birds & Bees and be nearer to Mom and the rest of my family.

I couldn't get much nearer to Mom. We shared an apartment above Birds & Bees.

My flock and I waited for traffic to clear, then moved as a group across the street to Jessamine's Kitchen, a homey Southern-style restaurant that had recently opened. I had called Jessamine Jeffries yesterday to let her know our group would be coming in.

A high school girl I knew greeted us at the entrance. "Hello, Ms. Simms. You're early." She had a laminated menu in her right hand.

"Hi, Lulu. It won't be a problem, will it?" Lulu Nowell was a chipper young blonde who worked weekends, and occasionally after school on weekdays when her strict mother and father would let her, to pick up some spending money.

"Not at all. Jess has your table all ready."

"Great."

The layout of Jessamine's Kitchen was simple, and the décor was as cozy as the food. The furnishings included Shaker-style tables and chairs. Blue-and-white checkered tablecloths covered the tables. In the evening, the wait staff placed beeswax candles on the tabletops in small cut-glass bowls shaped like tulips. The floor was old pine, reclaimed from a local barn that had been torn down. The local lumberyard sells tons of the stuff.

There was a black cast-iron woodstove near the center of the room, though I hadn't seen it lit yet. With winter around the corner, I was sure it wouldn't be long.

I followed Lulu. Several tables in front of the window overlooking the town square had been pushed together. Two vases near each end of the joined tables held fresh bouquets of sunny yellow coreopsis.

I took a seat at the far side. Floyd and Karl opted for spots against the window, looking inward.

"That sun is bright," Karl said. "Hurts my eyes." He made a show of removing his eyeglasses and vigorously rubbing his eyes with his fists.

Floyd agreed. "It is kind of bright." I had a feeling both men were more interested in having a good vantage from which to view Jessamine than they were in protecting their eyes from the sun's rays.

Steve held out a chair for Otelia facing the window. Sally sat at the opposite end of the table. Kim squeezed in beside her, and John Moytoy sat beside me.

A flamboyantly dressed man and woman, who appeared to be in their late fifties or early sixties, sat at the small round table nearest us. Their plates were piled high with fried chicken and hush puppies. My mouth watered just looking at them.

A lanky waiter, approaching forty by my guess, came to the table and took our drink orders. Karl and Floyd ordered beers, and the rest of us settled on a shared endless pitcher of iced mint tea.

As the waiter set down our drinks, Tiffany came hurrying in. "Sorry I'm late!" Floyd scooted over, and she took a seat beside him.

"Have some tea." I filled Tiffany's glass.

She pulled off her sunglasses and unbuttoned her green sweater. "Aaron was telling me all about the work he's been doing on his truck." She jiggled her brow. "The man about talked my ear off."

"Is he having a problem with it?" bellowed Steve from across the table. Steve wasn't much for whispering, a trait I was trying to instill in him if he was going to go bird-watching with us. Birds have a way of disappearing if you go thrashing about and talking at the top of your lungs. "Maybe I can help!"

"Thanks, Steve, but there's nothing at all wrong with it," called Tiffany from the other end of the table. "He's getting it ready for the car show." She picked up her napkin and unfolded it. "Polishing thingies, tuning the engine, replacing parts." She laid the white cloth napkin in her lap. "You name it, he's doing it."

"Don't tell me Aaron is all caught up in the car show this year, too," I groaned.

Tiff smiled my way. "Oh, yeah. Big time. I can't believe it. Just my luck, I go from being married to a car dealer to dating a car nut!" She laughed as she said it.

"Hey," Steve said, "I resemble that remark." He grinned. "I've been parading my car every year in the car show. It's fun." He picked up his iced tea. "Besides, we raise a lot of money for charity."

The stranger at the next table barked out a laugh. He leaned over and touched my arm. "I can't help hearing you all talking about the car show," he said loudly. "That's what me and Belle come for, isn't it, doll?" He winked at his wife, who beamed in return. "That and to see a man about a car."

His *doll* nodded. "Like the man says, I'm Belle," the woman said with a quick smile. Her unnaturally orange hair was tucked neatly atop her narrow head. She wore a yellow knit sweater and jeans. "This handsome devil with me is my husband, Emmett."

The handsome devil in question laughed uproariously. "Emmett Lancaster," he said, thrusting out a hand. We shook.

"Pleased to meet you both," I replied. His fingers were icy cold, probably from the soda his hand had recently been wrapped around. His cheeks were puffy and pink, and he had a cleft chin. His eyes were pulled close to his bulbous nose under which grew the beginnings of a sparse mustache. He wore a baggy tweed jacket. Its mottled white-and-brown pattern reminded me of a wood thrush's belly.

"Are you local?" I asked. The pair didn't look familiar, and I was certain I'd remember if I had seen the two of them before.

"Nope." Emmett tugged at the linen napkin tucked into his collar. "We drove up from Trenton. That's out east. We love cars and car shows. Don't we, Belle?" He reached under the table and patted his wife's knee.

"That's right," agreed Belle. "We go to as many as we can."

"Have you got a classic car yourselves?" asked Floyd.

Emmett puffed out his chest. "Do I have a car?" He laughed loudly. "Hear that, Belle? He wants to know if we have a car?" He laughed once more. "I've got a car all right." He laced his fingers over his belly. "And before we leave your little town, I expect to have another."

Steve coughed and reached for his iced tea. John and I looked across the table at one another and suppressed our grins.

"You hoping to buy a car from one of the folks showing at the festival?" asked Karl.

Emmett shook his head. "Nope. Not that I won't keep my eyes open for the right car at the right price." He shook his head. "No. I've arranged to meet a man named Hernando offering a car on one of the classic car websites."

"Em's been drooling over that car for weeks," added Belle.

"Hernando?" Karl pulled at chin. "Can't say as I know the man." He looked around at our group, and we all shook our heads in the negative.

Emmett chuckled. "Yeah, like Belle says, I guess I have been overanxious about this deal. We've been dickering back and forth over the internet for weeks. We finally agreed on the price. Now all I have to do is make sure the car checks out and is everything Hernando promises she is." He leaned toward me. "And it better check out. I sent the man a ten thousand–dollar deposit."

Floyd whistled softly. "That's a lot of money for a car you haven't seen."

"Tell me about it," said Emmett's wife. "But that's my husband."

She grabbed her coffee cup. "He's always been the impulsive type. We got married after courting for only two weeks!" She brought the cup to her lips and smiled at her husband as she drank.

"What model car you buying?" demanded Karl.

Emmett smiled enigmatically. "Oh, no," he said with a wagging finger. "I can't tell you that. You might just try to outbid me!"

I didn't think there was much chance of that. "What car are you driving now?"

"We have a 1939 Oldsmobile Business Coupe," Emmett said proudly. "I bought her when I was eighteen years old with my very own money. It took me five years and two layers of skin off of these two hands—" he thrust out his hands palms up, and the sleeves of his jacket rode back to reveal a pair of slender, hairy arms, "—to restore her."

"I'm not familiar with the model," Steve said, clearly intrigued.

"Me either," admitted Karl.

"Let me tell you," began Emmett.

"Now look what you've done," Belle said with a chuckle. "You've done set him off." She waggled her fork at her husband. "Once you get Emmett cranked up on the subject of his Business Coupe, you'll like as never get him off it!"

"Now, now. The man asked," replied her husband. "It would be rude of me not to answer." He swirled his cola, sipped through his paper straw, then twisted his chair at angle to our table. "Let me tell you, the Business Coupe was, and still is, a real beauty.

"She was a favorite of traveling salesmen because of her large trunk and reasonable price."

"Yes," added Belle. "The car has no backseat, but the trunk is big enough to hold an elephant. And seeing how we don't travel light and Em is a traveling salesman, the Olds is perfect for us." She removed a tube of red lipstick from a skinny black leather purse on the edge of the table and ran it across her lips.

"What line are you in?" inquired Steve.

Emmett shrugged his sloped shoulders. His ginger hair was thinning at the front. "Like Belle says, I'm a salesman. You name it, I've sold it." I noticed a cellophane-wrapped cigar protruding from his pale blue breast pocket.

Steve worked his lower jaw back and forth. "Would you consider selling the Olds?"

Emmett barked. "Not for all the corn in Iowa! But if you'd like to see her, come around to the motel. Me and the wife will take you for a ride."

"I just might take you up on that," Steve replied.

"Great. You show me yours and I'll show you mine," Emmett belted out with a lascivious grin.

"Good luck with that," Otelia said. "Steve here won't even let me see his precious car lately. Says he's keeping it clean until the parade."

Steve's face turned red as a scarlet tanager. "I spent twenty hours detailing her, Otelia. I've got to keep her spick-and-span."

She pulled at his sleeve. "I'm just teasing. Steve."

Emmett Lancaster turned to his wife. "Ready, doll?"

Belle tucked her lipstick back in her purse and nodded. Emmett rose and helped her with her chair. He withdrew a fat black wallet from the inside pocket of his sports coat and tossed a few bills on the table. "See ya at the show, folks." He waved a meaty palm in farewell.

The smell of fried chicken and gardenias lingered in the hole they'd left.

Steve watched them maneuver out the door, then dug into his sandwich.

"Sounds like that fella has a real classic," Sally said.

Steve looked put out. "I suppose."

"I've always admired your car, Steve," Floyd said, pulling at his mustache. "My pa had a '42 DeSoto. I wish I had it now."

"Well, mine's not for sale," Steve said. "I've owned her for twenty years and put twenty years of my life into restoring her."

"She's a fine car, all right," Karl said with a touch of envy. "But me and Floyd have a car of our own that we plan on showing this year. Don't we, Floyd?"

Floyd jerked to attention. "We do?"

"Of course we do." Karl shook his head. Both men had gray hair, though Karl's was by far the thicker of the two. "My pal here is a little senile."

Karl rubbed his hands together. His gray eyes seemed to say that they held a secret. "Just wait and see what we've got. Boy, she is something. I tell you."

Karl Vogel and Floyd Withers were retired. Both lived out at Rolling Acres, a senior living center. Karl was the former Town of Ruby Lake chief of police. Floyd was a retired banker who had lost his wife in the past year.

"Dan's planning on showing his Firebird, so I feel your pain, Tiffany," Kim said from across the table.

"Really?" Tiffany actually looked interested. "What year is it?"

"It's a 1980 Firebird Trans Am. He bought it from Robert a few years back as a project car. He gave me a ride in it once. Mostly we take my car or his truck because the Trans Am's parts are spread around his garage."

Tiffany laughed. "If he bought it from my ex, I'm sure *project* is the right word for it."

"What color is it?" asked Steve. "Red?"

"Black," answered Kim. "With pinstriping."

"A muscle car, eh?" Steve nodded appreciatively. "Well, all I can say is good luck if you think any of you is going to win a ribbon this year." I sensed some good-natured ribbing in Steve's voice.

John turned to me. "Wasn't this supposed to be a luncheon in which we talked about the birds we had seen this morning?" He riffled through the notebook he'd been carrying on our two-hour walk. John was a fastidious note taker. He'd even added tiny pencil sketches of several of the birds, a sparrow, a mockingbird, and the chickadee.

"That was the idea." I shot Karl and Floyd each a *behave yourself* look.

"Uh-oh," Karl said, nudging Floyd with his elbow. "Looks like you're in trouble."

"Me?" gasped Floyd. "What did I do?"

The former police officer ignored Floyd's agitation. "You have to admit, Amy, that '57 Chevy was something."

I looked down my nose and across the table. "I barely saw it. *I* was watching the birds."

"Like you always say, Amy," Karl retorted, "a good birder keeps his or her eyes open for anything, anywhere." He picked up his beer and drank it half down, then smacked his lips with satisfaction. I wasn't sure whether that satisfaction was with his beer or with having thrown my own words back in my face.

Two or, in this case, three could play that game. "I'll have you know," I said, folding my arms across my chest and clamping a hand down on each upper arm, "Derek and Paul are also planning to enter a car in the competition this year."

"They are?" Steve and Karl replied as one.

"Yes, they are."

"What kind of vehicle have they got?" demanded Steve.

"Now, now, Steve," Otelia interrupted. "Like John said, we're here to talk about birds, not cars." She patted his knee. "All this shop talk can wait." She giggled.

Unfortunately, I couldn't resist a little good-natured trash talk myself. "It's a 1961 Chevrolet Impala SS convertible."

Steve whistled through his teeth and brought his hands to his cheeks, making him look like a chipmunk with indigestion.

"That's some car, ain't it?" Karl remarked.

"Can we see it?" asked Floyd. "Please?"

"Sorry, Floyd. Derek and Paul have sworn me to secrecy." The two men had been huddled out in the detached garage at Paul's unfinished house practically every night for the past month. Plus weekends. I barely saw Derek, at least when his hands weren't covered in grease and grime and he wasn't smelling like an auto repair shop. "To tell you the truth, I haven't seen it lately myself."

"A '61 Chevy Impala convertible," Steve said, his voice just above a whisper. "That's some car, all right."

"An Impala *SS*." I couldn't resist correcting him.

Steve nodded. "Yeah. SS." He looked at Karl. "We've got some competition this year."

Karl twisted his lip. "We ain't worried, are we, Floyd?" He turned to Floyd, but Floyd's eye and attention had been drawn elsewhere.

ABOUT THE AUTHOR

J.R. Ripley is the pen name of Glenn Meganck. In addition to the Bird Lover's mystery series, he is the critically acclaimed author of the Maggie Miller mysteries and the Kitty Karlyle mysteries (written as Marie Celine) among other works. He also serves as an Audubon Ambassador. Visit his website at www.JRRipley.net.

CPSIA information can be obtained
at www.ICGtesting.com
Printed in the USA
LVOW11s1631110917

548293LV00001B/358/P